Nude Awakening II
Still Naked

A Novel by

Victor L. Martin

This is a work of fiction. Names, characters, places, and incidents either are the product of the author's imagination or are used fictitiously, and any resemblance to actual persons, living or dead, business establishments, events, or locales are entirely coincidental.

Wahida Clark Presents Publishing
60 Evergreen Place
Suite 904
East Orange, New Jersey 07018
973-678-9982
www.wclarkpublishing.com

Nude Awakening II by Victor Martin
ISBN 13-digit 978-1936649389
ISBN 10-digit 1936649381

Library of Congress Cataloging-In-Publication Data:
LCCN 2013914913
1. Porn Industry, 2. Coconut Grove, Florida 3. Modeling, 4. Street Lit, 5. Miami, Florida 6. African American Fiction 7. Urban

Cover design and layout by Nuance Art.*.
Book design by Nuance Art.*.
Proofreader Rosalind Hamilton
Sr. Editor Linda Wilson

Dedication

To you, my Fans, my Readers, my Supporters.

Without you there is no me.

Thank you.

Acknowledgments

Truth told, I'm far from where I want to be in this business. It was never about the amount of books I've written. My focus is quality over quantity and that will never change. Though I'm still with my faults, I give thanks to God for my talent to do this. Title #9!

To start out, much thanks goes out to my editor, Linda Wilson. Without you this book would not be as it is. I enjoyed your honest input and I mean that. My business manager and friend Jae L. Imes and his wife Allyson M. Deese-Imes, thank you both for all you are doing out there, and I've yet to reach my peak. Detra A. Young, Me Tova Hollingtonworth, Angie Moore, and all the others at the Sistah Reading Sistah Bookclub, thank you for your true support and I'll be waiting for y'all's review on NA2.

To my fans that took the time out to write me. Anne McArthur-Burt, April Torain, Carlene Crumpton, Harriet T. Davis, Yolanda Patterson,

Catherine Thomas, Janice X, Theron 'Smyre' Mosely, Jolene Paige, Patt McGee, Desi King, Ganesha Knight and Ian Mance. Shouts out to my supporters behind bars with me. My true homeboy, Arthur Little. I gotcha my nig! Darian N.I.C.E. Jones, Roderick M. Davis-El, Don Juan Smith aka Grime, Charles Horton, Roderic Gatling, Robert Regins, Roddricus Neal aka Dreek, J.C., Pysco, my barber, William C. Spease, Chauncey Evans aka Salafi, Nathan Smith, Rab aka Nice try . . . wrong guy, Quran aka Killer Ru, Chris B. Taylor, Jacques Floyd, Darrell Anderson, S. Suggs aka Stick, Mack Hunter, Marquis Myers aka Quavo, and Kareem Locke. And I can't forget Quentia Whitley and Tremaine Fonville aka Tiger.

A round of applause to the entire staff and team at WCP. Brenda, by now I hope you've read at least one of my books (smile). Mia Evans, thank you for all you do. Nuance, thank you for everything. To all the authors repping WCP! @ NeNe Capri, Cash, Mike Jefferies, Anthony Field, Tash Hawthorne, Missy Jackson, Charmaine White, Sparkle, Gloria Dotson-Lewis, Sereniti Hall, Intelligent Allah, Mike Sanders, Jason Poole, Shawn 'Jihad' Trump, Al Dickens, and of course (smile my friend), my Boss Lady. The Queen . . . Wahida Clark! Mere words can't express the love I have for you. But I will still say it. THANK YOU! Much props to DJ Kay Slay. I hope we can network.

DJ Ski Money at 101.9 FM in New Bern, NC. Thank you for your support. Teresa Terry, Big Mike Saunders, and Keith Combs, I hope you all will spread the word on my books. Felicia Moore, thanks for holding me down. You will not be forgotten. Jennifer Willis, thank you for being you and counting this trip down with me.

To my fam', the McMillans in Selma, NC and the Martins in Miami. I love and miss you all. Cuzo, Tykeva Dixon, stay focused and Cuzo, Eric Green, hold it down, fam'. I'll be home soon. Quovadis . . . what else do I need to say? Smile. Get mad b/c it's already written. LaShaun Terry, you're as real as it gets. I hope you'll enjoy this. If (which I know I have) I forgot to mention anyone, blame it on my limited space and not my heart. I'll make it up in book #10! "Motive for Murder." Thank you all for your support. I love you Mom, sis, niece, and nephew.

SOCIAL SITES

www.victorlmartin.com

TWITTER

@Victorlmartin7s

FACEBOOK

Email@victormartinsocial@yahoo.com

KEEP YOUR EYES DRY
AND
YOUR HEART EASY

Theme Song:

Kendrick Lamar

"Don't Kill My Vibe"

CHAPTER One

Ain't No Future Right for Me

January 20, 2012

Friday 3:10 PM – Miami, Florida

This some real live bullshit!" Trevon muttered behind the wheel of his newly painted gem green 2010 Jaguar XJL. "I knew they was gonna find that bitch ass homo thug not guilty!"

Seated next to Trevon, LaToria aka Kandi settled back into the black leather seat with her arms crossed. "Swagga ain't worth the stress," she muttered, tight-lipped with a frown.

"I know," Trevon replied, staring at the courthouse up the busy street. "I just can't get over what he did to you . . . or what he did to us!" he added, punching a tight fist into his right palm.

LaToria closed her eyes for a moment. "We got to move on from this."

"It ain't easy," Trevon said, slumping back into the seat.

She turned her head, looking into his eyes. “You got too much to lose. Ain’t trying to raise this baby by myself, Trevon.”

“I wouldn’t dare risk my freedom for that bitch ass coward!”

“Well, we both need to move past this and focus on us and our baby.” She laid a hand on his knee. “Ain’t trying to lose you.”

Trevon looked at her belly. In the month of June, she would bare his firstborn, and it was a moment that he was looking forward to. “What we gonna do about this film?” he asked.

LaToria shrugged. “I don’t think anyone will really care about Swagga fucking that tranny. With our luck, he’ll find some way to make it blow up in our faces. Besides, with Chyna dead, I don’t see nobody giving a damn, and that’s just how I feel.”

Those words fell hard on Trevon. In truth, he had too much at stake to focus on any type of revenge toward Swagga. Money had proven stronger than truth, and it had set Swagga free. Not guilty was the verdict of the kidnapping charge against Swagga. His high-powered team of attorneys argued heavily that no one could firmly prove that Swagga had actually kidnapped LaToria and taken her aboard his yacht. They turned their focus on Swagga’s former bodyguard, Yaffa.

Trevon had to accept the reality and remember the chance he was being given behind killing Yaffa in that warehouse. Even still, he was having trouble letting shit ride behind his beef with LaToria’s ex. As she had just mentioned, they were still in possession of the two video clips of Swagga and Chyna. LaToria was leaning toward the idea of moving up to Atlanta with Trevon, leaving

Swagga and the stress and past behind. Exposing Swagga's homo tastes would only bring drama back into their lives.

"I wanna go home," LaToria said, gazing out the tinted window at a black couple sitting at a bus stop. Both were in their own world, chatting away on a cell phone.

"You ain't going to Amatory with me?"

"Nah." She shook her head. "I'm tired, and plus my feet are hurting."

"Told you not to wear them heels so—"

"Look," she interrupted. "He's coming out!"

Trevon sat up the moment Swagga made his exit from the building. A roar of cheers went up from the mass of spectators that awaited Swagga's appearance. Trevon's tight jaws flexed at the sight of Swagga standing on the top step with his skinny arms raised joyously in the air. He was surrounded by his legal team and ten-deep entourage. The bright sun danced off the pricey diamonds that filled Swagga's mouth.

Trevon took it all in with silence. He could see Swagga taking a pose on the steps in front of a group of photographers while the crowd worked itself into a frenzy.

LaToria turned her head, forcing herself to let go of her anger. All that mattered in her life was the baby and loving Trevon.

Trevon pulled the XJL from the curb with the tinted windows lowered two inches. He didn't speak until he reached the first stoplight on Biscayne Boulevard.

"You thought about what we spoke on last night?"

LaToria sighed. "Don't make a big deal of it, Trevon. You signed the contract, and it's business, so I'm okay with it."

Trevon glanced at her, trying to understand how she was so at ease with him going forward with his contract with Amatory Erotic Films. He was willing to opt out of the contract for the strength of his relationship with her. LaToria assured him that she wouldn't trip. She told him she saw no wrong with him doing five more films.

"You gonna be okay?" he asked, reaching for her hand.

She nodded. "I just need to lie down, that's all."

When the light turned green, he drove the sleek sedan past a Burger King on his left. Looking ahead, he switched lanes while pushing his thoughts to the bright side of his life. His biggest joy was his freedom. He knew he had a rare chance to live the life he did by doing adult porn. How many ex-cons could boast of the life he had? Damn few! Trevon refused to risk his freedom again. Killing Yaffa last year was done in a rushed rage. But even now he held no regret, nor a touch of remorse. He had killed for a woman he was deeply in love with.

Reaching Coconut Grove, he parked his Jag behind LaToria's brand new soft-top diamond black Aston Martin DBS. After walking her inside, he glanced out into the backyard to check on his bullmastiff, Rex. He lay on his side in the shade, asleep. Kissing LaToria on the cheek and giving her plump ass a squeeze, he turned to head for the door.

"Trevon." LaToria stood in the living room with an odd, troubled look.

"Yeah, what's up?" He turned, standing in the door.

She just stood there, unable to speak what was on her mind.

"Baby, you sure you're okay with me—"

"I'm fine," she said in a rush. "Just bring me something to eat on your way back home."

"Pizza or chicken?" he asked, grinning.

She forced a smile. "Both," she replied. "I'm eating for two, remember." Trevon paused at the door with an inkling that Latoya was lying through her teeth. Though she wore a high voltage smile, her eyes told him differently. Not wanting to stress her out, he kept his view to himself.

***

Twenty minutes later, Trevon was seated in front of Janelle's office desk inhaling her light peach-scented body spray.

"I heard the news about Swagga," she said after Trevon was comfortable in the chair.

"Yeah, LaToria didn't take it too well."

"I'm not surprised about that."

Trevon removed his smartphone from his pocket to make sure the ringer was off. "Sorry 'bout that," he said, keeping his eyes above her breasts. The purple satin blouse clung tight against her perky twins. She was dressed professionally in a pantsuit that did little to cover her natural sex appeal. He managed to avoid any lustful looks at her.

"Well," she said, leaning back in her chair. "Are you ready to discuss your future here with Amatory?"

"It's why I'm here."

"So, what have you decided?"

Trevon wanted to make the right choice. "I'll finish out my contract and do the rest of the films."

"I assume you and Kandi have discussed this at some length?"

"Yeah, but mainly I was the one stressing it. She said it won't bother her for me to continue to do porn without her."

Janelle nodded at the wall to Trevon's left. "Don't take this the wrong way, but Kandi knows how to draw the line between her emotions and business."

Trevon looked at the cover art posters of the DVDs that were produced by Amatory. "She told me that herself. But being honest, I told her I couldn't stand to watch her be with another man. So you know I'm happy about you allowing her to opt out of her contract."

"I already knew that, Trevon. I won't force you to do the films. I'm really happy for you and Kandi, but at the same time, I don't want to leave money on the table. By you doing the last five films, I promise you that you'll be set financially."

"I don't doubt that," he said, thinking of the money still being made off the fast-selling DVD he made with LaToria. With each DVD sold, he earned $1.80. Trevon's future looked straight if his next five DVDs could sell like the first. Last week, Janelle had sent him and LaToria an e-mail to inform them of the success of their DVD ranking number one in sales. In less than four months, the DVD had reached a number of 375,000 copies sold! He was looking forward to his first royalty check.

"Have you read the latest reviews on your DVD?" she asked.

"Nah, been too busy with going to the gym and running errands for LaToria. Umm, did someone post something bad?"

"Nope. Far from it." She smiled. "Each day your female fan base is growing. Anyway, a fan posted a review saying how she loved the film and how much she envied Kandi. She gave the DVD five stars and asked if there would be more DVDs with you in it."

Trevon, in all truth, tried to stay grounded and humble. From ex-con to porn star was not an everyday switch. "Umm, I guess we gonna grant her request, huh?"

"Most surely!" Janelle replied, motivated.

Trevon adjusted his thoughts to focus on his actions as just business. He was sure of his love for LaToria. It was an issue he didn't doubt nor question. "When do we start filming?" he asked.

"Later next month." She reached for her laptop. "Here, I want you to look at something."

Trevon found himself briefly dwelling on whom he would be making his next film with. His thoughts were broken when Janelle turned the screen of the laptop in his direction.

"This is Chelsea Kelliebrew. I signed her last month to a four-film deal right before the Christmas holiday, and I'd like her debut film to be with you."

"She looks young." He observed.

"She's only twenty-two, and she's a very nice girl. Being with her will cover your venture into interracial films."

"She a true blonde?"

"Yep. She's five-foot-six and a former swimsuit model. She looks so much like Lindsay Lohan."

He nodded in agreement. "What will the theme of the film be?"

"It's still up in the air right now. But I did inform my screenwriters that I want it to be outdoors. The bedroom scenes are becoming the norm," she explained. "Also, I want you to do an anal scene with her. Are you okay with that?"

Trevon sat up, rubbing a hand down his face. His conscience was tearing at him. Even if it was just *business*, he felt wrong to be casually making plans to fuck another female. He looked at the image of Chelsea modeling a two-piece yellow string bikini. There was no need to deny how sexy she was, even for a white girl. “I’ll do it,” he finally said, after thinking on it.

Janelle lifted her arched eyebrows. “I’m not getting the vibe that you’re *sure* about doing this.”

“Uh, have you told her about me yet?”

“A little. By now she has viewed your video with Kandi. Trust me. If you want to be a top-seller, you have to do interracial films. Though it’s not my favorite.” She shrugged. “It’s business and business is money.”

“I don’t doubt you one bit. It just feels like I’m doing LaToria wrong,” he admitted. “I guess I need to stop mixing my work with my private life.”

“Just do what’s in your heart, Trevon. If you need some time to rethink—”

“Nah, I’m good.” He sighed heavily, allowing his shoulders to slump. “I said I’ll stick to the contract, and that’s what I’m gonna do.”

Janelle hoped his actions would match his words. “And I won’t doubt that, Trevon.”

“So, when will I meet her?” He nodded at the picture of Chelsea.

“Sometime next week. She’s moving down from Orlando and should be settled in her new spot soon.”

“Ai’ight. So what’s the deal with the other films?”

“I’d like to have you doing a different class of subject with each film. With Chelsea, you’ll be doing interracial like I said, so the other films will differ.”

“How?”

“Well, I’d like you to do a film with a plus-size female and one with an older woman. Also, I think a threesome is a good idea as well. I have a few more ideas, but the interracial film with Chelsea is a must do. For the record, interracial films are always top sellers."

Trevon turned his attention back to the picture of Chelsea.

"She looks even better in person," Janelle commented. "And FYI, she has never been in front of a camera, so this time you'll be the teacher."

"Hell, I'm still learning the ropes myself." Trevon leaned back in the chair. "Oh! What does FYI mean?"

Janelle smirked. It had slipped her mind that Trevon was still a newbie when it came to today's terms. "It means for your information."

"I'll have to remember that." He grinned.

Janelle turned the laptop off and then fingered a loose tress of raven black hair over her shoulder. "So how's life really treating you?"

Trevon shifted in the chair. "This drama with Swagga gettin' off free has me pissed! I know I did my dirt as well behind what went down in that warehouse. But still, Swagga tried to burn LaToria alive, and I just have to stand by and watch this nigga ease off the hook."

"Would you feel better if he went to prison?"

Trevon balled up his hands. "I can't ever wish prison on anyone. Not after doing all that time I did."

"You can't let this problem get the best of you. Like you just pointed out, you yourself were lucky with not being charged with killing Swagga's bodyguard. Just move on, Trevon. Let it go. Focus on your future with LaToria and the baby."

"I swear I'm trying," he said, being honest with himself.

"Try harder. Do it for yourself, Trevon."

He nodded.

After a few exchanged words about the new film, the meeting came to an end. It was official. Trevon would continue his career in the adult film industry with Amatory Erotic Films.

"Is there anything else that's troubling you that you'd like to talk about?" she pressed.

Trevon wasn't sure if he should open up to Janelle. The truth was yes. He had another issue troubling him, but he assumed she would view him differently if he spoke on it. Biting his words, he lied and said that everything was all good.

***

Strolling to the back of Amatory's private parking lot, Trevon continued to dwell on the choice he made. It was only business, he reminded himself. Nearing his Jag, he took a glance at Janelle's Lamborghini Aventador, wondering if he would one day own a high-priced whip as such. Not downing his XJL, he was content with it and the triple chrome Rucci rims 24's it sat on.

Easing behind the steering wheel, he reached for his shades off the dashboard. Times such as now, he was filled with a peace of mind. It bothered him that he couldn't feel this way when he was with LaToria.

After making two stops to pick up LaToria's food, he headed home with the system reverberating in the trunk. Tupac's "So Many Tears" came alive inside Trevon.

This ain't the life for me, I wanna change

But ain't no future right for me, I'm stuck in the game.

He kept the song on repeat until he pulled up in his driveway. To his surprise, LaToria's Aston Martin was gone. Slowing to a stop beside her black Escalade, he was suddenly caught off guard when his smartphone rung. He took notice of the unknown number on the screen.

"Hello?" he answered.

"Hey handsome!"

Trevon leaned up in the seat. The voice sounded familiar, but he wasn't too sure. "Who is this?"

She laughed. "Turn around and you'll see."

Trevon twisted in the seat and was moved beyond words from the sight that greeted him.

CHAPTER
Two
Why We Stressing!

Journee!" Trevon said when he stepped out of his ride.

"Surprise, surprise!" she cooed, strolling toward him in a pair of denim hip-huggers. She gave him a hug.

"Why didn't you give me a heads up you were dropping by?" he said, easing his arms around her tiny waist. "LaToria told me nothing."

"That's because I didn't call her," she replied, taking a small step back in her heels. "So what's going on? Where's Kandi?"

Trevon shrugged. "Out, I guess. You um . . . with someone?" he asked, nodding at the tinted lipstick red Benz SLS.

"No, honey. I'm alone. And who is Kandi with? I see her truck is here."

"She has a new ride like you."

"Really? What did she get?" she asked, propping a hand on her ample hip.

"A damn Aston Martin DBS."

"What! Is it black?"

"Yeah, how did you know?"

Jurnee smiled. "I guessed. You know black is her favorite color."

"You wanna come inside? I'll call LaToria to see where she's at. I'm sure she'll be shocked to know you're here."

Jurnee hadn't seen Trevon and LaToria since Christmas of last year. The three were still friends, and Jurnee didn't see that fact changing. She followed Trevon inside, helping him carry the food, but Jurnee glanced back at the empty parking spot with suspicion. *A black Aston Martin, huh?*

"How are things with ole dude you met?" he asked when they entered the kitchen.

"Didn't work out," she said, sitting at the table.

"Word! I thought you two were perfect."

"I'm good," she said, sounding sad. "I ended the relationship before things got out of hand."

"What went wrong?" Trevon asked after turning from the counter.

"He put his hands on me, and I don't play that shit."

"He hit you!"

"Yep. It was the first and last."

"That's fucked up. But you did right to leave him. So what are you doing now?"

Jurnee ran her fingers through her thick mane of curly black hair. "I need to relax. I think I'll get my job back at Amatory as Janelle's assistant. I know she's gonna flip when I tell her what happened."

"Why would she?" Trevon took a seat at the table across from Jurnee.

"Because she told me not to get involved with the bum. Oh well, that's a lesson I had to learn." She shrugged.

"Fuck that lesson! No man should be hitting you."

Jurnee stared at Trevon, thinking how lucky Kandi was to have a man like him at her side. A moment of awkwardness flashed through Jurnee when she looked around the kitchen. Memories popped in her mind back to the night she shared Trevon with Kandi. Only oral sex was given, and even now she caught herself craving to have her lips easing up and down his flesh. *Damn, I'm tripping. This is my bestie's man, and I'm up in here thinking about fucking his sexy ass.* "When you call Kandi, don't mention I'm here. I want to surprise her, okay?" she said, forcing the lust from her mind.

When Trevon pulled out his smartphone, she excused herself to go to the bathroom. Leaving the kitchen, she couldn't help but hope his eyes were glued to her shapely ass.

Trevon's nature had his eyes following Jurnee down the hall. He too had thought back to that night with Jurnee and LaToria. Shaking his head, he dialed LaToria's number. On the fifth ring, she answered.

"Hey baby. Where you at? Your food is gettin' cold."

"I'm in front of the Omni Mall waiting for the bus."

"Quit playing." He grinned.

"I'm not fucking playing!" she shouted. "Can't you hear the damn traffic in the background?"

Trevon was used to her mood swings, but today she was tripping. "Why are you waiting for a bus, LaToria? Where's the car?"

"I don't have it no more!" she snapped.

"Was it stolen?!"

"Fuck that car, okay! Are you coming to pick me up or not?"

"Yeah, but why the hell didn't you call me?"

"Now is not the time, okay? Are you coming or not?"

"Baby, you know I'm coming. But when I get there, you need to tell me what the hell is going on! Are you okay?"

"I'm fine. Just . . . please hurry up and come get me." Her voice broke, sounding as if she was near shedding tears.

***

Silence clogged Trevon's XJL with LaToria seated beside him with her head down. Physically she was fine.

"What the hell is going on, LaToria?" he asked, slowing for a red light on 14th Street. "You gonna tell me what happened to your car?"

She stayed silent.

"Oh, so now I'm talking to myself," he said without raising his voice. "I told you how I get when you go out without telling me nothing! And yet, you up and do it anyway like it's cool and then—"

"I'm not a fucking child, Trevon!"

Trevon's grip tightened on the steering wheel. Clenching his jaws, he fought hard to manage his temper. "Ain't gonna sit here and argue with you," he stated while staring straight ahead.

"Good, then don't!"

"I got the food you asked for." He forced himself to stay calm.

"I'm not hungry!" she snapped.

Trevon shot a quick glance at LaToria. "You ai'ight today? If this is about me sticking to my contract with Amatory then yes—"

"Trevon, listen!" she shouted. "I told you I don't give a fuck about that shit! I don't care who you fuck or who sucks your dick, okay! I just don't care . . . I don't care what you do!"

Before Trevon could respond, a horn blew behind him. The light had turned green. They made the rest of the trip without saying a single word. LaToria's emotions were so pent up that she paid no attention to the red SLS parked in front of her crib. Shoving the door open, she struggled out to her feet and rushed to the front door, leaving Trevon behind.

***

Jurnee knew there was tension between Kandi and Trevon the moment Kandi stormed inside the house.

"What the hell are you doing here?" LaToria shouted at Jurnee in the living room.

"I came to surprise some friends," Jurnee replied calmly. "But I didn't expect you of all people to welcome me like this."

LaToria rolled her eyes. "Whateva!" she huffed, stomping to her bedroom.

"And what's gotten up your ass?" Jurnee asked.

LaToria waved Jurnee off, slamming the bedroom door.

A few seconds later, Trevon eased into the living room, flopping down on the purple crescent-shaped leather sofa. "From the look on your face, I see that Hurricane LaToria just blew through here."

Jurnee nodded. "Were . . . you two arguing?" she asked.

"I won't call it arguing," Trevon replied, picking up the remote for the 70-inch 3D flat screen TV.

"Well, she sure as hell ain't happy." Jurnee looked at Trevon and sat down beside him crossing her legs. "She wasn't happy to see me at all. Maybe I shoulda called," she said, looking worried.

"Nah, you're good. She just going through those pregnancy mood swings or something." He flipped idly through the channels.

Jurnee shrugged. "If you say so."

Trevon lowered the remote. "Why do you say that?"

". . . I don't know. Maybe she has something on her mind."

"Yeah, and talking to her now will only stress me the fuck out."

"I hope I'm not being too intrusive about your personal business. But how long has she been having these mood swings?"

Trevon turned the TV off. Silence. Leaning his head back, he stared up at the high arched ceiling. "Shit seemed to change after we got back home from the holidays," he murmured, feeling dejected. "I'm just dealing with it because I know our relationship won't be perfect."

"Want me to go back and talk to her?"

"It's on you if you want to," he replied with no expression on his face.

"Ay, papi. I'll go and see what's got my girl in a bitchy mood." She adjusted the form-fitting corset over her lush breasts. "Be right back." She stood, consciously aware of her tight gear that catered to her toned figure. Still, at the age of forty-one she was proud to flaunt what she had to display.

Trevon picked up the remote as Jurnee sauntered out of the living room swishing her hips. By chance, *Access Hollywood* was doing a segment on Jennifer Lopez.

Trevon smirked at the strong likeness Jurnee had to Jennifer Lopez, and of course, he stole another glance at Jurnee's thick, succulent ass. She was a Dominican goddess, a tasty piece of eye candy.

***

Jurnee gave a warning knock on LaToria's bedroom door as she breezed inside.

"I don't feel like being bothered!" LaToria said before Jurnee had a chance to close the door. She lay out on the bed with her back facing Jurnee.

"What in the hell is going on with you, girl?!" Jurnee stated.

LaToria turned over to face Jurnee, who stood at the side of the bed looking pissed. "Ain't nothing going on with me!"

"The hell it ain't!" Jurnee fired back. "I know damn well you're not doing what I think you're doing."

"I dunno what you're talking about," LaToria remarked with a slight roll of her neck.

"That Aston Martin!" Jurnee shouted.

LaToria smacked her lips, shoving the pillow aside, so she could sit up and confront Jurnee. "I don't have it no more! Happy now?"

"You shouldn't've had it in the first damn place!" Jurnee lowered her voice. "I can't believe this mess. After all Trevon has done for you, you have the guts to—"

"Stop assuming shit that you don't know what the hell is going on!"

"Then tell me, so I won't have to assume!" Jurnee crossed her arms, waiting for LaToria to speak.

"It's none of your business," LaToria said, rubbing her temples.

Jurnee raised her arched eyebrows. "Now it's none of my business, huh? Why wasn't your ass saying that when this issue came up when we went to New York last year? If I can recall, which I easily can, mind you! You made it my business by coming to me, and I made it my personal business by doing what I did for yo' ass!"

"I don't wanna argue." LaToria lowered her chin.

"Fuck what you *don't* wanna do! I wanna know why you're doing this dumb shit, girl? That man in there loves your ass to death!" Jurnee pointed in the direction of the living room. "S'pose he was doing what you're doing to him, huh? How would you feel then?"

LaToria wanted to scream. Instead, she began to cry. "It's not like that, Jurnee. I would never—intentionally hurt Trevon."

"Oh, so it's all good to hurt him by mistake? What is wrong with you?"

LaToria's watery eyes sent a line of tears down her cheeks. "I'm trying to make things right." She sobbed. "You just don't know the fucked up position I'm in right now."

Jurnee wasn't moved to feel sorry for LaToria at the moment. "Does Trevon know how you really got that car?"

"No."

"Girl, what are you getting yourself mixed up in?" Jurnee sat next to LaToria and eased her arm over LaToria's shoulder. "You're pregnant with Trevon's baby, and I don't want you to mess up what you two got going. You'll only regret it, baby."

LaToria closed her eyes, leaning against her friend for the support she so desperately needed.

"It's gonna be okay," Jurnee said, gently.

LaToria wanted to believe in Jurnee, but deep down she knew differently and kept the truth of the matter to herself. She knew her past actions would not be understood by Jurnee nor Trevon. *If* she could make things right she would do so without a hint of hesitation.

"Now, what's up with this sour mood you got?" Jurnee asked after a brief spell of silence.

LaToria shrugged. "Just . . . I don't know."

"You and Trevon were so happy last month. Do you need to share something with me?"

"No, I'm okay. Just got a lot on my mind and stuff." LaToria wiped her eyes with the back of her hand.

"So you're telling me that nothing is going on with you and Mar—"

"No!" LaToria sat up, unable to look Jurnee in the face. "What happened up in New York is over, okay? Just, let me do what I got to do. I'll fix it all, and I did that today by gettin' rid of the car."

"I still don't understand why you even had the thing in the first place."

LaToria sighed. "It's done and over with, Jurnee, so please drop it," she pleaded, sounding tired.

Jurnee wasn't easily convinced, but she decided not to press any deeper.

"I'm sorry about snapping at you earlier," LaToria apologized.

Jurnee kiddingly rolled her hazel-brownish eyes. "Just don't let it happen again." She nudged LaToria. "You know it's all good, but who you really need to be making up with is that man of yours."

"I know," LaToria whined at hearing the truth.

"Well, getcha phat ass up and go do it." Jurnee laughed.

"'Ho, don't get it twisted, 'cause I'ma snap this body back ASAP after I have this baby," LaToria promised. "Okay, enough about my man. Where is yours? I—"

"We broke up." Jurnee's mood instantly turned sour.

"OMG! What the fuck happened?"

Now it was Jurnee's turn to build up a wall around her matters that dealt with her heart. "I'll tell you later. And before you start to pester me, I need to ask if I can spend the night?"

LaToria frowned. "So now you gonna hide stuff from me?"

"No. Ain't hiding nothing from yo' ass. I said I will tell you later and that's just what I'm gonna do. So can I chill here or not?"

"Yeah, you can chill. And I don't know why you even felt you had to ask. But anyway, I'ma take your advice and go make up with my man." LaToria smiled.

"Good, 'cause that's all yo' sassy ass need is some good dick!" Jurnee laughed.

"And my man has plenty of it!" LaToria boasted, giving Jurnee a high-five.

Neither felt at ease to speak on the oral threesome they shared with Trevon. By an unspoken agreement, both women figured it was simpler to pretend it never happened.

***

LaToria's three-bedroom crib gave Jurnee the comfort of her own bathroom. Standing at the sink, she gazed at her reflection. Heavy cosmetics hid the discolored bruise around her right eye. She was at least thankful the swelling had lessened to a point where shades weren't needed. Feeling the signs of an oncoming throbbing headache, she squatted down to search the cabinet under the sink. To her surprise, she discovered an opened box of panty liners. She found it odd for the box to be in the guest bathroom. Moving it aside, a white folded piece of paper caught her attention, sticking out the top of the box. The form drew more attention from Jurnee when she spotted LaToria's name on it. Eager to read the form, she removed it and then reached over to lock the door. Unfolding the medical form, she gasped at what she read.

"Why?" she muttered, shaking her head. *LaToria wants an abortion?*

Jurnee stayed silent, her mind running too fast to grasp any thoughts. She read the medical form carefully, specifically checking the dates. Closing her eyes, she wondered why LaToria was planning to have an abortion later in the month. Jurnee replaced the form back like she found it, knowing LaToria wasn't being honest with her nor Trevon.

CHAPTER Three

Gotta Pay You Back

"Where is Marcus?" Kendra demanded, using Swagga's real name.

Swagga's new bodyguard, thirty-three year old Rick, knew it was a wise choice to lie. "I'm not sure." He shrugged his beefy, tatted shoulders.

"Bullshit!" she said, throwing her wine glass to the floor. "You're his damn bodyguard, so shouldn't your black ass know where the fuck he's at? I'm not going through this shit today. Now where is he?"

"Please calm down, Kendra. It's his party. He's around here someplace."

"Uh-huh, probably with that pink-haired bitch I saw all up in his pocket a minute ago!" She scanned the crowd, not giving a damn about the sideways looks she was getting. None of the guests were her friends. All the people within her view stood in the lanes of 'dick riders' or straight up groupies. Both made her sick. All they cared for was Swagga's money. Kendra was fed up with

Swagga's bullshit constantly being thrown in her face every day. Shit started out sweet when Swagga appeared willing to keep it official within their relationship. It lasted all of three short weeks until she busted him with a thirsty ass 'ho in the gym sucking his dick. Kendra forgave him but she didn't forget. Fuck the money, the mansion, and fuck Marcus aka Swagga. Kendra refused to be dogged out by any man. She tried to give Swagga a chance on the strength of their daughter, but she could only deal with so much. Spinning on her toes, she rushed the exit with Rick on her heels, Kendra ignored his pleas to calm down.

Stomping up the stairs, she was glad her daughter wasn't with her today. She left Rick at the bottom of the stairs, and then stormed inside the spacious bedroom she shared with Swagga. It took her five minutes to stuff two large Gucci suitcases full of her shit. Today should have been a happy day for her. She no longer had the fear of her man going to jail. She knew he was cheating on her with a bottom ass bitch that wasn't worth shit!

Rolling the suitcases down to the garage, she headed straight for the brand new lightning silver Bentley Continental GT coupe. Slamming the trunk, she headed for the driver's seat to put Swagga in the rearview mirror. Just as she slid inside, Rick ran up to the window holding up his cell phone. He gestured her to lower the glass.

"Swagga wants to holla atcha," he said, catching his breath.

Kendra snatched the cell phone. "What!"

"Shit, dats what I need to be askin' yo' ass! What the fuck is wrong wit' you?" Swagga yelled in her ear.

"Where are you?" she asked, raising her voice. "Better yet, who is with you?"

"Huh?"

"Nigga, you heard me. So stop trying to play me! But you know what? I'm tired of your funky bullshit, so have fun with that skank bitch you fooling with!"

"Yo, why you trying to act all foolish and shit! I just beat a fuckin' charge that coulda laid my ass down, and you buggin' 'bout dis dumb shit! I swear I'ma—"

"Goodbye, Marcus!" She dropped the phone in Rick's palm, and then slid the tinted window up. She had no more words to exchange with Swagga.

***

"Dumb ass bitch!" Swagga yelled after Rick told him about Kendra leaving. Leaning his head back, he closed his eyes on the sofa in the game room.

"You okay, sweetie?" a soft voice asked.

Swagga nodded. "Just finish what you was doin'," he said, running his fingers through the pink hair of the groupie he just met. She smiled, lowering her soft wet lips back down his shaft. Swagga couldn't recall her name, but he knew her measurements—34B-26-42! Remembering his past, he made her get butt ass naked before anything jumped off. Of course, he hid his true reason for asking her to strip because he was still ashamed of his slip-up with Chyna. Focusing on the pleasure he was getting, he assumed Kendra would bring her ass back once she calmed down. Swagga opened his eyes and locked in on the sight of the groupie doing her best to swallow him whole. Up and down she slurped on his raw, stiff meat while cupping his balls.

"Eat it up, baby. Dis yo' dick fo' tahday." He reached down to squeeze one of her pointy nipples that jiggled with her movements. Without being asked, she ran her wet tongue up his shaft and then back down to his balls.

Her head work was on point. Swagga moaned and lifted his ass off the cushion. Four minutes later, her head was still bouncing over his lap without pause.

Swagga asked her to slow down when he felt a nut building. He wanted to be on his feet when he came. “Yo, what’s yo’ name again?”

“Nashlly,” she cooed, rubbing her lips against the tip of his erection.

“Okay, Nashlly. Now show me why I should let you be in my next video.”

She did so by taking him deep inside her mouth while palming his ass.

***

Later that night after the party ended, Swagga and Rick had a trip to make. With Rick driving Swagga’s new pearl-blue Rolls-Royce Ghost, they ended up at an empty public park in West Palm Beach.

“Is this nigga official?” Swagga asked, working on his third Newport.

Rick nodded. “I’ve known him for a few months. So yeah, he’s official.”

“A few months! And you trust dude to put in this type of work?” Sawgga asked with doubt creeping in.

“Relax, okay? Shit, you’ve known me less than three months, so what’s the big difference? Let me handle it like I promised you.”

“I hope this ain’t no bullshit.” Swagga settled deep into the soft, plush leather seat, wincing from the smoke burning his eyes. Looking ahead, he only saw darkness. “I know dis fool ain’t gonna be late! My time is money.”

“He won’t be late,” Rick replied, waiting for a pair of headlights to appear. “We’re early, remember?”

Swagga rubbed his nose, clearly showing he lacked patience. "Yo, you see that pink-haired bitch I bagged? I might feature her in my next video. Ass soft as hell!"

"Yeah, I saw her," Rick said. "And I think Kendra saw her too."

"I 'on't give a fuck! She just on some bullshit right now. By next week she'll be back wit' a nigga," Swagga claimed, full of pride.

Rick slid the sunroof back, allowing the smoke to clear.

"My bust," Swagga said, inching the glass down to thump the cigarette out. "I forgot you don't smoke."

Before Rick could respond, his eyes were drawn to the rearview mirror. "Here's our man," he said, removing a chrome .40 from his hip.

Swagga didn't question Rick's actions. If he felt some heat was needed, he would roll with it. A level of trust was still being built on Swagga's end, but so far Rick hadn't set off any ill vibes.

"Let me make sure everything is all good first." Rick was all business now.

"Do whatcha do," Swagga replied, hiding his nervousness.

Rick filled his palm with the .40, and then he exited the Ghost. Swagga leaned up when a dark colored sedan pulled alongside them with the lights off.

"I'll be a minute," Rick informed him before easing the door shut.

* * *

Slowing the dark gray Mercedes S550 was a Bahamian by the name of Fritz. Seeing Rick, he unlocked the passenger side door.

"Long time no see," Rick greeted Fritz.

Fritz loosened his black silk tie looking straight ahead. "And time a keep ah movin' wit' out us. So what is it that I can do fah you?"

"My boss needs to smooth out a few bumps in his path."

"Bumps eh?" Fritz rubbed his chin. "How many?"

"Just one," Rick told him.

"He know me price?" Fritz said, sitting a black cigar box on the dashboard.

"Money ain't an issue here," Rick told him.

Fritz smiled. "That be one of me favorite sayin'. So, how do ya boss want dis bump taken care of?"

"Make it look like an accident. Anything else will have the police looking our way."

Fritz nodded, keeping his face in the dark. "Dat can be done. And when does dis bump need my attention?"

Rick rubbed a palm over his freshly done cornrows. "By June."

"That won't be a problem," Fritz replied. "Can you meet me tomorrow at the Fontainebleau? You should bring all the details you have on dis issue you wish for me to take care of."

"What time?"

"Noon."

"Okay, I'll call once I get there."

Fritz nodded. "See you tomorrow."

Rick exited the Benz and then slid back inside the Ghost.

"What dude talkin' 'bout?" Swagga asked, the moment Rick was seated behind the wheel.

"Gotta get up with 'im at the Fontainebleau, tomorrow at noon."

"Y'all got all that shit in order that quick?"

"Fritz is 'bout his biz." Rick turned the headlights on, and then he pulled away from the parking spot. Fritz's Benz had already pulled off.

"Did you tell 'im how it needs to look like an accident?"

"Relax, yo. I got this. By June that nigga gonna be a memory."

Swagga ran his fingers through his long dreads, releasing a deep sigh. It was hard to relax due to his issues, but Swagga was set firm on keeping his hands clean. Pulling out his cell phone, he dialed up an urban model who was eager to get up on his dick again.

Rick drove with his mind dealing with his actions. He knew the risks that rode with hiring Fritz to commit murder. Those risks were overlooked by the twenty racks *($20,000)* that Swagga would drop in his pocket. Easy money in his view. Being Swagga's bodyguard had many perks that Rick worked hard to gain. He would do his job and get money. He stood at 6 feet 5 inches, 315 pounds. Rick was imposing, even without the sight of his licensed weapon. Added to his immense size, he easily favored the brawler, Kimbo Slice.

"How's the new track coming in the studio?" Rick asked when Swagga later ended his call. They were cruising down I-95 South entering Dade County.

"'Nother banger, I hope," Swagga responded with the seat reclined.

Rick slowed the Rolls-Royce when the radar started to beep. Lowering the speed to 85, he switched lanes to ease by a slow traveling van in the lane ahead. "You still need me to run that security check for your video next month?"

"Yeah go head an' do that." Swagga inhaled, yearning for another Newport.

When the two vehicles were side by side, the van seemed to match the speed of the Ghost. Turning his head, Swagga noticed the cargo door was cracked. He continued to study the van. The driver was hidden behind a poorly done tint job on the window. Glancing back to the cargo door, he suddenly sat up. Seeing a hand gripping the cargo door gained Swagga's full attention. Before he could shout a warning, he was nearly face to face with a masked gunman holding an AK-47 with an extended clip.

Swagga's panicked screams filled the interior as the hail of bullets rained against the passenger side door and window.

Rick instinctively jerked the wheel to the right, veering hard against the van. The action threw the gunman on his ass. Before he could regain his balance, Rick floored the pedal, weaving past a small sedan. Cars in their wake swerved and locked their brakes.

"You okay!" Rick shouted, pushing the Ghost near triple digits.

Swagga had his eyes shut with his chest heaving. "Why the fuck you do that shit?" he panted.

"Had to throw his aim off!" Rick glanced up at the rearview mirror trying to spot the van. "The car is armored but the tires ain't."

Swagga twisted around in the seat, feeling embarrassed. He forgot that his ride was bulletproof. "You see 'em?"

Rick shook his head. "Nah! I think they weren't expecting this shit to be armored."

Swagga turned back around. "Take me home," he said. "Niggas done fucked up fo' real now!"

Rick nodded. "I think you'll need more protection. Let me get my full team with me until we find out who is behind this."

Swagga's fear stood deep in uncertainty of who could be behind the attempted hit. Whomever it was, the motherfucker was bold and knew about his movements.

"Did you recognize anything about that van?" Rick was still speeding along the interstate with the hazard lights flashing.

"Nah. Nothing but that AK." Swagga turned in the seat again. "Damn, it's like they knew where to find me . . ."

Rick glanced at Swagga and then back to the road. "I think we were followed somehow." He hated to admit it because it was his duty to be on point and observant at all times.

"We got company!" Swagga pointed to the rear.

Rick didn't need to look behind him. He could hear the sirens and see the flashing blue lights in the side mirror. Someone had called the police and Swagga's Rolls-Royce was easy to spot. Slowing down, Rick removed his .40 and laid it in plain view on the dashboard along with his gun permit to carry a concealed weapon. "Call your lawyer and tell 'im you gonna need his assistance. When I pull over, let me do the talking." Rick stayed calm, despite the two Florida State Troopers filling the rearview mirrors.

Swagga fumbled his cell phone twice before his nerves settled. He had no reason to worry. Rick had a strict code of not driving dirty with drugs that were used daily by Swagga. Willing himself to match Rick's calm stance, Swagga hit the speed dial to get up with his lawyer with hopes that Rick knew what he was doing.

***

An hour later, the banged up van pulled into a vacant building with the headlights turned off. The driver slowed to a squeaking stop while watching his partner in the side mirror rolling a rusted metal door shut. All was quiet in the seedy area of Overtown.

"What the fuck went wrong!" the driver shouted, his voice echoing off the bare stone walls. "How the hell ain't nobody tell me about his car being bulletproof. We coulda gotten our asses fucked all the way up!"

"Bruh, I'm just as surprised as you. I hit that nigga at point blank range, and the shit just bounced off the glass."

"Fuck!" The driver shoved the door open and stood with his arms at his waist.

"What do we do now?"

The driver sighed. "Get rid of that AK and this van. I'll call you later on. Gimme a few days to think shit out."

CHAPTER Four

Sexing You

Uhhmmm . . . take this pussy, Smooch!" Jurnee heard Kandi moan through the partially opened bedroom door. Biting her upper lip, she continued to massage her left olive-toned breast while smearing the heavy wetness between her parted thighs. Focusing on the sounds, she matched the strokes against her clit with Kandi's constant pants. Hunching her hips up and down, she shoved her middle finger between her wet folds. Rocking against her digit, she pinched her nipple. With her eyes shut, she vividly fantasized about a union with Trevon. She envisioned herself riding the full steely span of his dick. He was pulling at her long hair while slapping her jiggling ass. Staying with that idea, she continued to please herself.

She slid another finger inside her tight slit and arched her back, driving her fingers deep. "Ahh fuck!" she whined, longing for someone to touch her all over. Releasing her nipple, she started to use both hands on herself. Reaching that higher level, she became lost with her self-pleasurement. The sounds of Trevon and Kandi had since ended five minutes ago. With her eyes still tightly shut, she finished herself off by stirring two fingers over her clit. Turning her face, she muffled her moans in the pillow.

Just as her body started to turn soft, she felt someone moving across the bed.

"Shhhh. It's me," Kandi whispered in the dark. "Trevon is taking a shower, so we got to be quick and quiet."

Jurnee smiled. "Did he cum inside you?" she asked, reaching to her right. To her delight, she filled her hands with Kandi's large D-cups.

"Yeah, why?" Kandi replied, reaching between Jurnee's legs.

"Let me taste you."

"Let's sixty-nine side by side," Kandi suggested.

In the dark, the two quietly licked and sucked each other's pussy, getting their fill. The act was unique for Jurnee. She slurped loudly between Kandi's soft thighs, relishing the warm cum that Trevon left behind. Mixed with Kandi's juices, Jurnee became high off the taste that saturated her tongue. She swirled her tongue between Kandi's meaty pussy lips, making her moan and quiver.

Lifting her leg up, she gave Kandi more access to swipe her tongue over her hairless sex. Their climax came in a rush. Both hated to untwine their limbs, but it was done with Kandi rolling quietly off the bed. In the dark, the two shared a quick kiss with their soft warm melons mashed together.

"I need to talk to you in the morning," Kandi whispered lightly, rubbing her palm over the sides of Jurnee's hips.

Jurnee crushed her urge to question Kandi of the abortion papers she discovered. Maybe Kandi would explain herself tomorrow.

"Okay," Jurnee said before sliding her tongue back inside Kandi's mouth. Ending the kiss, LaToria eased out of the bedroom with guilt riding on her shoulders. Entering her bedroom, she was greatly relieved to hear the shower still running. It was still a fact, even with Trevon in her life: LaToria was still a bisexual at heart. Pushing the bathroom door open, she joined Trevon in the steamy shower. Just for the hell of it, she reached between his legs to rub his soapy penis.

"I thought you were sleep," he said, pulling her closer to his wet body.

"I'm hungry," she purred, licking her upper lip.

"For what?"

"Some more of this dick," she admitted, shamelessly making him hard with the touch of her hand.

Trevon squeezed her ass and then lowered his mouth to her breasts. LaToria moved her grip back and forth over his dick, making it stretch to its full measure. Parting her legs, she moved a step back, releasing him. "Fuck me from the back and hold my waist while you do me."

Trevon lightly slapped both of her ass cheeks when she turned around to bend over against the wall. "Make it clap fo' me."

"Okay, Smooch," she said, looking over her shoulder. With a sexy look, she made her ass bounce and clap for her man. Her lust was burning to have him back inside her. Teasing her, he slid his dick between her ass cheeks while she continued to keep him in a trance.

"Now!" she moaned. "Put that dick in me. Gimme all that dick!"

Trevon slapped his erection up against her pussy four times before he pressed the tip against her opening. Looking down at the union, he held his breath until he was fully piercing her insides. His first thrust made her titties swing. Her ass began to jiggle and clap against his wet skin. Being raw inside her was a sensation that he would never tire of.

"Dis how you want it?!" he asked, stroking her with a smooth long dicking that had her chanting his name. Every fifth stroke, his palm would slap against her bouncing ass.

LaToria loved the dick. She wasn't acting, her pleasure was real. Being with him made her feel desired beyond sex. Catching her by surprise, she jerked up on her toes when he pushed his thumb inside her ass.

"Yeah, Smooch!" she shouted. "Fuck my ass and pussy! Oooo you fucking my ass and my pussy!"

They stayed joined together for nine and a half minutes.

"Shit! I'm cummin'!" she shouted with two fingers rubbing her clit. With the water pelting her ass, she shoved hard against Trevon, gasping and feeling weak. His arms circled her waist, holding her up while he jabbed in and out of her creamy hole.

***

"Damn, that was the bomb," she later purred, spooning in the bed naked with him.

Trevon grinned. "That pregnant pussy got a nigga open."

"Boy, shut up." She smiled, snuggling closer against him.

A brief silence fell between them. Trevon closed his eyes, inhaling the strong coconut lotion that coated

LaToria's soft skin. He felt lucky to have her. Sure, she had her faults just as he did, but he loved her. Even with LaToria's strong Nicki Minaj resemblance, he was able to respect her beyond the stance of mere looks. Most evident to him, she took him in with all his faults and scarred past. Their future? In truth, it scared him. Was he ready to be a father? A husband? With a hand lying on her belly, he reminded himself to take it day by day. The moment now was perfect, and that's a life he sought to have with LaToria.

***

While Trevon and LaToria found rest, trouble was wide awake up in Washington, D.C. Tahkiyah Bradford sat inside a dark silver BMW 640i convertible parked outside The Park at Fourteenth Club with its engine running. Tonight she had no plans to enter the club, even with the lure to mingle with a celeb or two. Behind the tinted window, she scanned the parking lot. She wore a heavy padded dark green L.L. Bean leather coat that hid her soft feminine contours. What couldn't be hidden was her ageless beauty. At the age of fifty-four, she easily fooled many to believe that she was in her mid to late thirties. With her light skin tone and doe-like hazel eyes, her looks were seldom compared to Sanaa Lathan. Shifting in the leather seat, she removed her designer glasses and rubbed the bridge of her nose. Her hair was pulled back into a bun, showing that she wasn't out to mingle. Sliding her glasses back on, she skimmed her fingers over the two items in her lap, a smartphone turned off because she wasn't expecting any calls. The second item was a fully loaded black and chrome 9-millimeter. A horn blew behind her. She ignored it, keeping her gaze focused at the entrance of the parking lot. She wanted some good news tonight. What she craved even more was peace and some sentiment of closure in her life. Just when her tolerable patience began to waiver, a black Dodge Durango pulled into the parking lot with dirty snow caked up around the wheel wells. Tahkiyah placed her smartphone on the dashboard and then thumbed the safety off the 9-millimeter. Two minutes later, she had company.

"Cold out, ain't it?" a white male with a full salt and pepper beard intoned, closing the door.

Tahkiyah sighed. "Do you have the information I requested? I didn't drive all the way out here to discuss the weather!"

"Yeah, I got it," he replied, unzipping his brown-hooded parka. "Here, take a look at this." He handed her a sealed manila envelope.

"Thank you," she murmured, eager to view the contents.

"Mind if I light one up?" the man asked, reaching inside the parka for his cigarettes.

"Yes, I do mind," she replied stiffly without looking at him.

Sighing, he waited until she broke the seal on the envelope. "The pictures that I mentioned in my e-mail are enclosed."

"I would hope so since I paid you sixty percent up front." She shifted through the papers until she reached a stack of pictures.

"That's her house," he explained, after seeing which picture she held.

"And you're sure it's here? I can't afford any mistakes with this."

"Without a doubt. I ran a full background check, and the birth certificate and social security number you gave me were a match."

Tahkiyah stayed silent until she picked up a second picture. To get a better look, she reached up to turn the interior light on. "Is this her?" she asked with her heart racing.

"Yeah. That's as close as I could get."

Tahkiyah couldn't remove her eyes from the photo. "What's her name?" she asked quickly.

The man cleared his throat. "LaToria Nicole Frost."

"LaToria," Tahkiyah repeated to herself.

"Yeah. I can find out more about her if needed. Starting with her job and stuff like that. She also—"

"You've done well enough," she said. "Our terms of business end here."

"Are you sure? I can easily—"

"I said our terms end here!" She made an unnoticed shift that placed a firm grip on the 9-millimeter wedged between the door and the seat.

"Fine with me." The private investigator zipped up his parka. He then made a rude exit without saying goodbye.

Alone once again, Tahkiyah was now faced with a choice. It took her several minutes to make up her mind. Doing so, she reached for her smartphone. Doubting her boyfriend Anthony was awake, she elected to send him a text message.

I'm okay. Will call u soon. Please manage things in the office until I return. Promise 2 explain. XOXO

Making it hard to change her mind, she pulled out of the parking lot and headed south. She wasn't packed for the trip to South Florida, but time nor money stood a matter with Tahkiyah. She could buy clothes when she reached the end of her trip. Leaving D.C. behind, she kept the 9-millimeter always within reach. Driving in silence, she softly whispered LaToria's name with tears rolling down her face. Tahkiyah was unable to let the past rest. She would face LaToria and worry about the results of it later. Mile after mile she drove down I-95. She willed herself on, refusing to stop and turn around.

***

Haters tried 2 make me a ghost in my Ghost!

Swagga tweeted when he finally made it home at two in the morning. He was still jumpy from the shooting, so to ease off the edge, he filled his lungs with some killer weed.

"I feel like Scarface up in dis bitch!" Swagga said and kicked back on the new brown and black gator sectional sofa in the huge living room. He took a hard long pull on the joint while his manager Harry Storm shook his head, frowning.

As promised, Rick had beefed up Swagga's security with an addition of four men.

"I need me a new ride." Swagga's voice dragged.

"Shouldn't you be more concerned about who tried to—"

"Can you handle it or not?" Swagga bassed on Harry. "Dat's the fuckin' police job, not mine!"

Harry removed his glasses. He hated how Swagga tried to play the gangsta role every day of his life. "I'm your music manager not your personal assistant, Swagga."

Swagga sat up, staring at Harry. "Muthafucka, you work fo' me! It's my name dat push yo' checks, so you better switch up that—"

"Swagga, chill," Rick said, rising up from the stool at the bar. "He has a point. This some serious shit we dealing with."

"Man, it is what it is." Swagga sat back reaching for the bottle of Crown Royal Black.

Harry slid his glasses back on. "You need to get back in the recording booth soon," he said, absently looking at Swagga filling his glass for the third time.

"I know," Swagga slurred. "Cain't you see a nigga is stressed? You a good ole white boy, so I doubt nobody eva popped no slugs atcha."

"And I hope to keep it that way," Harry replied.

Swagga looked up from filling his glass. "See what I mean, Rick? Harry don't back down, yo! He gonna have the same drive to get me back on top of the rap game!"

Rick rubbed his tired eyes, feeling the need for an energy boost.

"What are your plans?" Harry asked just as Swagga lifted the whiskey to his lips.

"I'ma be ready Monday." Swagga lowered the glass. "Lemme clear my mind of all this shit."

Harry stood. "Good."

"Why don't cha spend the night?" Swagga offered.

Harry shook his head. "Wife is waiting up for me."

Swagga shrugged, and then he raised the glass to his lips.

"I'll have one of the guards see you to your car, Mr. Storm," Rick said as Harry picked up his leather briefcase.

Swagga continued to get high in the comfort of his mansion. Rubbing his forehead, he found it odd that he was missing Kendra's company. Maybe it was best that she had bounced out. He couldn't imagine the pain of losing her because of some hating ass nigga. Smiling, he thought back to last year and how he hated so much on Trevon all because of Kandi's phat ass. Thinking of her made his dick hard.

"TV on," he said, turning the new voice activated 100-inch smart TV on. "Video six."

Three seconds later, Kandi's naked, oiled up, 48-inch ass filled the screen. She was outside by a pool with two black men that would fuck her endlessly for the next forty minutes. Swagga owned all of Kandi's adult films, all but her last that included Trevon.

"Bitches ain't shit," he slurred, watching the two men rubbing Kandi's ass while she stroked them below their waist. Swagga held no guilt about trying to kill Kandi to keep his deeds with Chyna a secret. Watching the porn easily reminded him of his times with Kandi in bed. Not wanting to spend the night alone, he picked up his cell phone to call up one of his many groupies.

CHAPTER Five

This Can't Be Real

January 21, 2012

Saturday 10:14 AM – Coconut Grove

"Since when do you get out of bed before noon on the weekend?" Kandi startled Jurnee as she attempted to quietly close the front door.

"Hey girl." Jurnee smiled nervously at Kandi lying on the sofa. "I had to run to the ATM right quick," she said, slipping the yellow leather strap of her Coach bag off her shoulder. "I didn't wake you up, did I?"

"Nah," Kandi replied, sitting up and yawning. "I just got up about ten minutes ago. I came in here to watch the news, but I fell asleep."

Jurnee grinned as she sat down on the sofa. "Trevon put that ass to bed last night, didn't he?"

"Naturally," Kandi answered. "And you helped me out too."

"I take it that you didn't mention what we did to Trevon?"

Kandi nodded.

"It's not good to be keeping secrets from your man," Jurnee warned, crossing her jean-covered legs.

"It ain't a big deal. Besides, he knew I was bisexual before we hooked up, so I won't stress it, okay?"

"That ain't the point I'm trying to make, girl."

Kandi rolled her eyes. "What's up with you and your man?"

"We broke up," Jurnee flatly stated, crossing her arms.

"Over what?"

Jurnee's foot rocked up and down. She sighed, and then cleared her throat. "He hit me and yelled in my face, and you know I don't play that shit. So I left his ass!"

"Are you okay?"

Jurnee shrugged and turned her head toward the floor. "Just need some time to get my life in order about what I want to do."

"You talk to Janelle yet?"

"Nah. But I plan to do so on Monday."

"Well, you know you're welcomed here."

Jurnee looked around the living room. "Is Trevon up?'

"Not yet."

"So, what did you have to talk to me about?"

Kandi tugged at the edge of the T-shirt she wore with no panties. "Have you ever done something that you regret doing?"

"Uh . . . yeah?"

"What was it?"

"Well, I guess my biggest regret is not allowing myself to fully open up to a man. It's not a day that goes by that I don't think about what it would be like to be in your shoes."

"My shoes?"

"Yeah. I think about having a child."

"Really! Shit. You ain't never tell me that."

"It's true," Jurnee confessed, rubbing her nose. "I know life isn't perfect, but I want the best for you and Trevon and the baby."

"Life ain't never perfect," Kandi muttered with a pout.

Jurnee could see that something was troubling her friend. "What do you feel is wrong? You have Trevon, right? And the baby—"

"Things just ain't perfect, okay!" Kandi said, standing up quickly. She paced the floor, her eyes welling with tears.

"What am I missing, Kandi?" Jurnee stood. "Ever since I've been here, you've been acting funny. Why aren't you happy?"

"It's real fucked up right now."

"What's fucked up?"

Kandi didn't answer.

Jurnee glanced down the hall before she spoke. "Is Trevon cheating on you or something?" she whispered.

"No," Kandi groaned, wiping her tears away.

Jurnee walked up to Kandi and laid her hands on her shoulders. "You need to tell me what's going on with you."

Kandi lowered her chin. "I can't." She sobbed.

"Yes, the hell you can!" Jurnee pressed, her voice filled with exasperation. She was fighting hard not to mention the abortion paper she found last night. Her hopes stood high on Kandi being open with her about her problem.

Kandi turned from Jurnee to sit back on the sofa. "It's about what happened up in New York."

Jurnee shook her head. "I thought you said you took care of—"

"Dammit, I lied, okay!"

"I'm starting to notice that."

"You're not being helpful!"

"How can I when you are keeping shit from me?"

Kandi ran her fingers through her hair, sighing. "It's about the baby."

"What's wrong with the baby, Kandi?" Jurnee replied mildly.

"When we were up in New York, I—" Kandi paused when her cell phone rang. Hearing the special ring tone, she answered quickly. "Martellus! I told you not to call this number!"

Jurnee shook her head upon hearing Martellus' name. She made no effort to conceal the disappointment on her face as Kandi got up to take the call into the kitchen.

***

"Fuck you, okay!" Kandi said, seething. "Didn't I make things clear to you yesterday?" She sat alone in the kitchen.

"You know you're wrong, Kandi! How the hell did you expect me to just let this shit go? My views are just as important as yours!" Martellus said.

"No, they're not! I told you I'll take care of this. So now you won't have to worry about breaking your wife's special little heart. And plus you—"

"I'm getting a divorce, Kandi. I was trying to tell you yesterday before you ran out on me," he said desperately.

"Bullshit!"

"It's true, baby. The papers have been filed, and I've told you you're the woman I need and want in my life."

"Don't be telling me a lie," Kandi whined, gripping the phone.

"I'm serious. I do love you, and I'm willing to prove myself to you beyond mere words, baby. But to make this work, you have to give me—give us a chance. Do you love me?"

Kandi sat down at the kitchen table with her lips quivering. "Why are you doing this to me?"

"All I know how to do is love you. Now, if I'm wrong for that. Then it's something I can't explain."

"I'm with somebody." She sobbed.

"You don't love him. We have a strong past, and if given the chance we can have a stronger future. He can't make you happy like I can. Why pretend? I'm leaving my wife for you because I've grown to care for you, and I love you, baby."

"But—"

"Ain't no buts. I've done all that you've asked of me, and I did it out of love, not lust. Think about what we did when you came to New York. It wasn't lust and you know it. I . . . don't want to have an affair with you anymore. I want you firmly in my life, no bullshit."

". . . I don't know." She cried at the table.

"Baby, listen to me. My flight leaves tonight at nine. I need to see you before I go. Can you do that for me?"

"Yes," she said, wiping her eyes.

"Promise?"

"I promise."

"I love you, Kandi."

Kandi closed her eyes and spoke the words he wanted to hear. ". . . I love you the same."

***

It wasn't until noon when Trevon finally rolled out of bed. Hearing the TV in the living room, he assumed he would find LaToria. To his surprise, Jurnee was sitting alone on the sofa watching *Notorious.*

"Hey, what's up?" he asked, having forgotten that Jurnee was visiting.

"Good afternoon, sleepy head." She smiled at the sight of him wearing nothing but a pair of black satin boxers.

"Damn, it's that late?" He yawned.

"That it is," Jurnee answered, fingering a lustrous curl of hair that hung near her left breast. She was digging Trevon for sure.

"Um, where LaToria?"

"Left for a nail appointment about an hour ago." Her eyes moved over his thick muscular torso and descended below his waist. The boxers did little to hide his dick even when it was soft.

"She say when she comin' back?"

Jurnee shook her head. "Why don't you call her?" she suggested, since she felt Kandi had lied to her.

"Nah. Ain't tryin' to argue with her today."

"Just trying to be helpful."

"Thanks," he said, scratching his baldhead. "Um, lemme put some clothes on and start my day."

"You going somewhere?"

"Wasn't planning to," he answered. "Just gonna feed my dog, then make breakfast."

"Let me cook for you." She stood, pleased to see his eyes moving over her body. Blushing, she smiled. "Something wrong?"

Trevon returned her smile. "Umm, don't get upset, but I was just thinking how—like—you um, sorta favor

Jennifer Lopez. But seeing you now, you look more like Paula Abdul."

"I hope it's in her sober state." Jurnee smiled, doing all that she could to keep her eyes above his waist. Sure, she had seen him naked and sucked his dick, but it was *before* any feelings were noted between him and Kandi.

Later, she stood in the kitchen frying bacon and eggs while Trevon took a shower. She bit back her words again on what she had discovered in the bathroom about the upcoming abortion. Things weren't right. She wasn't fooled by Kandi's lie. Deep down she knew her friend had rushed out to visit Martellus. Anger started to consume her. *Why do women dog out good men?* She could see the love that Trevon held for Kandi, but behind his back he was being played. This placed Jurnee at the crossroads. Tell Trevon the truth, or stay quiet and respect the bond and friendship she had with Kandi?

***

Kandi forced herself to think she was doing the right thing. Sneaking out to see Martellus had her heart twisted. He had spoken the truth earlier about the past they had together. Kandi had met Martellus Hart when she was only nineteen and dancing at the strip club up in Atlanta. Back then she wasn't up to speed on the game that men played to get inside her. Meeting Martellus was a new adventure for Kandi. For starters, she was drawn to him by the way he carried himself in a professional manner. He was twenty years older and married, but Kandi ignored both and dived heart first into an affair that would span over the next five years.

Kandi showed no guilt when she entered Martellus' suite on South Beach. Looking into his brown eyes, she saw the need that drove him to unbutton her blouse.

"I'm glad you came," he said, brushing his lips against her ears. "Let me make love to you, Kandi. I'm at the point where I can't share you anymore."

Kandi raised her hands up to his naked waist. He was warm.

"Touch me, baby. Look at what you're doing to me."

Kandi slid her hands down to grip his solid erection. With her eyes shut, she stroked him slowly. It all felt so right to her.

"Show me how much you love me," he said, removing the red bra she wore. "I need to feel those soft warm lips. Please, baby."

Kandi pushed him backward until he fell back on the bed. Going down to her knees, she moaned out his name and then slid her tongue up the underside of his swollen flesh. Unable to stop herself, she wrapped her glossy lips around his dick, bobbing up and down at a slow pace while massaginghis balls.

***

"Is it good?" Jurnee asked, standing at the stove. She already knew the answer since Trevon was asking for seconds.

"Hell yeah! How did you know I like my grits with cheese?"

She shrugged. "Lucky guess."

"Hey. Did LaToria tell you about the film we got on Swagga?"

"Um, no," she answered, filling a glass with some milk. "Only thing she said about him is that she was upset about him beating the case."

"Well, you won't believe it until you see it. But our boy Swagga has some homo tendencies."

"Stop playing!"

"Nah, for real. It's the reason he went after LaToria. For some reason he thought she had the film of him with a he-she by the name of Chyna."

"And you got the film?"

"Yep. It's on my phone."

Jurnee looked down at her food.

"Yeah, you might wanna eat first," Trevon suggested.

"Does Swagga know you got it?"

"Nope."

"How long have you had it?"

"Since Christmas."

Jurnee reached for the pepper shaker. "What do you plan to do with it? I assume that Swagga doesn't want it to be made public."

"Not sure right now. LaToria don't think it will do any harm to him. She feels that the public's view on being gay isn't the same as it used to be."

"She has a point. Look at the gay marriage laws being passed in some states. And I myself can't dog Swagga, because I'm bisexual myself."

"Yeah, but you don't do it in secret and put others at risk. Swagga on some down low homo thug shit."

Jurnee shrugged. "How are things at Amatory?" she asked, moving to a new topic.

"Good. I went to see Janelle yesterday, and I'm up for five more films. She has my next film being an interracial one with a girl by the name of—"

"Chelsea Kelliebrew." Jurnee jumped in.

"You know her?"

"Not really. But I did her interview at the office last year. And if Janelle didn't mention it, doing an interracial film is a good move for your career."

"She said the same," he replied, failing to keep his eyes off her soft line of cleavage.

After they finished eating, they went outside by the pool. It was now ten minutes past 2 PM.

"Have you and Kandi come up with a name for the baby?"

"Nah." He smiled. "She wants the gender to be a surprise.

"What are you hoping for?" Jurnee asked, sitting on the pool chair across from Trevon.

"A girl." He beamed. "Look, don't tell LaToria, but I'ma ask her to marry me after the baby is born."

"Seriously!" she asked, shielding her eyes from the bright sun.

Trevon nodded. "I just wanna do right by her and do-"

His words came to a halt when his smartphone rung. Seeing the call was coming from LaToria, he answered it. Before he spoke, he reminded himself not to trip over any small shit.

"Hey baby, what's up?"

"Nothing," she replied tersely.

Silence. Trevon cleared his throat. "Um, I missed you this morning. You coulda woke me up with a goodbye hug or kiss."

". . . I'm sorry, Trevon."

"It's all good, baby. You know how I don't like to wake up without you in my arms. And since that didn't happen, I'ma put it on you when you get back—"

"Is Jurnee still there?"

Trevon frowned. "Yeah."

"I need to talk to her right quick," she said, impatiently.

Trevon again fought within himself not to check LaToria. Biting his words, he handed the smartphone to Jurnee. Trevon stayed close by to listen in on the one-sided conversation. It turned out to be useless. Jurnee was speechless from the words that filled her ear. This drove Trevon over the edge. He was tired of LaToria and her funny style actions. When Jurnee held the phone out, he snatched it back.

"LaToria, what's going on with you?" he said, raising his voice.

"Trevon, I'm sorry," LaToria cried.

"Sorry about what, baby? Why are you crying? Better, why aren't you home with me?"

"Don't hate me."

Trevon turned from Jurnee. "What is going on with you, baby? You are starting to scare me, okay. Just . . . come home and we'll talk things out together."

A brief spell of silence stood. "Trevon, I'm not coming back home. What we had between us . . . is no more. I'm sorry, and I never meant to hurt—I can't do it no more."

CHAPTER
Six
Ain't This a Bitch?

Where the fuck this fool at?" Swagga muttered to himself after glancing at his icy Rolex for the fifth time in thirty minutes. He sat up in the black leather seat inside Rick's white BMW 760Li to scan the Fontainebleau Hotel across the busy street. Overlooking the bikini clad women filling the sidewalk, he searched for any sign of Rick. His effort was a waste.

Becoming annoyed, he yanked the white towel off his dreads. Then he turned to look at the empty key ignition. "Fuck!" he shouted.

At least the tinted windows were cracked, and it was needed due to the heat. Swagga ignored the beads of sweat on his forehead. He couldn't step out of the car without taking the risk of being recognized. Sighing, he wondered what in the hell was taking Rick so long. It was only ten minutes past 2 PM, and the ever prompt Rick had arrived on time at noon. Swagga picked up the loaded 9 millimeter that Rick left behind. His sweaty hand squeezed the black polymer grip. Ten more minutes rolled by.

"I got nineteen in the clip an' one in the chamber. I'm bustin' on you fool like my name is anger. Hatin' on me. Nigga, it's easy—" Swagga paused in his freestyle when he caught sight of the black couple exiting the hotel. Wide-eyed, he peered through the window thinking his mind was fucking with him. "Now ain't this some real live bullshit!" Swagga shook his head at the clear view of Kandi in the arms of Martellus. "That greasy, baldheaded, snake ass muthafucka!" Swagga gripped the 9 millimeter tighter at the sight of Martellus all hugged up with Kandi. Swagga's finger itched at the idea of dumping the clip against Martellus' smug ass face. As for Kandi, he'd save the one in the chamber for her phat, pretty red ass. His gaze stayed on them up until the valet rolled up in a roofless glossy black Aston Martin DBS. Swagga didn't have time to assume that Kandi was cheating on Trevon. He saw them just yesterday at his court hearing. Knowing that Trevon was being played eased a crooked grin on Swagga's face. As for it being a fact that Kandi was dogging Trevon, Swagga had a trick to bring that to the light. When the DBS drove off, Swagga turned his attention toward the packed beach. Flat asses were the thing of the past. Real or fake, Swagga was open off a nice swollen ass. From where he sat he could see two white women sunbathing side by side on their stomachs with their pale, bare, sandy feet facing him. Both were topless, wearing a thin bikini G-string.

"Damn, them asses phat!" he murmured, knowing his chances were high that he could fuck them both just off his fame and status. Building a taste for the *white* kind, he figured he could hook up with another groupie that happened to be a cheerleader for the Miami Heat.

Turning back to the Fontainebleau, he was relieved to see Rick jogging across the street.

"Damn, bruh! What the fuck took you so long?" Swagga asked when Rick was inside. "Hot as hell up in here!"

"Shit like this can't be rushed," Rick replied, removing his Smith & Wesson .40 from his waist. "Fritz is not a man to rush."

"So er'thang good or what?" Swagga asked, hoping against the latter.

"All we gotta do is go about our biz." Rick placed the .40 inside the custom built door panel. "Let Fritz do what he do. Trust me on this."

Swagga waited to speak while Rick removed his backup piece from a holster strapped under his left pants leg. "What kinda heat is that?"

Rick held the sub compact black polymer frame pistol near the steering wheel. "It's a Sig Sauer nine with a 2.9 inch barrel."

"Shit small as hell," Swagga retorted, frowning.

Rick shrugged. "It holds six rounds, and it's a major upgrade over the thirty-eight." Rick nodded at the larger 9 millimeter he left with Swagga. "You done with that?"

Swagga's interest in guns ranked at the bottom of his list. Handing the loaded nine back to Rick eased a heavy weight off Swagga's mind.

"Ai'ight, where we headed?" Rick asked, pulling from the curb. "If it's not back to the crib, I'ma need to call the whole team, and plus we need to switch—"

"Just take me back home 'cuz I ain't tryin' to go through all that shit."

"You heard from Kendra?"

"Nah. And I ain't gonna call 'er ass!"

"You should if you want my view."

"Yo, I've been thinkin'." Swagga was brushing Rick's last words off. "Look, while you was up with ole boy. Three rides came by thumpin' and none of 'em were bangin' my shit. Them niggas Lil' Wayne, Future, and Rick Ross are eatin'! Here I am on some bullshit when my ass need to be in the fuckin' studio!"

"So get on your grind. Let me handle your safety. You do you and handle it, bruh. Yeah, I don't always agree with things you do, but I got your back and that's on my hood."

Swagga slid the towel back over his head. "You ain't seen shit yet! I know I can put this rap game on smash. Wayne nor Ross can see me word fo' word off the dome!"

"What up with you going in the *Backroom* on BET?" Rick asked, constantly checking the rearview mirror for anything suspicious.

"Harry 'pose to be workin' on it," Swagga replied, trailing his thumb along the fresh crease of his acid-washed Red Monkey jeans. "Yo, can I trust them other niggas you got working wit' you?"

"Relax, bruh. All of them are proven."

Swagga *tried* to relax inside the sedan while Rick took the long road home by avoiding I-95 North. They rode in obscurity inside Rick's BMW, which was needed for today. Running the AC was also needed, even in the month of January.

"I still need a new whip to replace the Ghost," Swagga reminded Rick when they reached the city limits for Fort Lauderdale.

"Yes, still got your eyes on the Panamera?" Rick asked, driving through a green light.

"Nah. I think the Aston Martin Rapid look betta—matter of fact. Guess who I saw at the Fontainebleau?" Swagga sat up.

"Um . . . Rihanna?"

"Fuck no! She ain't neva' hit me back, but anyway I saw that nigga, Martellus. I told you about that."

"Word?" Rick nodded at hearing the name. Upon taking the job as Swagga's chief bodyguard, Rick requested a list of names of people that Swagga had beef with or any type of issue. Those names were on Rick's alert list, and none would ever be within arm's reach of Swagga, nor would they get on RSVP to any function hosted by Swagga. Rick was aware of all beef that Swagga had, with whom and why.

"What is he doing down here?" Rick asked.

"Creepin' wit' Kandi, of all people."

Rick glanced at Swagga. "Your Kandi?"

"Bitch don't belong to me, but yeah, her. I guess she steppin' out on Trevon."

"Want me to see what he's up to?"

Swagga cracked his knuckles. "That might be a good move. I know Martellus will do some grimy ass shit, so I ain't puttin' shit pass that nigga. What I wanna know is how long he been fuckin' Kandi?"

"I'll look into it and make some calls."

"You do that," Swagga said, narrowing his eyes and looking straight ahead. "'Cause if our boy Fritz come through. I might add Martellus to the menu too."

CHAPTER Seven

Moving Forward

Back down in Coconut Grove, the dead silence frightened Jurnee for Trevon's safety. For the last ten minutes she stood anxiously at the locked bedroom door.

"Please make a sound or something," she begged, her eyes wet from crying. "I know you're hurting over this mess Kandi has done, and I swear to you I didn't know anything about this, Trevon." She knocked. "Please open the door and talk to me, or just talk to me through the door so I'll know you're okay. Trevon, please . . . I'm really getting scared out here, so don't make me look crazy by calling the police to come kick this door down!" She crossed her arms. "I won't leave until you open this door or say something. C'mon now, Trevon. Please open the door." Ignoring the coming pain, she banged six times on the door as hard as she could. "I'm calling the police!" she shouted with new tears welling. Just as she pulled up the 911 icon on her touch screen phone, she heard the lock click. Jurnee froze with her heart jumping. Calming herself, she reached for the doorknob and slowly opened the door, taking things in. She stepped inside the bedroom and found Trevon sitting at the foot of the bed with his head down.

"Why do you care?" he asked, looking up at her with hurt showing on his face.

Jurnee closed the door. "I'm sorry this has happened to—"

"What did she say to you?"

Jurnee closed her eyes. She couldn't lie to him. "She told me not to try to talk her out of going back to . . . Martellus."

"Who the fuck is he!"

Jurnee opened her eyes. "Kandi met him when she was dancing up in Atlanta, and they started an affair back then. And—"

"He's married?"

"Was," Jurnee answered.

"So, she's been fuckin' this nigga behind my back since day one!"

Jurnee couldn't reply.

"How the fuck she just up and run off!" he shouted. "Ain't done nothing to be treated like this and yet—" He paused, turning his head away.

"I don't like this, Trevon. You gotta believe me, okay?" Jurnee sympathized.

"Where are they going?" he asked, looking up.

"I really don't know. He has a home up in New York and one in Denver."

Trevon shamelessly wiped his eyes. "Oh, the nigga get money, huh?"

She nodded. "Plenty. He owns a record label, and last year he tried to buy an NBA team."

"So she left me for money," he stated, shaking his head.

"Trust me, I'm not standing up for her, but I think it's more than that."

Trevon looked around the bedroom. Signs of LaToria were everywhere. A pair of her panties were folded up a top a stack of clean clothes. On the dresser, her perfume and cosmetics reminded him of how she would apply lip gloss in the nude. "This can't be real," he muttered.

"Don't let this break you." Jurnee moved across the room and placed a hand on his muscular shoulder.

"Ain't—" His words couldn't be found to express the pain over losing LaToria.

Jurnee sat down and waited a few seconds before she spoke. "Why was she going to have an abortion?"

"What!" Trevon came to his feet. "Who told you some bullshit like that?"

Jurnee shook her head. "No one. But I found this in the second bathroom." She reached inside her jean pocket and pulled out the medical form.

"What's this?" Trevon asked, unfolding the paper.

"She was—or is—still planning to have an abortion later this month."

Trevon's entire world was crushed. Losing LaToria was one thing, but for her to kill their child to lay under another nigga was out of order. "How the fuck can she do this to me!" He shook the form in Jurnee's face.

"I'm on your side—"

"Fuck being on my side!" he shouted. "She gonna kill my firstborn and push me out of the picture like my voice don't count! This . . . this some bullshit! How can she even look at herself in the mirror! *How*!"

Jurnee winced when he shouted.

Trevon, even in his rage, saw the sudden fear in Jurnee. She had tears in her eyes, but Trevon knew the deeper fear that made her jump. Dropping his hands, he went down on one knee. "Don't be afraid of me, okay? I . . . I shouldn't be yelling at you, and I'm sorry."

She nodded. "Kandi is wrong." She sobbed, reaching for his hand.

Trevon didn't know the words to speak. Doing what he felt was right, he took her into his arms. "I can't let her kill my child," he said, meaning every word. "I can go on without her, but I want my seed."

Jurnee could agree with him. Making a quick choice, she spoke what was dwelling in her mind. "I'll help you," she said, tightening her embrace around his neck. In his arms she felt safe. Their closeness also made her feel awkward.

"You don't have to—"

"No." She lifted her head off his shoulder to look into his eyes. "Let me do this. What she is doing to you. You don't deserve."

Trevon placed his hands on the bed next to her hips. Her arms remained around his neck, their faces only inches apart. "I don't even know what I deserve."

"You deserve better," she said with her eyes intent. "I know LaToria is my best friend and all, but right is right and wrong is wrong. It's like . . . I don't know who she is."

Trevon lowered his head, closing his eyes. "I don't know what to do, Jurnee."

"We'll figure it out," she assured him, easing her arms from his neck only to rub his arms.

"I gotta find a place to stay, and if—"

"That isn't Kandi's place, remember? It's Janelle's name on the title, and I'm sure she'll let you stay here once we explain what happened."

Trevon stood and then crossed the room. Stopping at the dresser, he saw a broken man in the mirror. "I was a fool to even think she really loved me." He picked up a picture that he took with LaToria last year.

"Don't think like that. She's the one with the issues, not you," she told him.

"Where do I start?" he asked.

"You start by moving on with your life. You can't let this eat at you, Trevon. I know it hurts because I know how you feel about Kandi."

He shrugged, placing the picture face down on the dresser.

"You still have your career—"

"I can't—"

"Yes you can!" She came to her feet. "Don't let this break you!"

He turned to face her. "Why do you even care?" he asked again.

Jurnee looked at him eyes to eyes. "Why shouldn't I care?"

"Don't answer a question by asking one."

"You want me to be honest?"

He shook his head. "No. I *need* you to be honest."

She crossed her arms, lowering her eyes to the floor. "I don't know why I care, but I do, okay?"

"LaToria said she cared about me too, so how—"

"I'm not her!" She looked up.

Trevon shifted his feet. "I'm sorry 'bout that."

"Are you gonna be okay?"

"I guess. It just seems like none of this shit is real." He shook his head. "One minute I'm about to get an engagement ring and the next . . . I just need to get outta this fuckin' house before I spaz out."

“Where are you going?” she asked, watching him pick up his keys.

He shrugged. “I don’t know.”

Standing in place, she wondered how he would feel if she spoke the truth on why she cared about him. Assuming the worst, she stayed quiet as he made his exit.

Trevon was trudging down the hall when Jurnee called out his name. Coming to a stop, he turned. She eased up to him, her eyes still wet from all her crying.

“Do you want me to be here when you get back?” she asked softly.

Trevon sighed. “I don’t care, Jurnee. I . . . I just don’t care.”

“That’s the last thing you should do is not care,” Jurnee said.

“So what do you suggest?”

Jurnee smiled. “Let me go with you. How about we get out of this house and grab a bite to eat?”

Trevon sighed and thought about Jurnee’s suggestion. “Why not?” he said as he fought to hide his pain over LaToria. “Let’s go before I lose my fuckin’ mind.”

***

“She’s not answering any of my calls,” Trevon told Jurnee as they later sat inside his XJL outside of the Sushi Samba Restaurant.

Jurnee could hear the pain in his voice. “She can’t hide,” she said, rubbing his shoulder. “Like I told you in the restaurant, Martellus has a record company, so we’ll just reach him—”

“And say what?” Trevon looked at Jurnee. “You think I’ma ask for LaToria back?”

“But I thought you wanted—”

"It don't matter no more. I mean, really. How can I stop her from having the abortion? Hell, I can't even leave the state without going through a ton of bullshit with my PO! If she don't want to be with me no more then fuck it. And fuck her!"

"Do you really mean that, Trevon?"

"Ain't got no choice," he said, looking up through the sunroof.

"You always have a choice," she pointed out.

"Do I really?"

Jurnee reached for his chin, turning it toward her. "Look at me, papi. You can waste your time running after Kandi, or move on with your life and become the superstar in this biz. Kandi made her choice, now you make yours."

Trevon released a sigh. "I guess this will be a life lesson learned, huh?"

"Damn right! Get money over pussy. Stick with Amatory, and you'll be rich and famous, papi. If Kandi was meant for you, or you for her, then this shit wouldn't be happening."

"But what about my seed?" he asked wistfully.

Jurnee turned in the seat. "I don't have all the answers, papi."

They both sat in silence, trapped in their thoughts. Trevon was thinking of the disappointment his mom and sister would feel over the news about the breakup.

As for Jurnee, her thoughts jumped back to weighing the option of telling Trevon the truth about why she really cared about him.

"It's getting late," she said, looking at her watch. "Don't you have a certain time to be in?"

"Yeah, by ten if I ain't working."

"I wouldn't mind keeping you company. We could order a movie and just chill if you want to," she suggested, smiling at him.

"To be honest," he said, seeing it was ten minutes past 8 PM. "I'd rather stop at the liquor store, get something to drink, and just get fucked up because being sober is the last thing on my mind."

Jurnee thought his suggestion over. "Sounds like a plan to me."

Minutes later, the XJL exited the parking lot with "Shot for Me" by Drake, pounding in the trunk. As Trevon drove with Jurnee sitting beautifully at his side, he willed himself to become cold-hearted toward that false item called love.

CHAPTER Eight

Blame it on the Henny

Killing someone was easy when it was fully thought out and planned. Fritz was alone at an undisclosed location in the Northwestern area of Miami. In the one bedroom apartment, the wall in the tiny bedroom was covered with pictures of his new target. Fritz was shirtless, smoking a thick, genuine hand rolled Cuban cigar. Smoke wafted up near the stained popcorn ceiling marred by three bullet holes. Sitting up on the queen-size bed, Fritz took a close study of the man in the pictures. Rick had supplied the pictures and all the vital information that Fritz had requested. In the coming days he would begin tracking his new target to get a deeper knowledge of his daily movements. Being close but unseen was an easy task for Fritz to accomplish. Committing an act of murder seemed the norm for Fritz. There were men and a few women who took their last breath with Fritz's grinning face in their vision. The others died by what was deemed as an accident. From the ungoverned streets of Zimbabwe, to the flashing lights of

Hollywood, California, Fritz had proven his talent. A professional killer is how he viewed himself. At times he couldn't determine what drove his urge to kill. The money, or the rush of stalking his target and seeing fear pooling in their eyes when they realize their life on earth has ended.

Yeah, killing was easy in Fritz's mind. The muted TV on a fake wooden stand was tuned on a bland sitcom that Fritz gave no attention. The cheap, outdated TV was being used for lighting in the stuffy bedroom with brown carpet torn in various spots. This dwelling was only temporary for Fritz. It would suit his needs until the job was done.

Inhaling on the cigar, he picked up his cell phone. After dialing a local number, he placed the cigar in a chipped glass ashtray. His call was answered after the third ring. Knowing his number was known on the other end, he made no attempt to introduce himself. He also knew the person on the other end was strictly business as himself.

"I need a new vehicle by tomorrow night," Fritz explained. "And I don't need anything flashy." Fritz was flawlessly speaking without an accent now.

"Not a problem. You'll find what you need parked at our normal spot tomorrow at 7 PM. The keys will be taped inside the front left wheel well."

Fritz ended the call and then massaged the tight tendons in his neck. He was reaching for the cigar, when a knock rattled the iron cage on the front door. In the blink of an eye, a silenced Glock 19 appeared in his right hand. Easing off the bed, he moved quickly into the unlit living room with the Glock held in a steady two-handed grip.

"I gotcha chicken, so hurry da hell up and lemme in!"

Fritz relaxed his grip on the pistol upon hearing Jenny's irritating voice. "Show some patience!" he shouted, thumbing the safety on the Glock and tucking it away behind his back.

Unlocking the two doors, he stepped aside as Jenny flounced into the apartment in a glinty pair of black leather five-inch spiked booties. A heavy, cheap pineapple perfume and fried chicken filled his nose, causing his stomach to growl. "Anybody follow you?" he asked, scanning the streets outside.

"Nooo . . ." she complained, rolling her green contact covered eyes. "Ain't nobody important, and I don't have no pimp runnin' after my ass. Now let's eat. And maybe we can have some fun after we finish." She whirled her wide ass, unaware that her blonde wig was slightly crooked on her head.

Fritz locked both doors and then joined Jenny on the tattered green cloth sofa. Like every man, Fritz had likings that he filled his downtime with. In Fritz's case, his mind was at ease when he could entertain himself with a willing prostitute and chicken.

***

"This was an excellent idea, papi," Jurnee said, curled up on the sofa with her heels off. She kept her eyes on Trevon while sipping her third glass of Ciroc and Sprite.

"Life's a bitch, ain't it?" he said, lounging back on the sofa with a bottle of R my Martin VSOP between his legs.

"Life is what you make it," she replied, raising her glass in the air with a small grin. "Words from my girl, Mary J. Blige."

Trevon lifted the bottle to his lips to finish it.

"Easy, papi," Jurnee warned as Trevon gulped the drink until it was empty.

Trevon savored the sweet cognac and the airy feeling it induced over his mind and body. He was feeling mellow. "Wh-what's that song you got on?" he asked Jurnee. "Sounds so relaxin'."

"It's called 'Nothing Can Come Between Us' by Sade," she said, softly.

"I like it," he said with his eyes low.

"Really?"

"Yeah, but—" He paused, sliding a hand down his face.

"But what?"

"Nah, I was 'bout to say sumthin' stupid." He grinned.

Jurnee giggled. "Are you drunk?"

"Not yet, but I'm damn shole' tryin'." He sat up, placing the empty bottle of Remy Martin VSOP on the floor. "What that Ciroc taste like?"

"Like me," she flirted, knowing full well that the cocktail was making her tipsy.

"You're crazy." He smiled, reaching for a second bottle of Remy on the table.

"Hey. I got a question," she said, handing him her empty glass. "Say, if you were like . . . alone on an island with one famous woman . . . um, who would she be?"

Trevon paused a second from opening the bottle of Remy. "Um . . . just one?"

"Yes." She giggled, tucking her feet up under her body.

With a wide grin he said, "Um, I'll have to pick the MSWA, Paula Abdul."

Jurnee exploded into a fit of laughter.

"Why is that so funny?" he asked, enjoying the sight and sound of her mood.

Jurnee couldn't speak until her giggling ceased. "You're just saying that because you said I favor her." She nudged him on his knee.

"So." He shrugged, removing the wooden cork from the bottle.

"And what does MSWA mean?"

"Most sexiest woman alive," he said, filling her glass with the new drink.

"You love yourself some Paula Abdul," she teased him. "Well, if I was alone on an island. I swear I'd love to be with Tyrese, and it ain't because you look like him," she lied.

"Yeah, whateva." Trevon handed Jurnee her glass.

"Thank you, papi." She waited until he filled his own glass before she spoke again. "Let's um make a toast."

"For what?"

"Um . . . to the future."

Trevon lifted the VSOP that filled his glass. "Why not? 'Cause the past ain't shit."

"Moving forward," she said when their glasses clinked.

They kept the mood laid back while consuming glass after glass of Remy. "What time is it?" Jurnee asked, rubbing her forehead.

Trevon had to study his watch for a moment. "Uh, ten minutes past ten."

"I can't drink another drop." Jurnee stretched her legs out in Trevon's direction. "Rub my feet." She wiggled her neon blue coated toes.

"What I look like?" he asked as she laid her feet on his lap.

"My personal masseur," she said with a slight slur.

"Ain't nothing free."

"And what is your fee?" she asked, lifting her eyebrows.

"I'll let you know when I'm done."

Jurnee pulled her feet back, grinning. "Well, if I have to pay then I might as well get my money's worth and um . . . enjoy myself." She giggled easily.

Trevon remained seated as Jurnee slowly eased to her feet. His eyes roamed over her plump ass and small waist. "Hey. What are your measurements?"

"Hold that thought, papi," she said, steadying herself on the cushioned arm of the sofa. "Relax and give me a few minutes."

"Ain't movin' from this spot."

"Who said I wanted my foot rub in here? Since I have to pay, I get to set the um—guidelines and stuff like that," she said with a sexy smirk.

Trevon nodded. "Fine by me," he said, undressing her with his eyes.

Jurnee tottered with her first step, but caught herself, giggling. "I'm okay." She motioned for Trevon to remain where he sat.

When he was alone on the sofa, he kicked his shoes off and leaned his head back, closing his eyes. His pain over LaToria was slowly drowning by spending time with Jurnee. His eyes stayed closed. There would be no more tears. Even in his current intoxicated state, he realized that Jurnee had spoken the truth about moving on through his loss of LaToria. Stress kept his eyes shut. Sleep crept up on Trevon several minutes later.

Within fifteen minutes, he snapped awake when his smartphone rung. Sitting up rubbing his face, he retrieved the ringing phone off the table between the three empty bottles. "Yeah?" he answered, without taking the time to see who was calling him.

"May I speak with Señor Trevon?" Jurnee giggled.

"Speakin'," he replied, grinning at the seductive tone of her voice.

"I'm ready for my massage, and I hope you won't keep me waiting."

Trevon could see where the night was heading. "I guess I should go and handle that, huh?"

"That would be a good idea. I'm in my bedroom waiting for you."

***

Jurnee lay on her stomach when Trevon entered the bedroom. She had taken the time to set the mood by lighting seven mango passion scented candles around the room. After a quick shower, she coated her skin with some luminous gold dust body lotion that had her glowing.

"Smells good in here," he said, closing the door.

Jurnee didn't speak until she felt him sitting on the bed. "You like what you see, papi?" she asked as "Sweet Lady" by Tyrese played softly in the room.

Trevon nodded at the sight filling his eyes. Jurnee was clad in a black honeycomb lace and fishnet teddy that exposed the bottom part of her phat bare ass. Looking at her back, he didn't see a bra strap.

"Can you start on my shoulders?" she asked, turning her head on the pillow in his direction.

"I think I can do that," he said, moving up on the bed.

Jurnee knew she was putting herself on front street by wearing the sexy short teddy without any panties. She told herself she wouldn't shelter any regrets tonight. No matter how far things went.

"Mmm, that feels soooo good," she moaned when his hands began to knead the area around her neck and shoulders.

"Been a crazy day, ain't it?" he voiced, kneading her shoulders.

"Life ain't never perfect," she said with her eyes shut.

"Shit. We both back to being single."

"I won't miss him," she said, being honest. "Nor the sex, because I was making him wait."

"For real?"

"Yeah. I guess he assumed I was easy since I'm a former porn star."

Trevon pressed his thumb along her shoulders, moving them in circles. "Um, when is the last time you had sex with a man?"

"That would be eight months ago."

"And women still do it for you?"

She shrugged. "Why do you ask?" She opened her eyes.

"Just wonderin'," he said, grinning at her.

A few moments moved between them. Jurnee spoke first.

"You ever think about that night I schooled you on the art of oral sex?"

"Puttin' me on the stage, huh? But yeah, it crossed my mind from time to time."

Jurnee smiled. "Mine too, papi, and I can still taste your cum sliding down my throat. I really, really, enjoyed sucking your big dick that night. Did it feel better when I sucked it slow or fast?"

Caught off guard by her bluntness caused him to stutter. "I-I um—guess I'll say both."

She blushed. “I wanna tell you something, papi.” Jurnee turned over to her side. “That night I was with you. I wanted to feel your dick all up in me, but your contract wouldn’t allow it.”

“You know you’re so damn sexy, right?” he said, sliding a hand up her thigh.

Jurnee sat up. “Can you take your clothes off? I want to see all of you tonight.”

“We don’t have to do—”

“Shhh . . .” She laid a finger on his lips. “It’s just the two of us tonight, and I know you want to fuck me, Trevon.” Smiling, her lips brushed against his ear. “We can do it all night long, papi. I wanted you the very first day you walked inside my office at Amatory.” She stuck her wet tongue out and licked the back of his ear. Without warning, she lowered a hand between his legs, gripping his solid erection. Keeping the mood going, she pushed him to his back, pushing her fingers under his clothes. In the scented candle lit room, their lips met in a long, slow, tongue-clashing kiss.

Trevon found the softness of her breasts within seconds of their contact. By her heavy breathing, he knew the line of friends was about to be crossed. With their hands moving quickly, Trevon was undressed piece by piece. They met in the middle of the bed.

“I want you so bad, papi!” Jurnee exclaimed, reaching for his dick. She was tired of fingering herself, or using the vibrator, or a detachable shower head to bring her pleasure. Her body wasn’t just asking for any man. It was asking for Trevon. Countless nights she had been fantasizing about feeling all of Trevon inside her. Unknown to anyone, just the sound of his voice would make her hot and want to throw the pussy on him that he would never forget. Slipping the teddy off, she was delighted to see the spark in his eyes. She licked her glossy lips and then took his dick back into her hands. She caressed him while pressing her nipples against his arm.

Trevon gasped when Jurnee lowered her beautiful face between his legs, taking his balls into her mouth. He closed his eyes, enjoying how she slurped and popped his balls in and out of her wet mouth. Her soft hands massaged the length of his dick, making his back stiffen. She took her time pleasing him with her mouth. Seeing a drop of precum at his tip, she worked her way up his shaft with her tongue. She licked him clean, moaning with the sweet taste of his precum in her mouth. She licked all over it like a lollipop. Coming up on her knees, she lowered her soft lips down the length of his stiff, hard dick. With her titties pressed against his thigh, she bobbed up and down, slurping around his meat.

Trevon ran his fingers through her hair, and then he held it up and out of her face so he could see. With his free hand he palmed, squeezed, and spanked her soft, golden ass. Gently, her soft lips rose and fell on his long, hard dick.

She continued to do her thang, waiting for him to pop his delicious whip cream inside her mouth. Up and down she deep throated his flesh while caressing his balls. For eight minutes she had him feeling like a king.

Allowing her to lead, he showed no hints of wanting to stop her when she mounted him. Squatting on her toes her titties swung in his face.

"I need this dick, papi," she moaned. Licking his neck, she raised her ass up a few inches and then reached down his body to hold his dick straight up. With nothing between them, she slid down on his throbbing hot meat, losing her breath. Her pussy was wet and surprisingly tight. Slowly, she moved herself up and down. "Fuck, this feels good, papi!" she moaned heavily. Balling up the sheets in her hands, she moved faster, her soft ass clapping against his flesh. Each time she went up, she squeezed her pussy muscles to grip his long dick.

Trevon was in a trance, watching her breasts jiggle and the erotic way she was dancing on his bare dick. He encouraged her to keep going by telling her how good the pussy was. No thoughts of LaToria filled his mind as he later pounded Jurnee from the back while pulling her hair. They had a wild marathon of fucking that lasted fifty-five minutes. Jurnee had cum twice in that time, and was gasping and out of breath when Trevon finally came deep inside her.

CHAPTER Nine

Can I Hit in the Morning?

January 22, 2012

Sunday, 12:30 PM Miami, Florida

I need your help," Tahkiyah said over the phone while closing the door behind a female hotel attendant.

"I thought our terms ended—"

"I'm not in the mood, Mr. Staton," she said, interrupting the private investigator. "Do you wish to be paid, or not?"

"What's your problem?"

Tahkiyah sat on the edge of the bed. "Why didn't you tell me that LaToria lives in a gated community?" she complained. "Quovadis Estates."

"I didn't feel it was of any relevance."

"Well, it is. How did you manage to get those pictures?"

"I got my sources. Uh, by any chance are you down in Miami?"

"Yes. I'm at the Mondrian Hotel. Now, can you help me or not? I need to get on the visitors' list somehow without LaToria knowing it."

"All right. I'll make a few calls, and I'll call you back around five or six."

"I'll be waiting," she said dryly.

Ending the call, she sat in silence for a few moments. She had to go through the plan she had set before herself. Her options were limited. Ignoring the truth was an issue she could no longer live with. Still somewhat exhausted from the road trip, she elected to take a long relaxing soak in the tub. Stripping her name brand, tailor-made clothes, she stood naked in the middle of the bathroom. Closing her eyes she licked two of her fingers and then lowered them between her legs. Her folds were warm and slightly moist. Anthony liked it when she touched herself in front of him. Doing it alone didn't bring her the same satisfaction as it did when she was being watched. She pushed two fingers between her delicate folds and then imagines she wasn't alone. "This isn't working." She said and gave up on pleasing herself. Her breasts were full, well rounded and youthful looking. She found delight in the way she still had a sex appeal that could turn Anthony on with little effort. She also craved it when he would caress or suck her nipples when he was stroking hard inside her.

She knew she didn't have a large ass. She was content with being viewed as somewhat petite. At her age, she didn't have a damn thing to cry or fuss about. Hell, she herself would proudly point out that her body could double for Gabrielle Union's and Tahkiya had no ill views of showing off her body. Even with all the pressure she was facing, she held a slim hope of visiting the beach wearing a bikini. Sex was a major element in her life. She was open-minded toward sex but was wise to play it safe.

Relaxing in the hot, scented water, she closed her eyes after placing her glasses to the side. She hoped Staton would be able to get her through the gate at LaToria's home. The trip to Miami was for a reason, a reason that Tahkiyah was steadfast on seeing through.

***

At the same time, Trevon and Jurnee were just waking up in bed together. Across the room the sun threw its beam through a slit in the curtain.

"My head killin' me," Trevon complained, rolling to his back.

"That's your fault, Mr. Drink From The Bottle," Jurnee kidded, with the sheets up to her neck. "You um, want something to eat?"

"What's on the menu?" he asked, with his voice raspy.

"Name it," she said, feeling the warmth of his body next to hers.

"Uh. How 'bout some bacon, eggs, toast, and grits."

"That's simple, papi." She turned to her side, hoping he wouldn't push her away.

"About last night," he said.

"What about it?" Jurnee moved closer, placing her hand on his six pack stomach under the sheets. "You have some regrets about what we did?"

"Nah. But I don't want you to feel that I took advantage of you."

"Please." She rolled her eyes. "I was in my sober mind when I *gave* you this pussy, and I'm in my sober mind now. What we did last night was natural, papi, and I enjoyed all of it."

Trevon slid his hand down her back until he reached her bare ass. "Okay, it's all good then."

Jurnee looked into his eyes, slowly inching her fingers down. When she discovered that he was fully erect, she smiled. "You're gonna spoil me with this." She took him inside her hand and then leaned up to cup her swollen nipple to his mouth. Closing her eyes, she tossed her head back moaning his name while his tongue circled her nipple. Under the sheets, she squeezed his dick, pressing her body closer.

"I need to be inside you!" he groaned between her soft breasts. Jurnee released his erection, and then rolled over, parting her legs. Trevon shoved the sheets back, so he could view her body. She gazed up at him, rubbing her clit with two fingers. He took her legs and placed them up on his shoulders and slid in deep and slow.

"Damn, you got some good pussy!" he moaned, taking full length thrusts inside of her warm pussy.

"Shit . . . papi. Fuck me! Go faster . . . ahhh . . . I love your big dick!" she cried underneath him. "Do it! Fuck this pussy! Aaahhh, right there!"

Up and down he fed her soaked pussy with his manhood. The bed started to squeak from their weight and movements.

"You like it like this?" he asked, grinding between her legs.

"Yesss, papi! Ahhh. This dick is so fuckin' good!" she screamed, digging her nails into the back of his arms. Closing her eyes, she entered a state of pure euphoria. Trevon pounded hard and steady at a pace that had Jurnee fighting to catch her breath. He filled her thoroughly, causing her legs to tremble with each and every stroke. The wetness between her thighs became heavy, allowing

Trevon to easily slide in and out. Churning her hips, she murmured his name continuously, matching the tempo of his thrusts.

"You love this pussy, papi!" She breathed as their bodies smacked together. Trevon changed the angle of his thrusts by leaning up and pressing her legs back near her ears. Groaning, he kept fucking her with no regrets.

"Turn over," he said minutes later.

Jurnee rolled to her knees but kept her head on the pillow.

"Mmm. This ass looks so damn good!" he said, caressing her ass.

"Gimme that big dick, papi," she purred, wriggling her hips and ass. Reaching back between her legs, she wrapped her hand around his dick and began to jack it. She felt his hands moving all over her ass, making her shudder with lust. Teasing him, she placed his tip against her syrupy pussy lips, and then moved it up and down its length. They both moaned.

"Make me cum. Please fuck me good and hard, papi." She released her grip and then pushed herself back while biting her bottom lip.

Ecstasy stung her from her nipples to the center where Trevon was splitting her. She wiggled her ass as he fucked her. "Fuck! Papi, you feel so good in me! Yes . . . gonna cum all over your big dick!"

"Shit!" He smacked her jiggling ass. "Pop that pussy fo' me!"

Trevon had a firm grip on her hips, pounding in and out of her sweet pussy. He couldn't stop if he wanted to. No regrets.

"Aww fuck, aww fuck! Aww . . . shit, it's so good, papi!" She shuddered.

"You love dis dick?" he shouted, running his length inside her.

"Fuck yes!" she moaned. "Owww . . . yes! I feel it in my stomach!"

"Mmm. You got my dick so wet!" he moaned, staring at her ass.

Jurnee squeezed the pillow, drowning in pleasure as Trevon stirred her insides. Staying face down–ass up, she took the dick happily, climaxing eight minutes later. She was speechless when he pulled out of her. No words were needed to meet his needs. Turning over, she slid off the bed, pulling him with her. She went down to her knees, wrapping both hands around his love tool. She jacked him off slowly with a twist on her upward trip. When a drop of precum formed before her lips, she flattened her tongue against it and then wrapped her wet lips around it. Her eyes stayed open while she sucked his meat.

Trevon ran his hands through her hair as her lips slid back and forth across his rod. "Shit. Suck it, baby," he groaned. "Mmmm. Work it good fo' me, baby."

Jurnee went to work, slurping and sucking on his dick until spit started coming from the corners of her lips. She loved how his large manhood stretched her jaws. "Mmm, you taste so good papi," she said, giving his balls a gentle squeeze. Showing it was true, she took him back inside her mouth, loving the taste of his precum. She sucked it hard while jacking him off. His tip popped in and out of her mouth with a loud wet snap. His head rolled when she gripped his ass and forced his rod to the back of her throat. She could feel his balls slapping her chin when she engulfed all of him.

Trevon closed his eyes, holding Jurnee's head with both hands while fucking her moist mouth. She hummed and moaned, giving him the best head in his life. Jurnee looked up at him when she felt his veins throbbing and growing thicker along the length that slid in and out of her mouth.

"Jurnee!" he moaned, curling his toes. His nut exploded in a sudden release, bursting inside Jurnee's mouth.

She took it all in, licking his dick clean after she slurped down every drop of his cream. Purring, she lifted his soft dick and suckled gently on his balls. When their eyes met, she twisted her tongue around his tip, smiling. "You ready for breakfast now, papi?" Sweat dripped down in between her titties.

Trevon nodded, and then helped her to her feet. Her body was too appealing to ignore. His hands slid down her back, coming to a stop to palm both of her succulent butt cheeks.

Trevon squeezed her ass, grinning. "You made a nigga feel real good."

"So . . ." she said, tilting her head. "I too can say the same in return because I really enjoyed having you all up in me."

"Too bad we couldn't film it," he said, rubbing her thigh.

"Them days are ova for me, papi. The only porn star under this roof is you, and I'm one lucky bitch to have this dick on tap." She smiled.

Trevon was grateful for Jurnee's company. She had forced LaToria from his mind and showed him that he still had a life to live.

Kissing her on her forehead, he left her alone, so they could take separate showers. They met in the kitchen, and Jurnee had indeed made his requested breakfast to replenish their bodies. At the table, it warmed her to see how Trevon couldn't take his eyes off her. She had her long hair piled up on her head with two stringy curls hanging on both sides of her face. Staying sexy was always an effortless task for Jurnee, who wore pink tight shorts and a matching V-neck tank top without a bra.

"So you think I rushed things with LaToria?" he asked, feeling natural to be at the table wearing nothing but his boxers. The easy flow of conversation with Jurnee seemed odd to Trevon.

"Sure. See, I think you needed to enjoy your freedom. Hell, I still do. To me, I just felt like you were moving too fast."

"What about now?" he asked as she got up from the table with the empty plate.

"It's your second shot," she replied over her shoulder. "Life is too short to stress, so fuck the bullshit and focus on today and tomorrow."

Trevon followed her to the sink with his eyes. He was thinking about how things would change between him and Jurnee after sex. So far, she wasn't acting too clingy nor speaking of any emotions that she was feeling. On his part, it was all about sex. Fucking Jurnee had been a ride that he was willing to enjoy over and over. Looking at her from behind pushed his mind back toward sex. Sliding back from the table, he crossed the black tiled floor and moved up behind her, placing his hands on her succulent hips. Closing his eyes, he kissed her lightly on the back of her neck.

"You smell so good," he said, telling her the truth.

"Thank you." She smiled with her nipples stiffening under the top.

"You got anything planned for today?"

She shook her head, pushing her ass against him. "I wanna tell you something, papi."

"What's up?" he said, sliding his hands down the front of her shorts.

"I"—she gasped—"wanted to be your first when you got out of prison. I wanted you so bad when I first saw you," she finally admitted.

"You got me now."

Jurnee leaned her head back, moaning softly as his fingers moved over her pounding clit. "Right there. Aaaahhh. Touch me, Trevon."

"Take your top off for me. Can you do that?"

"You know I will, papi. I'll do anything for you."

Trevon skated his fingers lightly across her clit, coating his fingertips with her wetness. When she removed the top, her heavy 36 DD's popped free. Sucking on the side of her neck, he continued to rub between her wet folds.

Jurnee bit her upper lip as her body responded to his touch. She could feel the hardness of his nature pressing against her ass. Knowing that he wanted her again had her floating. "Ahhh shit, papi . . . mmm that feels so good." She grabbed her titties, mashing them together and pinching her nipples.

"I can make it feel better," he said, kissing behind her ear.

"Better than this?" she breathed. "You'll have to show me."

Trevon removed his fingers from between her legs. "Turn your sexy ass around."

Jurnee obeyed, pleased with the attention he was giving her. Her titties shook when she turned to face him.

With her back against the sink, she was unable to move. Their eyes met.

"Now what?" she asked, rubbing his erection through his boxers.

Unexpectantly, he lowered his lips to hers. Jurnee squeezed his dick while kissing a man she wanted at first sight. He tongued her slowly, roaming his hands through her hair and rubbing the sides of her breasts.

"I wanna fuck you again," he moaned. "Gotdamn, that pussy is good, baby."

She nodded. "This pussy is all yours, papi."

Trevon lowered his lips to her nipples, kissing both. "Get naked and wait for me on the sofa."

"Okay, papi," she moaned. "But please don't make me wait too long."

Jurnee pranced out of the kitchen swaying her hips and ass like a model. Whatever Trevon had in store for her, she was down with it. Reaching the living room, she quickly peeled the shorts off her ass and then got comfortable on the sofa. Just as she was relaxed, Trevon came out of the kitchen butt ass naked with his imposing dick semi-hard.

"Let me suck that dick, papi," she said, reaching between his legs.

"Not yet." He grabbed her hand. "I'm runnin' shit today. Now lay back and bust that kitty open 'cause I'm still hungry." He smiled, licking his lips.

Trevon sat down on the sofa, staring between her legs. Once she was ready, he lowered her right foot to the floor and placed her left over the back of the sofa. Her pussy lips were puffy and bald. Her scent expelled a hint of cinnamon.

Jurnee's ass rose up toward his mouth when she caught on to what he was planning to do. "Mmmm . . . you gonna suck my pussy." She squirmed and moaned. He held her in place by her hips so he could feast. "Ahhh. Papi, dis your pussy now!"

Trevon went to work, sucking on her swollen clit and jabbing his lethal tongue in and out of her tight hole. Cursing loudly, she hunched her pussy with both hands on his head, smearing her juices all over his face. The sounds of his slurps were driving her wild. His tongue flicked between her slippery lips like a ribbon caught in a breeze. Trevon took his time pleasing Jurnee. Parting her lips, he forced his tongue deeper, making sure he pressed his tongue against her inner walls.

"You got some sweet ass pussy," he said between licking her wet folds all over.

Jurnee cooed his name in a slow chant as he went on tasting her. She could never tire of his sex, or just being with him. "Yesss, suck on my pussy, papi. I love this! Ooohhh gonna cum all over your sexy face!" she squealed with sweat beading up on her titties. It took twenty minutes for Jurnee to reach her climax. When she came, he made her scream in pleasure by making circular motions on her clit with his tongue.

"Shit, papi, don't ummm . . . stop," she said, damn near out of breath.

Trevon slid two fingers inside her wet hole, and then slid his tongue left and right across the clit. He could feel her muscles contracting around his fingers.

In a sexual daze, she touched his fine chiseled body as he moved on top of her, hooking her legs in his strong arms. Holding her breath, she reached down for his long dick and guided it back inside her slippery pussy, and then begged him to fuck the shit out of her.

CHAPTER Ten

Sloppy Seconds!

"You alive in there?" Trevon shouted through the closed bathroom door where Jurnee was taking a bath.

"What's up, papi? It's open," she replied, lying back in the tub.

Trevon entered the dimly lit bathroom and found Jurnee relaxing in a peach scented bubble bath. It was ten minutes past eight, and the two had spent their day fucking and enjoying each other's company. "Just wanted to let you know I'ma head out to the store right quick. You need anything?"

"Nah, I'm fine." She smiled up at him. "Your probation officer gone?"

He nodded. "Yeah, he left about five minutes ago."

"Do you still wanna go out tonight?"

"Might as well."

"Good. I have just the spot we can go to."

"Where?" he asked. "Lemme guess. Ah . . . Club Liv at the Fontainebleau?"

She grinned. "It'll be a surprise."

"Ai'ight. I'll be back, and I let Rex in. And yes, he's house-trained."

Jurnee waited until she heard Trevon driving off before she reached for her iPhone. Clearing her mind, she hoped she was doing the right thing by trying to reach Kandi. After the fourth unanswered ring, she was just about to hang up when Martellus answered.

"Hey, Jurnee."

She frowned. "I need to talk to Kandi if you don't mind."

"I hope you're not mad at me for being in love with Kandi?"

"If I wanted to talk to your ass I would have called you!" she said sternly.

"We don't have to be bitter. You should want what's best for Kandi, and it's a no-brainer that it's me. I Googled that ex-convict, Trevon, and I was alarmed by what he—"

"Who the fuck are you to judge somebody! I bet your wife isn't happy about you fucking around on her, now is she? Listen, is Kandi around or not? 'Cause listening to your dumb ass is giving me a headache!"

"Hold on," he replied through his teeth.

Jurnee only had to wait a few seconds before Kandi got on the line.

"Hey girl," Kandi said in a neutral tone.

"Are you on drugs or something? What in the hell is wrong with you!"

Kandi sighed heavily. "I'm grown, okay? And I don't need to explain nothing to you."

"It ain't about me!" Jurnee shouted. "It's about Trevon! The man you ran off on! The man whose baby you're carrying and you blocked his number so he can't call. That's who you need to explain this bullshit you're doing to! I thought I knew you as a friend, but I guess I was wrong. Okay. Tell me. Is your prince Martellus paying for your abortion too? He got your head so twisted that you're gonna kill the baby. Bitch, that's low!"

"Who—you don't know what—"

"Stop lying, Kandi! I found the damn abortion form under the sink. Now try to tell me I didn't!" Jurnee waited for Kandi to defend herself. When she stayed quiet, it only increased Jurnee's anger. "So it's true, huh? How can you do this to Trevon? Running off . . . and I–I don't understand nothing you're doing! You think Martellus is gonna be faithful to you?"

"You don't know him like I do!"

"And I'm glad I don't!" Jurnee shouted.

"Is Trevon around?"

"Why do you care? You got his number blocked, and I assume you'll do mine the same way after this call."

"Just—tell him I'm sorry and I—"

"He already knows you're sorry, and I ain't telling him nothing. You wanna talk to him, call 'im!"

"Oh. So you've been keeping him company?" Kandi asked with jealousy creeping into her voice.

"And if I have? What issue is it with you?"

"Did you fuck him in my bed? Ain't been gone two days and your grimy ass is in my house fucking my—what if this was all a test, huh? Both of y'all failed! You ain't shit, and it only proves my point to be with Martellus!"

"Nah bitch, you ain't gonna make us out to be bad people! You started this bullshit, and now you see yo' ass ain't gonna be missed. And FYI, hell yeah we fucked, and no he didn't utter yo' name when he was all up in me!"

"Fuck you, bitch!"

"Whateva, 'ho! Trevon *will* get over yo' ass, and I'ma make sure of that, personally!"

"Y'all can have each other! I don't give a fuck!"

"Good, bitch! I'ma enjoy bagging all your shit to toss in the trash 'cause we don't need no memories of yo' sleazy ass here! Trevon don't need you, and he'll be better off without you in his life—"

"And listen to you! We in the same boat, bitch. Only you had twice as many dicks up your funky ass than me! Fuck you! Fuck Trevon. And next time, get your facts straight before you toss it up in my face! Oh, have fun throwing my shit out, 'cause bitch I'm good and always will be! And always remember this! You can never be me, so settle for being second and having my leftovers!"

***

Kandi ended the call with Jurnee, and then immediately added her number to be blocked.

"Are you okay, baby?" Martellus asked, rubbing Kandi's arm. "Aren't you tired from the trip?"

"No! I'm fine. I just need to put this shit behind me." She frowned.

"Is it true what you said about Jurnee sleeping with Trevon?"

"It doesn't matter, okay!" she said, turning away from him.

"I just want you to be happy here."

"I am," she said, gazing out the bedroom window at the snow-capped mountains in the distance. Her life had changed instantly when she boarded the private jet to fly away to Denver with Martellus. He assured her that she would lack for nothing, and that she would be the only woman in his life.

"Do you need me to do anything before I go?" he asked her.

Kandi turned from the windows. "I haven't been here for a full day, and you're leaving me here!"

He grinned. "Relax, baby. I have a business meeting to attend, and you're more than welcomed to sit and wait until it's over. Or"—he reached for her hands—"you can stay here and explore your new home and kick back off your feet. I'll be back before nine."

Kandi sighed. "I'll stay here."

"Are you positive, baby?"

"Uh-huh," she replied, looking at the large bed across the room. She couldn't stop her mind from wondering if Martellus had slept with his wife on that very bed. *Of course he had,* she told herself. Sighing, she spoke her mind. "I'm not sleeping in the same bed you shared with your wife."

Martellus shrugged. "Okay, I can understand that. Uh, you can go online and pick out any new bed that you want."

"I need some clothes too," she said tersely.

"Use my credit card and get all that you need," he said, lifting her chin. "I'm going to take care of you, baby. All of your needs. I promise you." He kissed her, sliding his hands up and down her arms.

"I hope so," she said, nuzzling her lips against his neck.

"When I get back. Do you think we can find another place to do it since you'll be getting rid of the bed?" he asked, grinning.

Kandi licked his lips and then ran her nails lightly across the back of his neck. "I'll see what I can do. That big sofa downstairs looks like a good spot."

"Mmmm," he moaned, pulling her against his crotch. "That sounds perfect. And we can do it in front of the fireplace."

Kandi played the good girl, looking innocent. "Don't let your business come before me, because I'm gonna need some hot dick on this cold winter night."

Martellus roamed his hands over her voluptuous body, wishing he could take her right now on the bed. Kandi was familiar with the look in his eyes.

"What time do you have to leave?" she asked, rubbing the hard bulge between his legs.

"I can spare ten minutes. What do you have in mind?"

"I need you in my mouth, and I only need five minutes."

Martellus allowed her to unbutton his pants to free his dick. Standing in the middle of the bedroom, he was satiated with his dick easing in and out of her wet mouth. She quietly bobbed back and forth while massaging his shaft with both hands. On her knees she hummed around his flesh, doing all that she could to push Trevon from her mind. Three minutes later, he came inside her mouth and on her chin. This was Kandi's new life and her new home, one she would share with Martellus.

Later, when he left for the office, she headed down to the first floor after brushing her teeth. Martellus' home was a lavish custom built ranch with five bedrooms and four full bathrooms. Luxurious as it was, it wasn't something new to her. Trailing her fingers along the polished rail of the oak staircase, she paused halfway to fully view the elegant furnished family room with exposed wood timbers along the vaulted ceiling.

"Do you like the view?"

Kandi already knew she wasn't alone, so the sudden voice didn't catch her off guard. "It'll take some getting used to," Kandi replied, looking out the French doors that showed the expansive wooded backyard and snow-covered ground. "You must be Mrs. Biathrow. Martellus told me about you on our flight."

"Yes, I am. And is there anything you require, Ms. Frost?"

Kandi figured Mrs. Biathrow would be the one item that she would learn to live with. She had mixed emotions when Martellus first told her about his housekeeper. Kandi wasn't about to share her new home with no other bitch up her ass 24/7. She was somewhat calmed when Martellus further explained that Mrs. Biathrow's husband was his fulltime chauffeur whenever he was in Denver. He went as far as giving Kandi the right to fire the housekeeper if she wasn't comfortable with her, but first she had to agree to at least meeting Mrs. Biathrow. Kandi had assumed the housekeeper would be an attractive slut that Martellus favored. Upon meeting Mrs. Biathrow, Kandi saw the total opposite.

"You can call me Kandi," Kandi said, making a true effort to be friendly. The lady before her was dull looking with pale white skin that showed no hint of being under the sun. She was big boned with large breasts, wide hips, and a heavy ass. Kandi knew Mrs. Biathrow wasn't the owner of any two-piece swimsuits or thongs. Her dark brunette hair was pulled back in a bland looking ponytail, matching her less than average looks that would never earn a second look from a man.

In the large gourmet kitchen, Kandi elected to sit at the table with Mrs. Biathrow over a cup of hot cocoa. With a baby on the way, Kandi didn't see any wrong to have someone cater to her every need. Relaxing, she could see herself turning this house into a home.

***

Back down in Miami, Florida, Jurnee was trying hard to enjoy herself with Trevon. She was dwelling over that last harsh statement that Kandi had told her. For now she had yet to tell Trevon of the call. She wasn't too sure how he would react. Tonight she used her status to get inside the new trendy club, Taste Me, on Lincoln Road. Jurnee made heads turn by her stunning beauty and the black and gold catsuit with fishnet sides. Trevon was Gucci from head to toe in a tight-fitting shirt and a pair of loose jeans. Up in VIP they ordered a bottle of Grey Goose on the rocks.

"How'd you get us by that line?" Trevon asked Jurnee when they were seated at their private booth.

"I know the owner," she said, crossing her legs.

"Y'all go way back or something?"

"Yeah. I've known Tamika for about five years now."

"Maybe one day I'll be known like you."

"You gotta put in work, papi. Look at Mr. Marcus and how many films he made. He has his own company, and he's doing good."

"You ever did a film with him?" he asked, preparing to fix their drinks.

She frowned. "Don't tell me you haven't seen all of my films yet. And I thought you were a true fan." She pouted. "But yeah, I did a film with him when I first started out."

"You think I could reach his level?"

"Absolutely! I think you need to do a threesome with Cherokee and Pinky, because them two are really doing it right now."

"Wishful thinking, huh?" He grinned, thinking of the days he had jacked off to X-rated pictures of the two famous porn stars.

"It can happen, papi. Shit, I got both their numbers on speed dial. Just run the idea by Janelle and see what happens," she suggested.

"I'll do that," he said as three women breezed by the booth. The shortest of the three stared at Trevon but stayed silent.

"Do you know her?" Jurnee asked, after the women were gone.

"Nah. Never seen her before," he said honestly. "Maybe she's a fan."

She shrugged. "Oh yeah. I meant to ask you while you were driving. But why were you looking in the rearview mirrors so much?"

"You noticed?"

"Uh, yeah."

Trevon scratched his eyebrow. "I thought I was being followed for a minute. At first, I thought it was my probation officer, but he drives a Tahoe. I guess I was just trippin'."

Jurnee assumed it was Kandi or Martellus, since she had no idea where the two assholes were. Sure, Kandi had said she was leaving Miami, but right now Jurnee had no trust in Kandi. Biting her words, she refused to even mention Kandi's name. "Who do you think it was? And how long were we followed?"

Trevon handed Jurnee her glass. "Nah, it ain't nothing. I'm just buggin' out. Let's enjoy the moment."

"This will be my only glass for tonight," she told him. "So the rest of the bottle is all yours."

"What? You trying to get me drunk again, so you can take advantage of me when we go home?" he joked.

Jurnee laughed. "Papi, you know I don't need to do that."

"What's on your mind?" he asked after taking a long drink of the Grey Goose.

"Um . . . you ever had a threesome?"

He shook his head. "I uh, can't count what I did with you and—"

"Don't even mention her name," she interrupted. "So would you like to do a threesome?"

"Janelle has one set up in the making for me."

"I'm talking about your private life, papi. Being with two women is an art. What you did with me and you know who was just oral sex. When you have to split that dick between two women you better know what you're doing."

"And let me guess. You wanna show me how it's done?"

Smiling, she nodded yes. "I could hook it up."

"When? I mean, who would the other girl be?"

"Soon," she said, looking around the club. "You just sit back and let me handle it."

Trevon laid his hand on her leg and then whispered in her ear, "I never forgot your golden rule, so I'll remind you of it. Just go for what you know."

"That's so true, papi," She uncrossed her legs. "And I need you to keep that in mind as you move on with your life. Do what makes you happy. Enjoy your freedom most of all. And don't deal with matters of your heart too much." She pointed at his chest. "Many men would pay to be in your position, so don't blow it because someone else made a stupid mistake."

"You really care about me, huh?"

"Sure I do, papi. I'm just a real ass woman."

"And a gorgeous one too."

She blushed. "Let's do something wild tonight." Jurnee fingered her long, silky black ringlets over her left shoulder.

"What do you have in mind?"

Jurnee leaned closer, her soft moist lips sent a chill down his spine when she kissed his ear. "Let's get a room tonight, papi. I want to make your fantasy come true. Let me share you with another woman. It will make me sooo hot to see you fucking somebody else while she eats my pussy."

"With no regrets?"

"None." She licked his ear and then slid her hand down to his lap. "Mmm, I knew it would be hard," she cooed, rubbing his large erection.

"Damn, what would I do without you?"

She squeezed his erection. "Dream about me."

"You ready to go?"

Jurnee tilted her head. "We just got here," she pointed out.

"The club will be here tomorrow. All I got on my—" He paused, looking toward the exit.

"What is it?" she asked alarmed.

"Don't look, but Swagga's homeboy, D-Hot just came in through the back door."

CHAPTER Eleven

A Table for Three-Some?

Are you sure you wanna do this tonight?" Rick asked Swagga from the front passenger seat of Swagga's Bentley Brooklands.

"Yeah, bruh. I gotta get back on my grind! Fuck all these 'hos and all this bullshit. Them niggas at Cash Money and Maybach Music Group is munchin' in record sales. I 'on't give a fuck what time it is. I need to be in the studio."

Rick turned back, and then made a call to ensure the securing would be in place for Swagga's spur of the moment visit to the recording booth. The Bentley was being closely followed by two of Rick's men in a black tinted Tahoe. No chances were being taken. It was Rick's job to keep Swagga alive, and failure was not on Rick's list. Things moved fast and in accordance once Swagga reached the studio. Rick could see that Swagga was driven to be number one. It was all business tonight, not a groupie in sight. With the lights dim, Swagga went into a zone once the heavy bass filled his headphones. He bobbed his head, bouncing on his toes.

"Jeah! Uh-huh . . . Swagga in da buildin'! Jeah!" He went on hyping himself up for a freestyle flow. Nearing the microphone, he showed why he wasn't to be overlooked in the rap game.

I thank the Lord for my wrist. I just whip it and go
Cookin' crack is my hobby. I got dat straight drop dope
Sell it all by today. I'm tryna accomplish my goal.
Dat forty stuck on my waist just in case dey kick in my do'
Had a dream gettin' money, 'til I woke up an' got it
Much respect to dem junkies, dey help me double my profit
Daddy wasn't around. Momma strung out on dope
Went and copped a few yams, then I nevah seen broke
. . . I got dem racks—

Rick's focus on Swagga was broken when his cell phone rung. Pulling it from his hip, he moved quickly to the corner once the coded number for Fritz appeared on the screen.

"Is there a problem?" Rick asked, being pessimistic.

"None at all, mon," Fritz replied, using his accent. "Jus' lettin' ya know dat me caught up wit' ya issue. Me been him shadow an' him don' even know it. Tings not lookin' too heavy like ya explain. Me guessin' he not 'spectin' no trouble."

"He still in town?"

"Yeah. Clubbin' wit' a fine lady."

"Okay. Just do what you do, but don't forget how I want it done."

"I neva fahget da rules to me biz."

"Good. So is there anything else you need to tell me?"

"Naw. Just wanna give you an update."

"Okay. I'll relay the message to my boss."

"You do dat. Till next time."

Rick ended the short call with a sigh of relief. He didn't feel at ease discussing the hit over the phone, even if it was worded in code. Going back to his security post, he listened to Swagga's voice filling the studio. He figured he'd tell Swagga the news after everything was done here tonight. Rick wanted Swagga to remain focused on his music and not the bullshit concerning hiring Fritz to commit murder. Playing it safe, Rick pulled his cell phone from his hip again to delete Fritz's call.

***

Back at Club Taste Me, Trevon and Jurnee had managed to slip out of VIP without being spotted by D-Hot. Down on the dance floor, Jurnee had to pull Trevon along with her. Moving to the center of the crowded floor, she began to dance with him, using his body like a pole. Trevon enjoyed having Jurnee in his arms, and her moves defied her age of forty-one. With her arms around his neck and his hands glued to her hips, she danced like a stripper to Rihanna's "What's My Name?" Closing his eyes, he enjoyed the moment and his freedom. After staying on the dance floor through five songs, Jurnee motioned Trevon to lower his ear to her lips. "Hey," she shouted over a new hit by 2 Chainz. "Meet me over by the ice sculpture in thirty minutes. I see an old friend at the bar."

Trevon looked up over the crowd toward the S-shaped bar. A bounty of beautiful women were standing and sitting along the green LED lit bar. "Which one is she?"

"Stop being so nosey." She grinned. "Ain't forgot about our ménage, so let me do my thang, papi." Before he could reply, she rose up on her toes to tongue him down. When they parted ways, Jurnee danced her way off the dance floor headed straight for the bar. She prided herself on her unique talent of being able to point out a bisexual woman at first glance. There were certain traits that couldn't be hidden nor overlooked by Jurnee's proven eye. In truth, she had told Trevon a small white lie. She knew none of the lovely women lined up along the bar. Jurnee was hunting, stalking for someone special that would cater to her needs tonight. Three times she was stopped by men seeking her attention. She turned all of them down. The women in her view came in so many assorted sizes and colors. It was at the end of the bar near the waterfall when her intuition went off. Smiling, she sauntered up to the cute Tamar Braxton look-alike with a friendly, confident smile. "Care for some company?" Jurnee asked over the loud music.

The woman gasped when she got a clear look at Jurnee. Her reaction caught Jurnee off guard to say the least. "OMG!" The woman stood, staring at Jurnee with both hands up to her mouth.

Jurnee frowned. "Ummm . . . are you okay?"

The woman blushed. "Yeah! I know who you are, and if I'm wrong . . . But you're that porn star. Honey Drop, right?"

Jurnee couldn't recall the last time she was noticed in public by a female fan. "Yes, I'm Honey Drop and—"

"OMG! I can't believe this! I have *all* of your films and I'm like—your biggest, biggest fan! And to finally meet you in person! Gosh, you're so beautiful too!"

"So I guess I can buy you a drink?"

"Not in a million years! But I'll buy you one."

Jurnee's plan would now have to be played by the moment. Sitting at the bar, she ordered a glass of vodka and cranberry juice. Before the drink arrived, she learned her new friend was only twenty-five and her name was Ariana. Around them, the club was rocking to Flo Rida's "Wild Ones".

"So you're a fan of porn?" Jurnee asked Ariana in her effort to break the walls between them.

"I love it!" Ariana confessed. "I bet it's so wild to have sex with so many good looking men! And to be honest, I enjoyed those few girl on girl films you did a few years back."

"Really?" Jurnee smiled. "It's nice to meet a true fan, and being that you're a female is . . . special."

Ariana was beyond star-struck. "Can I get a picture with you? I'd like to post it on my social sites."

"I don't think it would be a problem," Jurnee said, leaning close against Ariana's ear.

"And could I pretty please get your autograph too?"

Jurnee nodded, showing no ego over her fame. "Relax, okay. Whatever I can do to make you happy tonight. Consider it done."

Ariana took a sip of her fruity cocktail in an effort to calm her excitement.

"You're a very beautiful woman," Jurnee said, facing Ariana. "Have you ever thought about doing porn? You know I know the right people." She winked.

Jurnee was being completely honest with her view. Ariana was on the slender side, but her small frame was curvy and nearly matched the looks of Kelly Rowland.

Ariana blushed. "It's my fantasy," she admitted. "But it's something I could never ever do."

"Why not? Is there a boyfriend at home?"

Ariana sighed. "No, I'm single right now. But the real reason is because doing porn wouldn't mix too well with my career goals. I'm studying for my DVM–Doctor of Veterinary Medicine."

"So you're intelligent and sexy."

"Thank you," Ariana said, being modest. "Um, are you really done with porn? Like, I really, really enjoy watching you."

Jurnee shrugged. "Those days are over for me, sweetie."

"Do you come here often?" Ariana asked politely.

"Not much. How about you?"

"Oh, about once a month."

"Just to unwind, huh?"

Ariana nodded. "A girl still has her needs if you know what I mean."

Jurnee took a sip of her drink and then crossed her thick legs. Just as she hoped, Ariana lowered her eyes to view her shapely legs. "Did you see the film I made titled, *Honey Drop for Two*?"

Ariana blinked. "It's one of my favorites! You and that other girl wore that one brother out!"

"Have you ever done a threesome before?"

"I did it in my dreams," Ariana said, fanning herself. "Like I mentioned, I live out my wildness by watching porn and doing my solo thang with my toys."

"Ain't no wrong in that, baby."

Ariana smiled. "Do you enjoy being with girls off the camera?"

"Yes, I'm bisexual, Ariana, and it's a part of my life that I don't hide. Does that answer your question?"

"Yes, it does."

"Have you been with a woman before?"

Ariana blushed again. "Why ask a question when you already know the answer?"

"It's not good to assume things."

"So is it true?"

"What?"

Ariana touched the back of Jurnee's hand. "That you really taste like honey when you climax?"

Jurnee eyed Ariana up and down with lust in her eyes. "Would you like to find out for yourself?"

Ariana suddenly felt lightheaded. Calming herself, she nodded yes. "I would love to have sex with you."

"How about I make tonight really special for you?"

"You're already doing that."

Jurnee looked at the revealing dress Ariana had on. With its deep, plunging neckline, she was able to see the sides of Ariana's small, but perky breasts. "I can make your fantasy come true."

Ariana waited a few seconds before she spoke. "I just need to have some fun with no strings attached. If you can help me with that, I'm down."

"Okay, before we leave, I'd like you to meet someone. That's if you don't already know him."

***

Trevon couldn't believe how his night was turning out. He had left the club twenty minutes ago, and was now following Jurnee and her new sexy friend, Ariana. When Jurnee arrived at the ice sculpture with Ariana in tow, he was speechless. The three got quickly acquainted, and Trevon was all smiles when Ariana proved she was a true fan of his debut film. They all knew the lust was heavy tonight, and each was willing to act on it. Trevon slowed his XJL when the brake lights lit up on Ariana's burgundy

2006 Escalade ahead. He was filled with wild sexual ideas in his head as he turned into the parking area at the Betsy Hotel. Jurnee and Ariana went up to the room alone, leaving Trevon down in the cozy lobby. Jurnee assured him that his wait wouldn't be long. She also explained how she wanted Ariana to be fully relaxed and ready before the threesome started. Trevon didn't mind the wait. He just hoped he would be able to please both women to their fullest content, while doing all he could to crush any and all thoughts of LaToria. Thirty minutes later, he received a text message from Jurnee.

Cum on up papi. We R ready 4 U

***

Trevon later entered room 37 at twenty minutes past midnight. He was greeted by darkness and the smell of perfume. Closing the door, it took a few seconds for his eyes to adjust to the dim lighting. Moving along a black leather sofa, he came to a halt when he spotted Jurnee's catsuit tossed on the arm. He picked it up, knowing how pleased Ariana must be feeling to have unwrapped Jurnee of her clothes. Down by his green gator shoes, he saw a pair of blue panties. He tried to picture the erotic image of the women kissing and touching each other as they removed their clothes. He was about to turn on the lights when he heard a faint moan coming from the back of the large suite. Dropping Jurnee's catsuit, he figured it was time to make his fantasy a reality. Rounding a section of the wall, he found Jurnee and Ariana on top of the rumpled sheets in bed. To his left he saw the shades were drawn back on the floor-to-ceiling glass doors that led to the balcony. The full moon threw erotic shadows created by Jurnee and Ariana against the wall.

Trevon moved closer to the bed as Jurnee slurped loudly between Ariana's slender, long legs.

"Mmm . . . right there! Right there!" Ariana cried while she tweaked her thimble-shaped nutmeg colored nipples.

Jurnee shook her head and lips against Ariana's wet pussy with her bare ass up in the air. She lapped her tongue between Ariana's thin pussy lips, relishing the new taste that filled her mouth.

Trevon removed his clothes as Jurnee continued to attack Ariana with her skilled, wet tongue. Once he was naked, he made his presence known by sliding his hand up between Jurnee's soft ass cheeks. She responded by wiggling and pushing her ass in his direction. Standing above the two women, he was unable to remove his eyes off them. Instinctively, he kept sliding his fingers up and down the length of Jurnee's ass. She began to buck wildly each time he pressed a finger against her asshole. His dick grew solid and throbbed with each beat of his heart.

"Do it!" Jurnee blurted, lifting her face from Ariana's triangle of dark wet curls. The look she gave Trevon, was clearly wantonness. Using his middle finger, he inserted his digit slowly inside her warm and wet ass. Her new moans were muffled between Ariana's sopping wet pussy.

Ariana couldn't believe what was happening to her. Jurnee's tongue was making her body twist and turn on the soft sheets. When she realized that Trevon had joined them, she fearlessly reached between his legs, wrapping her fingers around his long, swollen dick. Squirming from Jurnee's soft tongue, she managed to split her focus from Jurnee to jack Trevon off. His dick felt so large in her small grip. Up and down she caressed his flesh as her mind and body debated if she could take all of him inside her.

A break came only when Jurnee told Trevon to turn the lights on. It was then that Trevon was able to fully recognize how sexy Ariana was. With Jurnee taking charge, she invited Ariana to join her at Trevon's feet. Together they licked and nibbled a path up his legs, starting from his ankles. They met at the solid length of his dick. Jurnee started the honors by flicking her tongue lightly across his precum coated tip. Keeping her eyes open, she eased the helmet tip inside her mouth.

Ariana caressed Jurnee's cotton-like ass with her mouth watering and waiting for her turn at sucking Trevon's beautiful dick. Tonight she would do it all. Tonight she would be a porn star, and like she promised Jurnee before texting Trevon, she would hold no regrets.

Jurnee shared Trevon like it was natural. Pulling her lips away from his scrumptious dick, she kissed Ariana and then coached her how to take Trevon deep within her mouth. The minutes turned as they took turns sucking him. Trevon withheld his first climax by pushing Ariana's sucking mouth from his dick. He wanted to be inside both women before the night came to an end. Even in the height of carnal lust, Jurnee had the safe mindset to drop a thin ribbed condom in Trevon's hand.

Once he was ready, Jurnee told him to start with Ariana. At 5-feet 4-inches and 120 pounds, Ariana was dwarfed by Trevon's imposing 6-foot 4-inches, 245 pound muscular frame. Wide-eyed, she stared at his dick as he parted her legs. Jurnee tried to relax her by telling her that Trevon wouldn't hurt her. Closing her eyes, Ariana gasped when the blunt head of his dick pushed through her outer pussy lips. Trevon stayed braced up on his huge hands looking down at his dick easing inside Ariana.

"Take that dick!" Jurnee moaned, rubbing her titties.

Trevon moved easy and with patience. Minutes later, his slow incessant strokes had Ariana whimpering and withering in pleasure beneath him. Her heels bounced on his ass as he soon found a gentle pace. Screaming loudly, she urged him to fuck her harder.

Trevon, at one point had Ariana hopping up and down on his dick while Jurnee sat on his face. On the floor he pounded Ariana doggy-style for fifteen straight minutes while she ate Jurnee's pussy. Their chorus of moans was a new melody to Jurnee's ears. Watching Trevon filling Ariana with his manhood was such a delicious sight, one that left her breathlessly wanting him even more.

CHAPTER Twelve

She Came Back

January 23, 2012

Monday, 10:30 AM – Coconut Grove, Florida

For the first time since Friday, Trevon could consider himself as being alone. After waking up three hours earlier entwined with Jurnee and Ariana's soft, nude flesh, he began his week with more sex. Showing an insatiable sexual craving, the two women shared Trevon for an early morning workout. He catered to their needs by fucking them doggy-style, side-by-side as they knelt on the sofa. He started out with Jurnee, poking her fifty times before pulling out to slide up in Ariana's small-hipped frame. He lasted for twenty minutes, swapping between the two women several times before he came. Jurnee had sensed his climax and slid off the sofa to remove the condom. It was an act of Ariana's porn star fantasy as she helped Jurnee suck Trevon off. She slobbered all over his dick and balls until he nutted on her face, chin, and pointy titties.

Trevon was outside in the backyard under the cloudless blue sky lifting iron. His nude torso was covered in sweat due to the sweltering heat, and for that reason he stayed hydrated with water. He stood by the pool in a pair of white Nike shorts curling 80-pound dumbbells on each arm. Jay-Z and Kanye West's "Niggas in Paris" blared from the house on repeat as his source for motivation and to stay hype. After completing his last set of alternating dumbbell curls, he moved over to the bench where a 435-pound barbell awaited him. His pure strength was shown when he easily lifted the weight, and then lowered it an inch from his sweating pecs. He went hard, fueled by the performance enhancer pills. To stay fit, he knew he had to eat right. His breakfast had consisted of six eggs, two cups of oatmeal and two fresh oranges. Yeah, he loved that bacon, but he didn't eat it daily. Along with the enhancer pills, he also had two apples and two scoops of whey protein for his pre-workout meal.

Resting on the padded bench after his fifth set of benching, he fed his thirst with a cold bottle of Gatorade. Glancing at his watch, he wondered when Jurnee and Ariana would finish up their one on one at the hotel. He saw the strong new attraction Jurnee was building toward Ariana when she told him she would catch a ride home with her new *friend.*

Trevon was about to lay back and do two more sets when Rex suddenly lifted his large head. He growled, and then sprung to his paws, bolting toward the house barking. Just as he darted through the glass backdoor and into the living room, the doorbell chimed. Trevon knew it wasn't Jurnee since she now had the code and a key. Since he wasn't expecting anyone, he allowed Rex to make his fearsome presence known. Grabbing a towel off the back of the pool chair, he draped it around his sweaty neck, and then stopped inside as the cool air filled the living room. Rex continued barking and growling at the door. Approaching the front door, he called Rex off with a firm command. Rex looked back over his shoulder, but kept on barking. Trevon shook his head as he moved Rex aside with his leg.

“Move boy! And stop that damn barking.” Trevon wiped the sheen of sweat off his face. Then he closed his right eye, placing the left against the peephole. As soon as he realized who was standing outside, he became frozen. *I gotta be trippin’!* he thought, taking another look. Nope, what he saw was real.

***

Kendra was walking back to the curb when she heard the door open behind her. Turning, she felt something strange when she viewed Trevon. With his muscles rippling and the sweat coating his chocolate skin, she was unable to suppress her sexual thoughts. She had some comfort in the dark shades hiding her eyes that roamed yearningly over his upper body. She met him halfway in the driveway beside his shiny XJL.

“Hey stranger,” she said with her hands in the back pockets of her jeans.

“Just another day,” he replied, knowing there was an issue between them since she had gotten back with Swagga. With Swagga briefly crossing his mind, he looked over her shoulder at the silver Bentley GT. Seeing she was alone, he relaxed a bit, tripping off how much she still favored Jill Scott.

“Bet you’re wondering why I’m here?”

“Sumthin’ like that,” he said, remembering how soft her breasts were.

“I um, thought I should give you a heads up on something.”

"And that being?"

Kendra lifted the large shades off her eyes. "I'll be going back to work next week, and if you want me to, I can work some things out and get you back on my case load."

Trevon lifted his eyebrows. "Uh . . . that might not be a good idea since you are back with—"

"I'm not with Swagga no more," she told him. "I'm done with him and his games, and he cheated on me for the last time."

He shook his head. "Well, only on the strength of your little girl not having a dad around. I'm sorry to hear that."

Kendra smiled for the first time in two days. "That's a very considerate thing for you to say, Trevon. And if it's true, I'm sorry to hear about your breakup with Kandi."

"Damn. Where you hear that at?" he asked, wondering how the fact had gotten out.

"It's all on the porn news sites. What? It's not true?"

"Yeah, it's true. But hell—the shit just happened back on Friday."

Kendra lowered the shades back over her eyes. "They said it came from an unknown source that said they saw Kandi at a hotel with some other dude."

"Fuck it!" He shrugged. "It is what it is."

"Are you gonna be okay? I mean, you won't have to move out again. Will you?" she said, showing that she was somewhat concerned.

"I doubt it. But I'll know for sure when I go to see my boss later on."

"You still doing porn?" she asked, watching a bead of sweat trickle down the left side of his chest. She would give up every dime in her pocket to capture that one drop with the tip of her tongue. In truth she could see herself licking his entire chest and just letting herself go. Caught in a daze, she blinked out of the trance.

"You ai'ight?" he asked when she started biting her bottom lip.

Kendra smiled. "I'm okay. I was just thinking about something, and my mind got carried away. So are you still doing porn?" she asked again.

"Yeah. I just gotta get back focused now."

"That shouldn't be too hard."

Trevon wiped his face again. He noticed sweat forming on Kendra's nose. After running a thought through his mind, he went ahead and invited her inside.

"I'm on a tight schedule as it is. But if you can make some time for a big girl, I might take you up on that offer on a later date."

He grinned. "You ain't no big girl, so kill that."

"This ain't small, baby." She laughed, doing a pose for him. "But seriously, do you wanna go back on my case load or not?"

He crossed his large arms. "It depends. Will you be the mean ass PO that was trying to send my black ass back to prison? Or will you be my little secret again?"

Kendra couldn't resist the urge to touch him. She slid her fingertips down his left sweaty shoulder. "I'll gladly be your secret again."

Trevon recalled the times he had sex with Kendra. Remembering that night he fucked her raw in her bed, a sense of worry filled him. He wondered if and when she had fucked Swagga raw, and if she knew about Swagga and Chyna. Keeping that filling his mind, he promised himself that he would sit down and talk to Kendra before any sex popped off.

Before she left, she gave him her new cell number and e-mail address. Back inside the home, Trevon no longer had the drive to work out. After feeding Rex, he went to take a shower. It was hard for him to ignore LaToria's pink terry cloth bath towel hanging on the wall. It forced a vivid memory inside his head. The last time he saw that towel wrapped around LaToria was five days ago. Being in one of his freaky moods, he had removed the towel from her luscious frame after her nightly bubble bath. Placing her on all fours, he tongued her ass out while rubbing her clit until she shuddered to a climax. When he opened his eyes in the shower, he knew it wouldn't be easy getting over LaToria. Cursing his thoughts of her, he finished showering, and it wasn't until he was done that he noticed he was wearing a pair of shower shoes. Angered at still doing little things that stayed with him from prison, he tossed the shower shoes in the trash, hoping above all that his nightmares of returning, or being in prison wouldn't return come time for his rest.

***

Jurnee waited until she was relaxing in the tub before she called Trevon.

"Hey sexy. What's up?"

"You, papi." She smiled. "I'm back home. Just got here about twenty minutes ago. Where you at?"

"At the office waiting for the boss lady to call me up. I see you and Ariana finally let go of each other."

"She's something special. We're planning to go out this weekend. Oh, she told me to tell you hey and that she had a ball last night. And this morning."

"Yeah, it was wild."

"Mmm, did you enjoy it?"

"That's a crazy question, Jurnee."

"No it's not." She giggled. "But I'll say this, papi. You did your thing with us, and you're going to be even better when you do it for your film."

"Couldn't've done it without your sexy ass."

"I just want you to be happy and on top of your hustle, papi."

"Shit, maybe you should be my manager or something."

Jurnee laid her phone on the edge of the tub and then turned on the speaker phone. "You serious about that?" she asked, hoping he was.

"Yeah, why not? You know a lot more about this biz than me, and plus I know you'll push me to be the best."

"Run it by Janelle, and yes she knows I'm here. I talked to her this morning."

"You ah . . . tell her about the shit between me and LaToria?"

"She already knew."

"Lemme guess. She heard it on the web."

"Mm-hmm, how'd you know?"

He sighed. "I'll tell you 'bout it when I get home. But what did she say?"

"Nothing much. Just said she wanted to hear your side. I told her how it went down and all, and Janelle knows I'ma give it to her raw, and I did. I told her that Kandi is on some dumb shit, and that you shouldn't have to move."

"What she say?"

"She said I was right."

"You uhhh, tell 'er 'bout us having sex?"

Jurnee smiled, rolling her eyes. "Papi, Janelle ain't stupid or slow. She asked me if we did it, and I told her the truth. We ain't got shit to hide from nobody. And we didn't have sex yet. All we've been doing is fucking," she said, grinning.

"Did she trip?"

"Nope."

"You wild, yo."

"Hmph. You ain't seen wild yet, papi," she purred.

"What's the noise in the background?"

"I got the vent on in the bathroom. Don't want the place smelling like weed."

"You smoke!"

"Sure do. But I'm not a pot head."

"What else don't I know about you?"

"A lot."

"Well, we need to change that, don't we?"

"Sounds like a good move, papi."

"Ai'ight. Do this . . . let's go out to eat tonight. No sex. I just wanna get to know you as a person. I can't let you be my manager and all I know about you is your body measurements."

"You gotta point there."

Hey look. Umm, you still want me to run the threesome idea with Pinky and Cherokee by Janelle?"

"Yes! Don't forget that. Oh and here's another good power move for your career. I think you should do a film with someone that's a vet. I'm thinking like ummm . . . Janet Jacme, Cassidy Clay or Sinnamon Love."

"Or Heather Hunter?"

"That's if Janelle can convince her to come out of retirement."

"I'll see what she says."

"Listen, papi, about last night. When I gave you that condom, it was mainly because of Ariana. I know you're gonna be doing your thang, but you need to be safe. Now, I know how we've been doing it—but it's different."

"How?"

"Well, for one, you're the only man I'm fucking. But that don't mean you gotta commit to me. If and when you meet a girl you wanna fuck, do you. But save some of that raw dick exclusively for me."

"And why am I so lucky?"

"I'm feeling you, Trevon. Really, papi, I wanna see you on top. Fuck the past. Stay focused on getting paid, and you better be saving your money for your future. I know you look young, but you can't see yourself doing porn for thirty more years, so move wisely."

"And you're gonna help me?"

"I give you my word, papi. Take my advice. Live now. Love can come later."

"Was that your plan?"

Jurnee leaned her head back, closing her eyes. "I don't believe in love no more. All I do now is care about those that mean something to me."

"You shouldn't be that way."

"Too much heartbreak has made me this way."

"Well, I ain't trying to 'cause you no more pain."

"I know." She smiled. "Right now you're my sunshine."

"Good, let's keep it that way."

Jurnee sat up and reached for a rag. "Um, like I said. I'm all for the date tonight. But the 'no sex'. I might have an issue with that. I know I won't be forced to use my hands, will I?"

"Damn. You tryin' to wear a nigga out." He laughed. "But yo, you know I'ma take care of your needs."

"Now you're talking."

"Ai'ight. How wild you wanna get tonight?"

"Remember how you fingered my ass last night? Well, tonight I wanna feel your tongue back there."

"That's all?"

"There's more. I want you to fuck me in my ass tonight, and I don't want you to stop until you cum inside me."

"You won't have to ask me twice."

"Is your dick hard?"

"You know it is."

"Well, I can't—" She was suddenly interrupted by the doorbell. "Hold on, somebody at the front door."

"I heard."

Jurnee quickly got out of the tub. "Let me go peek out the window right quick," she said, leaving the phone behind. When she reached the curtains, she inched them apart, frowning at the sight of the dark silver BMW 640i parked behind her SLS.

CHAPTER Thirteen

Back to the Old Me

Trevon had to end his call with Jurnee before she was able to tell him who was at the front door. He was now making his way up to Janelle's office after getting a signal from the third floor receptionist. When he stepped inside the elevator, he nodded at a thick Black female with blonde hair. She had on a pair of yellow peep-toe heels and a form-fitting white sundress. Her large breasts were stretching the thin fabric of the dress, showing off her gumdrop nipple prints.

"The man of the hour," she said a second after the elevator doors slid shut. "Trevon. . . . Mmm, I finally get to see you in person." She extended her hand. "My name is Brooke Vee." She smiled. "Ms. Babin gave me the name since I favor Brooke Valentine. I'm a new fan. I saw that film you did with my girl Kandi."

Trevon still had a way to go before he was used to his new fame. "Thanks, I'm glad you liked it."

She played with the tips of her hair extensions. "It's fucked up how Kandi peeled out on you."

Trevon sighed. “She’s old news.”

“Shit happens,” she said, checking out how he was dressed. She was giving him points on his grown man attire. Trevon was sporting all white Gucci linen slacks and a button-down shirt with a pair of gators.

Trevon couldn’t help but stare at her cleavage. “You do porn?” he asked when he noticed she wore a similar rose gold necklace like his own. It also held a rose gold diamond encrusted AEF medallion.

“Yeah. But I’m just coming back from having a baby.”

“Boy or girl?”

“Girl.”

“So you’re new here or what?”

“Nah. I got a year and a half in the biz.”

“You like it?”

She nodded. “Wouldn’t trade it for nothing. I don’t lack for nothing and neither will my baby.”

“How many films have you made?”

“Nine.”

“Guess I need to check ’em out and support you.”

“That’s what’s up.”

“Who knows . . . maybe we’ll do a film together.”

Brooke Vee started grinning. “My contract is already filled, honey. But since Kandi done bumped her head I ain’t got no problem seeing you outside of this office.”

“You got a man?”

“No, I’m single. My baby’s daddy is in the NFL and married. I’m okay with it because I knew the deal before I got pregnant.” She shrugged.

“Ai’ight. I guess we can exchange numbers if you want to.”

“That’s what’s up for real.”

The two exchanged numbers just as the elevator slowed to a stop.

"I'll get up with you," he said before he made his exit.

"Make sure you do that because if you don't, I will." She winked as the doors slid shut.

Trevon wondered if his life would be better off without Kandi? Maybe Jurnee was right about saying he needed to enjoy his freedom.

"Hey, Ruby. What's up, baby?" he said, playfully flirting with Janelle's personal receptionist.

"You, with you handsome self," she replied, grinning ear to ear.

"The boss lady ready for me?"

"Yes. And I'm sorry to hear about you and Kandi."

Trevon forced himself to smile. "I'm good. If it was meant to be. Well, you know the saying."

Ruby nodded, pushing her glasses up her nose. Trevon didn't waste his time asking how she knew about his personal life. He was learning firsthand about the power of Twitter and Facebook when it came to speaking to the public about other folks' business.

As always, even though Janelle was expecting him, he paused to knock on the door.

"It's open, Trevon."

Entering her office, he was instantly drawn to her stunning looks. If Keri Hilson had a clone, it would be Janelle. Today she wore a green mesh blouse with an elegant pearl necklace. Her long natural hair was set in a spiral of large bouncy curls that framed her round face. Smiling, she motioned him to sit. "You're looking better than the news that comes before you."

"Talkin' 'bout my issue with LaToria?"

Janelle nodded. "I talked to Jurnee, and as shocking as it may be. It's life, Trevon."

"I'm learning that."

Janelle drummed her glossy fingernails on the desk. "Mentally, are you okay? Do you need to take some time off?"

"That's the last thing I need," he said, sliding to the edge of the chair. "I want to move forward. Yeah, I'm hurt over losing LaToria, but I ain't gonna let it drag me down. Ai'ight, you signed me because you really believe I can be a star, right?"

She nodded.

"Well, I think I need to do more than five more films. I want this to be my life. I want to be the best! And Jurnee can be my manager."

Janelle could hear the new determination in his voice. If his mind was set on his career and not love, then it was a change she would welcome. Her opinion of him and Jurnee fucking wasn't a big surprise. She had known the urge was on Jurnee's shoulders when she told her about the oral threesome. Janelle also knew how Jurnee could draw the line between business and pleasure. Making up her mind, she leaned forward, making direct eye contact with Trevon. "If you're ready to make a career of doing porn I'll back you one hundred percent."

Trevon thought about his future. He wanted his own shit, his own money, plus the freedom to do what pleased him. Things that he wanted most—true love and a family—he would have to store it away. Besides, didn't LaToria just prove that love was just a mere word? Moving off the hurt he still felt toward his loss, he told Janelle he was ready to be a star. Keeping Jurnee's suggestion of a future threesome film in mind, he also shared her ideas with Janelle. She said she would give the idea some thought. Several minutes later, Ruby interrupted the meeting causing Janelle to instantly frown.

"Ms. Babin, please forgive me. But there's an issue going on down in the lobby on the first floor!" Ruby's voice emitted from the intercom by Janelle's wrist.

"What type of issue? Isn't security on post?"

"Yes. But I feel you need to be made aware of who it is."

Janelle waited for Ruby to continue. "Who is it?"

"It's the CEO of Bigg Dog Records, D-Hot. He's down there with his crew trying to force his way up. I heard he's looking for Brooke Vee. It don't look good. Our security is really outnumbered."

"I don't need this shit!" Janelle muttered. "Listen, call the police and get Brooke Vee in my office ASAP!"

"I'm on it."

Janelle rubbed her temple as Trevon stood. "Where are you going?"

"Down to the first floor. Sounds like your boys need some help."

"Trevon, no—"

"Chill," he said, moving for the door. "Let me handle this."

Janelle did something she rarely did. She stayed quiet, going against her better judgment.

***

"Just tell that 'ho to bring me my fucking chain!" D-Hot shouted in the lobby with his ten man crew backing him up. He stood chest to chest with three AEF security guards that were trying to end the tension peacefully.

"Sir," the middle guard said, holding his palms up as he spoke. "Please lower your voice and explain what—"

"The bitch stole—I mean, she stole my muthafucking chain!" D-Hot shouted even louder. "Now, somebody gonna bring that bitch down with my chain, or I'ma go up and find 'er my damn self!"

"How and when was it stolen, sir?" the guard asked.

D-Hot balled up his fist. "Muthafucka, I ain't come here to file no gotdamn report! I came here to get my shit! I know that stealin' ass bitch is here because her ride is out back! Right now, I ain't the one to be foolin' wit'!" D-Hot grilled the evenly height white security guard. "Oh yeah." He sneered. "My crew got guns too, and I know you ain't trying to go there. Last chance. Get that bitch down—"

All heads turned to the elevator when it pinged. D-Hot started to rush ahead, but he paused when Trevon stepped out.

D-Hot remembered Trevon easily. "Where Brooke Vee!" D-Hot bassed.

"She around," Trevon said, walking up to D-Hot and his crew.

D-Hot shook his head. "Oh, you must be fucking that 'ho since you coming down here on some captain save-a-ho shit!"

"Nah, I'm just trying to see what's up. This is a place of business." Trevon crossed his large arms, staring at D-Hot's chubby face.

"Nigga, that He-Man shit don't hold no weight wit' me!"

"It must do somethin' for you to notice."

D-Hot glanced back at his crew. "Y'all see this nigga here?" He turned back to Trevon and then lowered his voice, so only Trevon could hear him. "Nigga, I ain't come here to play no games. Yeah, I heard 'bout cha. But know this. I ain't that lame ass nigga Swagga or his goofball Yaffa that you laid down. Now, that bitch gonna bring her ass down here, or there gone be some major problems."

"Bruh, I couldn't understand you 'cause I'm used to only females whispering in my ear."

D-Hot's nostrils flared. "Oh, you one of them smart mouth niggas!"

"Just trying to settle this shit, bruh," Trevon said, chancing that D-Hot was bluffing. A man of his status wouldn't risk the chance of a bullshit charge over a chain. Trevon stood his ground with the three security guards confronting D-Hot. Trevon was fully aware of the egos that had to keep their rank. D-Hot had to be the man. Trevon could feel it. He came down on the strength of Janelle, not Brooke Vee. Tension bounced back and forth, filling the lobby with the stench of bad vibes. Trevon uncrossed his arms. He would never underestimate the next man when it came to beef. Trevon remained unflappable as he stood showing no fear, keeping his temper in check.

"Yeah." D-Hot sneered, again grilling Trevon. "This a place of biz, my nig. But we both know that 'ho can't hide fo'ever. Now, since you wanna jump in this shit. Don't holler when it starts to stink."

Trevon was done exchanging mere words. His entire body was ready to spring at the slightest provocation from D-Hot. One of the guards on Trevon's left laid a hand on his shoulder, giving him a concerned look.

D-Hot saw the exchange. "Yeah, you don't want no problems, son." D-Hot eyed Trevon up and down. "But be sure to tell that bitch that I'll catch her around. And you can keep that in mind too, playboy." D-Hot sucked his teeth, backing away from Trevon and the three guards. When he was sure he had Trevon's attention, he lifted the hem of his large multi-colored Versace shirt revealing the butt of a gun.

***

Trevon later sat alone in Janelle's office while she was down on the first floor talking with the police. D-Hot and his team sped off a mere two minutes prior to the cops' arrival in a caravan of three Toyota Land Cruisers. Janelle didn't want Trevon to even be questioned by the police. On her call, she also made it clear to the guards that they weren't to mention anything about D-Hot having a gun. She didn't want any bad publicity raining on her company. Trevon was slumped deep into the chair staring aimlessly at the olive green wall. D-Hot had him unstable by flashing his heat in his face. He could feel his mind-set edging back toward his *I-don't-give-a-fuck* mode. Day by day, he was quickly learning the ropes of how unpredictable life could be. Things were faster, and the risk ran deeper than his time spent in prison. The taste of being helpless was sour over him. D-Hot could have taken things to a level that Trevon very well knew he wasn't prepared to handle.

"Never again," he whispered with conviction. Sighing, he rose and went to take a seat on the sofa to his left. He was preparing to make a call to Jurnee when Janelle pushed the door open.

"I can't believe D-Hot did this shit today!" She stood with her hands on her hips. "I knew I shouldn't have allowed . . . I mean . . . fuck!" She stomped.

"Now it's my turn to tell you to sit down and relax," Trevon told her.

Janelle sat down on the edge of her desk crossing her arms. “That was crazy what you did down there.”

He shrugged his big shoulders.

“From what I was told, you had a lot to say to D-Hot.”

“I was just trying to make things calm,” he said with a deadpan expression.

She cleared her throat. “Next time, let’s let the security do their job.”

“I feel you.”

Janelle slid off the desk and then sat down beside Trevon, turning slightly to face him. “Don’t get yourself caught up in no bullshit, Trevon. I can only imagine how you’re keeping it all together up here.” She tapped her head. “But you gotta do what’s right for Trevon from here on out. Now, about you and Kandi . . . I’ll leave that alone. Because from what Jurnee told me, I’m just at a loss of words on that. But anyway, you came here to speak on your future with Amatory, and like I said before, I’ll back you. Now as for Jurnee being your manager, that’s an excellent idea.”

“Ai’ight.” He nodded.

“So you’re really serious about this, huh?”

“My choices are limited right now.”

“Well, the ones you have in front of you are good ones. Trust me.” She smiled. “Everything will work out for you.”

Trevon had mad love for Janelle. She was one of the rare females he could count on without the topic of sex being in the mix. Staying true to her always-on-the-grind mission, she had to bring her meeting with Trevon to a close. Grabbing her iPad, iPhone, and car keys, she explained about an out of state business meeting with Wahida Clark.

"What do y'all two have going?" Trevon asked as he followed Janelle out of her office.

"A movie deal," Janelle told him. "If I can reach a deal with WCP, AEF will turn a WCP sex-driven novel into a movie."

Trevon raised his left eyebrow. "Be sure to keep me in mind for a part."

CHAPTER Fourteen

Having the Last Words

Trevon steered his XJL behind Janelle's Lamborghini Aventador until she turned off Biscayne. The sun was still holding claim overhead, making the scene fit for a postcard. Trevon's attention was focused. D-Hot was back on his mind, and Trevon was set on keeping his word. Instead of heading home, he made a left off Biscayne Boulevard when he reached 62nd Street. Inching all four windows to his eye-level, he turned the system on with "Everyday Struggle" by BIG ringing his ears. He was in his element behind the wheel, in control. He drove by the same bus stops along 62nd Street that he used to sit and wait for the bus with his mom and sis. Those days were over, but truth be told, he missed them. Nearing Liberty City, he saw it was still the same. Black people were living the very song he was blasting. Only their everyday struggle was life, not a verse in a rap.

Reaching his old stomping grounds of the Pork and Beans projects, he whipped his sedan to a known trap house that sat on a corner. Trevon's XJL stuck out like oil in water amongst the fleet of Donks and candy-painted four-door Chevy's parked up and down the block. A tall hustler with a mouth full of gold teeth slid off the hood of a pea-green '74 Caprice Vert sitting on 28's. Squinting hard at the XJL, he broke out into a crooked grin.

"If it ain't my muthafuckin' ace boon coon, Trev!" Twank shouted.

Trevon was all smiles at seeing his old schoolmate from Brownsville Junior High.

"Damn, bruh. You look old as fuck!" Trevon joked, giving Twank a thug hug.

"Shit. You just look young 'cause the pen kept yo' ass on ice. But damn, it's good to see you. I heard you was out, and I see you eatin' good, my nig." Twank nodded at the Jag parked under a mango tree.

"I got a little gig going," Trevon replied without saying much else.

Twank rubbed his hands together. "You know we go way back. So if you want some weight I—"

"Naw, bruh." Trevon shook his head. "I need something else if you can help me?"

"Holla."

"I need a burner."

Spending $100 cash, he now owned a chrome and matte black finished Smith and Wesson fifteen shot .40. Twank assured him it was clean and fresh out of the box.

Trevon was taking a major risk with his freedom. Pushing his XJL at the posted speed limit, he now felt weary about being pulled over by the police for some bullshit. Driving with the system off, he suddenly had an idea. LaToria was back on his mind. Knowing his iPhone number was blocked from LaToria's cell phone, he wondered if she did the same for the second number he used for the Bluetooth system. Steering with his left hand, leaning slightly to the right, he switched lanes to pass a city bus.

"Call LaToria," he said, turning the hands-free system on. A second later, a small picture of LaToria's smiling face appeared on the central display screen along with her phone number. Willing the call to go through, he was startled when it started to ring. Gripping the steering wheel, his heart began to race after the third ring that sounded from the small hidden speakers inside the cabin. Slowing for a red light behind a white late model Honda Accord, he swerved a bit when she answered unexpectedly.

"Hey, Trevon," LaToria's voice rang into his ears. "I know it's you because you're real funny acting about letting people drive your car."

Trevon had a million things to ask and a millions things to say, but the moment was too awkward to compose himself. "What's up with you? You gonna explain to me what's going on with us?"

She sighed. "It just wasn't working out for us."

"And you came up with that feeling overnight? What about the baby? Is it true you're going to have an abortion?"

"No."

"Oh, so it's just fuck me and on to the next nigga, huh?"

"It's a lot of shit you don't understand, okay?"

"Yeah, I bet it is. But guess what? It don't even matter to me no more. All I care about is the baby."

"It's not like that, Trevon."

"You told me that before."

"Do you hate me?"

He frowned, staring at the picture of her face. "Are you serious? You act like what we had wasn't shit. You dip out on me for another nigga wit' bread and now—"

"Jurnee tell you that?"

"Why does it matter?"

"Is she with you now?"

"No."

"Maybe y'all need to stop assuming shit 'bout me and—"

"Ain't nobody assuming shit 'bout you! We speaking off the bullshit you doing."

"And you can't say much since you didn't waste a damn second to fuck Jurnee."

"Well, least you *know* who I'm fucking!"

"Fuck you!"

Trevon's grip tightened on the steering wheel. "You know, I don't even know why I'm wasting my time talking to you."

"That makes two of us then!"

Silence. Any second now he was waiting for her to end the call. Fuming, he stayed silent as the line remained connected. He couldn't find the resolve to end the call himself.

"Shit is crazy," he heard her mutter.

"I guess you're just doing what makes you happy."

"You ain't answer my question. Do you hate me?"

Trevon rubbed his forehead with the light still red.

"You gonna answer me, Trevon?"

"Why does it matter how the fuck I feel? Your ass didn't have that in mind when you left with Martin!"

"Martellus."

"Martin, Martellus. Fuck him!" Trevon shouted.

Silence.

"I can't make you understand."

"Ain't shit to understand, okay? You been cheating on me, so fuck it. It is what the fuck it is, and trust me. You don't need to make me understand."

"It's not really like that," she tried to explain. "Please don't judge me."

"Whatever, yo," he said, glancing at the rearview mirror. His heart skipped a beat at the site of a Metro-Dade police cruiser two cars back.

"Trevon, I know what I did was wrong. But I—"

"It don't matter to me no more, ai'ight."

"I have to go, okay? But you can't call me at this number no more."

"Like that's a surprise."

"I'll call you later on in the week with a new number, okay?"

Trevon, with all the hurt he held inside matched it against the love he still carried for her. Frowning, he refused to be boyfriend number two.

"Nah, I'm good. Wouldn't want to make your *man* mad, so keep that new number to yourself. Or give it to somebody that wanna hear that bullshit you talking. I'm done." Pressing a button on the steering wheel, he ended the call. Six seconds later, the light turned green.

***

Jurnee was chatting with her new friend Tahkiyah when she heard Trevon coming through the front door. Excusing herself, she asked Tahkiyah to relax a second while she got up to speak to Trevon.

"How did things work out with Janelle?" she asked Trevon as he entered the code to turn the alarm system back on.

"Good and bad," he replied.

"What happened?"

"Just some crazy shit with D-Hot," he said, turning to face her.

"D-Hot?"

"Yeah. But it didn't have nothing to do with me talking to Janelle. It's all good on that subject, and she's down with you being my manager."

"Cool!"

"You ummm, got company. I see that BMW out front. Do I know 'im?"

"Yes, I got company." She smiled. "But you don't know her."

"Oh, my bad." He grinned.

"Hell, I just met her today." She glanced over her shoulder.

"Who is she?"

Jurnee quickly explained that Tahkiyah was in the neighborhood to view the house across the street that was up for sale. Wanting to know how the neighborhood was, Tahkiyah was just being friendly.

"She seems cool. C'mon and meet her. She said she'll be moving in next month."

"Ai'ight. Just gimme a second. I need to go post an update on my Facebook right quick."

"Hurry up."

"Okay gimme a second."

Going to his bedroom, he figured it wasn't a good time to ask Jurnee about her talking to LaToria. In truth, it was really starting not to matter. After stashing the .40 under the bed in a shoe box, he kept his word by joining Jurnee and his soon to be new neighbor in the living room.

"And here's the man of the house," Jurnee said when Trevon made his entrance.

Trevon was thankful that he couldn't speak his mind. His first sight and impression of Tahkiyah came quickly. *Damn, she fine as hell!*

"Tahkiyah, this is Trevon," Jurnee said, making the introductions.

Tahkiyah held out her hand as she stood to greet Trevon. "This is a nice home you have," she said, playing her lie out. *Whew! He is handsome!*

"Thanks," he said, wondering what Jurnee had shared with Tahkiyah.

"Tahkiyah's from up North," Jurnee said when they were all seated.

"What state?" he asked.

"Actually, I'm from D.C.," Tahkiyah replied.

"Too cold up there for me." Jurnee shivered.

"True, but it's something I'm used to," Tahkiyah said truthfully.

"She wants to know how the yard care is done," Jurnee told Trevon.

"Um, every other Thursday they have a crew to come out, but it's optional. Some homeowners like to do their own work, or just don't want any strangers on their property."

"Which option did you pick if you don't mind telling me?" Tahkiyah asked.

"I do it myself. But mainly it's because of bad ass over there." He pointed at the glass back door where Rex sat panting and fogging up the glass.

"He's just a puppy," Jurnee added.

"Yeah, and he don't listen." Trevon shifted on the sofa, lowering his eyes down the length of Tahkiyah's sexy legs. "So you're gonna make Florida your new home?"

Tahkiyah nodded. "I think it's time for a new change of pace."

"You have any family?" Trevon asked after noticing the big platinum ring on Tahkiyah's finger.

"Just two kids, and both are grown and my husband, of course. If you see two energetic little ones in my yard, they're my grandkids."

"Grandkids!" Trevon noted how young Tahkiyah looked.

"Guess her age," Jurnee teased.

"Now you're being rude." Trevon shot a look at Jurnee.

"Boy, I felt the same when she told me she's a grandmother. I know one thing. I hope I can look that good when I reach her age."

"I'm fifty-four," Tahkiyah told Trevon to prove she wasn't uncomfortable about her age.

"Hey, y'all excuse me for a second." Jurnee slid off the sofa and then sauntered to her bedroom. Without a forced effort, Trevon's gaze followed Jurnee's heart-shaped ass out of the living room. By sight alone, he knew she wasn't wearing a lick of panties under her pants. Being left alone with Tahkiyah had Trevon searching for a topic. Her beauty was just too stunning to let it go unnoticed.

"You got any more questions about the neighborhood?" he asked as she crossed her legs, forcing the pencil skirt to tighten around her thighs.

"Not much. I see it's an upper class area. And quiet."

"Yeah, it is."

"Jurnee told me you live alone now. She spoke briefly on your former roommate moving out just a few days ago."

Trevon's expression didn't change. "Yeah, and I'll be solo whenever Jurnee gets back in her own place."

"She told me that as well."

"What? Are y'all best friends now?" He laughed. "What all did you two talk about?"

"Just women things—clothes, shoes, and men."

"So what do you do for a living?"

"I own a public relations company up in D.C. And what about you?"

"I'm an actor."

Tahkiyah assumed he was teasing. "An actor? What movies have you been in?"

Trevon wasn't sure if Tahkiyah would respect his line of work. In his view she was a woman of highbred taste. Just as he started to explain, his iPhone chimed. Seeing an unfamiliar number, he was about to ignore the call until he realized it was Brooke Vee.

"Yeah, what's up?" he said after gesturing to Tahkiyah that he need to take the call.

". . . Hello? May I speak to Trevon?"

"This me. What's up?"

"Hey. I need your help."

"What is it?"

"That fool D-Hot had one of his groupie hoes cut all my tires, and now I'm stranded."

"Where you at?"

"On South Beach. About a block away from the Marlin Hotel. Can you help me out?"

"Yeah um," he said, looking at his watch, "I'll be there in thirty minutes."

"Where you coming from?"

"Coconut Grove."

"Okay. Just gimme a call back when you get on Washington Avenue. I'll be standing by my car."

Trevon ended the call just as Jurnee returned from the back. As he explained what was going on, Tahkiyah used the opening to make her exit as well. At the front door he assured Jurnee that their date was still set for tonight.

***

Telling lies was not a trait that Tahkiyah held close relations with. She hid her disappointment over LaToria's absence until she was back inside her car. She was back on the phone with the private investigator.

"She's gone!" she said, irritated. "I just left her house, but—"

"Slow down, okay. Where is she?"

"If I knew that I wouldn't be calling you!"

"Okay, what can I do?"

Tahkiyah was driving behind Trevon's Jag toward the exit. "I need you to get some details on someone. You have a pen?"

"Yep. Go ahead with what you got."

Tahkiyah sat up against the steering wheel, reading off the tag on Trevon's XJL. "All I have is his first name, and it's Trevon." She then went on to explain how Trevon was living with LaToria before she left.

"Okay, I remember seeing that Jag in the driveway, but I didn't know who drove it," the private investigator told her.

"How soon can you get something back to me?" she asked.

"Soon. I'll just reach my contact with the DMV and go from there."

"Please do that because I came too close to let go of this."

***

It was six minutes to 3 PM when Swagga rolled off of a groupie he had met last week. He had fallen at first sight of her coke bottle figure. Like all the rest, she would remain a mere addition to the number of women he fucked just for the thrill. Reaching for his boxers, he stared at her ebony sweat coated ass as she strolled naked to the bathroom. From the waist down, she reminded him of the urban model Cubana Lust.

Leaving her in his bedroom, he strolled down to the first floor to get a drink.

Rick was chilling in the living room with three other guards watching a Kevin Hart DVD on the wall mounted plasma TV. Seeing Swagga coming down the stairs, he got up and met him halfway. Rick smelled the scent of sex, weed, and liquor on Swagga from an arm's distance.

"You look like shit," Rick said as Swagga nearly tripped over his untied retro hi-top John Varvatos Converse shoes.

"No I don't." Swagga grinned. "I look like money."

"I got some news for you," Rick said.

"Whut up?'

"Martellus is back up in Denver, and ole girl, Kandi is too." Rick followed Swagga into the kitchen.

"I knew that bitch was on some bullshit."

"Yeah, but my main concern was Martellus."

"Fuck 'em both!" Swagga said as he opened one of the stainless steel doors on the refrigerator.

"I need to run something by you before you go back up."

"I'm listenin'," Swagga said as he reached for a bottle of Crown Royal Extra Rare.

"There was a little drama down in Miami at the Amatory office."

Swagga's mind clicked when he heard the mentioning of Amatory Erotic Films. He assumed it was something dealing with Kandi. "What kind of drama?"

"Trevon had some beef with D-Hot."

"And how you find that out?"

"Fritz was there. He's doing his surveillance, remember?"

Swagga nodded, closing the refrigerator with his elbow. "So what's that 'pose to mean to me?"

Rick didn't expect Swagga to see how things could be manipulated, so he pointed it out. "We can put Fritz to work early and turn that shit between D-Hot and Trevon into some major beef. Nigga can be dead this week."

Swagga shrugged. "Make it happen an' make sure he suffer."

CHAPTER Fifteen

I'm Listening. She's Watching

Did you fuck Brooke Vee?" Jurnee asked Trevon the moment he strolled through the front door. It was twenty minutes to 6 PM.

"No. I didn't fuck Brooke Vee," he answered truthfully.

Jurnee kissed him on the cheek. "Good because that means you'll have more stamina with me after our date."

"Yo, what if I did?"

"I would just hope you used a condom," she said, being straight forward.

Trevon laid his hands on her waist and then kissed her forehead. "I'ma always keep it real with you."

Jurnee circled her arms around his neck. "I need to tell you something."

"Speak your mind."

"I called Kandi the other day," she told him. "I just wanted to see what was up, but I lost my temper and told her about us. I didn't mean to start—"

"Listen Jurnee," he said, showing no anger. "Fuck her, okay? Whatever you told her don't matter. I'm done lookin' for love. And since you waited 'til now to tell me. I'ma punish this ass tonight."

Jurnee jumped on him, crossing her ankles around his back.

"Whoa girl!" He laughed, carrying her weight with little effort.

"Am I heavy?" She giggled as he carried her to his bedroom.

"A little bit," he lied.

Jurnee gasped. "You hurt my feelings, papi," she said, rubbing his baldhead.

"Well, do something about it," he said, kicking his bedroom door open.

Jurnee looked over her shoulder at the bed. "What are we doing in here, papi?"

Dropping her on the bed, he looked around the room. "I wanted you to help me get all of LaToria's shit up outta here."

Jurnee tugged her shirt down, thinking of how quickly things had changed since she arrived. "You sure about this?" she asked.

"Yeah. Let's start now, and then we can shower and get ready for our date."

***

Fritz was a man of trained patience when it related to his trade. Back at the apartment, he was alone tonight, preparing his tools. While sitting on a padded milk crate by his bed, he picked up a Bushmaster AR-15 fitted with a 12x50 riflescope. He had cleaned it twice, taking it apart down to the firing pin. Two 30-round clips loaded with brass 5.56 millimeter rounds were laid to his left near the head of the bed. On a bad day Fritz could knock a target down center mass at a distance of 500 yards with the AR-

15. With the assault rifle fitted with a silencer, it made Fritz a dealer of death at a distance. Lying to his right was a Mossberg blue barrel 12 gauge pistol grip pump. Fritz favored the Mossberg when he needed to get his point across in close quarters. On a job down in Belize three years back, he had kicked in a door and took down two drug dealers with a pump. Coming in fast and loud, shooting first was his markings.

Sitting on the bed with his tools was a small GPS tracking system monitor. With it, he knew when and where his target was moving in his vehicle. If the chance were given tonight, Fritz would make his move without a hint of hesitation. He had gotten the message from Rick about making the target suffer. To Fritz, that was just an added bonus with no extra fee.

***

It was five minutes to 8 PM when Trevon stepped out of the shower.

"Good news and bad news," Jurnee said, leaning against the sink. She bit her bottom lip at the sight of his wet, naked body. His hairless crotch and the way his wide upper body tapered to the V at his waist looked so erotic.

"Gimme the bad first." He reached for the towel to dry off as Jurnee shamelessly kept her eyes below his muscular stomach.

"I just got off the phone with Janelle."

"Damn, I don't want no bad news from her," he said, drying his arms off.

Jurnee's pussy twitched at the sight of his dick swinging between his legs.

"My face is up here," Trevon teased.

"Umm, we can't go out tonight," she said, snatching the towel from him.

"Why not?"

Jurnee started to dry him off as he waited for her to explain what was up. "She wants you to go on this live radio show tonight."

"What for?"

"Exposure, papi. You're a porn star, and you have a brand to build. If you want to shine you gotta stay on your grind."

"What kind of radio show is it?" he asked as she toweled off his chest and stomach.

"It's a late night sex talk show called *Climaxx* hosted by this dude from Queens, New York. Last week he had Tahiry Jose up there talking about her sexual fantasies and stuff. Turn around."

"And I have to go tonight?"

"It's business, papi. You wanna boost your DVD sales you gotta stay in the public. I think it's an excellent idea. Mmm, I love your sexy build."

"So no date tonight?"

"Nope. We have to be at the studio in Coral Gables by 10:30. The show starts at midnight."

"Ain't never been on—"

"I know, papi," she said, caressing his ass with her bare hand. "I'm your manager now, and I'll walk you through the process. Just relax. Be yourself, and it will all be okay."

"Um, I think my ass is dry now," he said over his shoulder.

"Be quiet," she purred, reaching around his waist. "I know what I'm doing."

Trevon felt her breasts mash up on his back just as she circled her soft fingers around his dick.

"You like this, papi?" She slowly jacked his meat as it throbbed and grew in her gentle grip.

"You know I do."

"I still want you in my ass tonight. I can't wait for it." She stroked him from the flared tip to his thick base that she couldn't circle her fingers around entirely. Just the thought of her ass being stretched by him had her clitoris bulging under her panties.

Wanting him to save all his vigor for later, she unwillingly released his dick to prepare for the radio talk show.

Jurnee switched into her business mode as she coached Trevon on a few pointers related to doing interviews.

"If they ask you something stupid, let me handle it. You *do not*"—she emphasized—"want to lose your cool and make a fool of yourself. If you do, this will be your first and last interview. And remember, you represent Amatory Erotic Films."

Following Jurnee's advice, Trevon later stepped outside sporting an all-black Armani suit. By habit, his head tilted up toward the dark star-lit sky. Moments such as now meant a lot to him. While in prison, he was always forced to go inside before nightfall. For fifteen years he was never able to view the moon and stars in its true form. Seeing it from behind his Plexiglas cell window was not a joy to remember.

He turned back toward the house when he heard Jurnee's Jimmy Choo stiletto sandals clacking on the tiles.

"You look yummy," she said, standing in the doorway putting her earrings on. She squeezed her tantalizing frame into a mango-red Ms. Kat catsuit that accentuated her curves.

"Thanks," he said as a soft surge of wind rustled the pencil thin palmetto trees in the front yard.

As Jurnee locked the door and turned the alarm on, Trevon asked if it would be okay to ride in her sleek SLS. Keeping his still, somewhat paranoid feelings of being followed to himself, he got her to say yes with no suspicion on her part.

When the gullwing doors lowered in place, Trevon glanced over at Jurnee in the passenger seat. "You ready?"

She nodded with a high gloss shine on her succulent lips. "Let's make history, papi."

***

LaToria had gotten the mass e-mail from Janelle's personal receptionist about Trevon's radio interview an hour before the show started. Dealing with conflicting emotions, she ended up getting away from Martellus by taking a bubble bath. Behind the closed door, she carefully eased into the soothing hot strawberry water with a touch screen tablet. She couldn't pass up the opportunity to hear Trevon's voice.

***

"Me say . . . yahhhhh! Dis yo' boy Grime comin' live fo' another night of the realest talk show swingin'. You're tuned in with me, Grime. Me say . . . yahhhh and my sexy co-host Chanel! Dis is the *Climaxx Late Night Talk Show,* and tonight is fo' my ladies. Wit' me in the studio, I have a special guest that I'll let Chanel introduce."

"Hey y'all. This your diva Chanel, and I wanna welcome everybody to another night of *Climaxx*. In the studio we have Trevon, who's an adult film star, and yes I posted a link to his video on our site. Tonight we're gonna interview Trevon and find out what it's like to be a porn star."

"Oh, for the fellas," Grime jumped in. "I'ma Instagram a picture of his fine ass manager, former adult star, Honey Drop. Me say . . . yahhh!"

Trevon was seated in the small studio wearing a pair of headphones, forcing himself to relax. Jurnee was seated to his left on a small leather sofa near the door. The studio was dimly lit with most of the lights coming from the switchboard that Chanel and Grime sat behind. Trevon sat facing them with a thick padded boom mic a few inches from his face.

"So what's happening with you?" Chanel asked, starting the interview off.

"I'm good," Trevon began. "Just taking it day by day and enjoying my freedom and the job I have."

"That's how you view doing porn—a job?" Chanel asked.

"Shit. I get paid for it." He laughed. "But seriously, it's a job because at AEF that's how it's run. Do I enjoy it? Hell yeah!"

"I watched your debut film on my phone, and whew. You got it going on!"

"Thanks. And thank you for your support too."

"You're more than welcomed. Okay, give our listeners a brief bio about yourself and speak up a lil' bit, baby."

"Uh-oh!" Grime said into the mic. "Bruh, she called you baby, so she might try to toss that big booty on you. Me say . . . yahhhhhh!"

"Grime, hush!" Chanel playfully shoved her co-host, and then gestured for Trevon to speak.

"Well uh, I was born in Miami back in '79 on July 25."

"Ladies, this man does not look like he's thirty-three," Chanel said, staring at Trevon with a sultry pout.

"I um, did some time in prison, which isn't a secret. All you gotta do is Google it. Ah, I just got out of prison last year, and I was given a chance to do adult films by Janelle Babin."

"Was the film with you and adult film star, Kandi, your first time having sex in fifteen years?"

"Yes, it was."

"Do you have any kids?"

"Nah."

"Okay. In your films, do you have any control over what kind of sexual acts you do?"

"At AEF Janelle will not force anyone to do anything they're not at ease with. Speaking for myself, but not downing the bisexual males in porn. I'll never take that path."

"Can you see yourself still doing porn . . . say, five years from now?"

"It's possible."

"Ah, let's say if you were to have a sex tape leak out with someone famous, who would it be?"

"Hmmm. I think it would be Maliah Michel. It's just something about her sexy ass that gets me going."

"You heard it here first y'all. Mr. Trevon Harrison has a thang for, Maliah Michel. Now, let's open up the phone lines and take a live caller. Is that okay with you, Trevon?" Chanel asked as Grime signaled that a caller was on hold.

"Yeah. I'm good with that," Trevon replied.

"Okay. Our caller is, Nashlly from Fort Lauderdale. What question do you have for our guest tonight?"

"Yeah um, I wanna know what the deal is on the whole issue with Kandi stepping out on you? Also, is it true that she's pregnant by you?"

Trevon cleared his throat. "First off, it's personal, but I'll address it since it's all over the web. As you all know, I um, did my debut adult film with Kandi. She also became the first woman I had sex with in fifteen years."

"So she had you pussy whipped?"

"I won't put it like that," Trevon said as Jurnee gestured for him to end the call.

"So how would you put it then?"

"Nothing in life is perfect," Trevon went on after mouthing to Jurnee that he could handle the call. "Yes, I had feelings for Kandi, and it was beyond just sex. Maybe I rushed it or maybe I wasn't ready for a relationship."

"So, did you get her pregnant when y'all did that film?"

"No. All Amatory Films are strictly safe sex, and if you were a true fan of AEF then you would know that. What happened between Kandi and I was personal, and I don't regret one moment spent with her."

"One last question. How did you manage to avoid any legal issues for killing Swagga's bodyguard last year?"

Jurnee was on her feet, wildly gesturing for Chanel or Grime to cut the line. Trevon shook his head, knowing it was best to face the facts before rumors took over.

"Nashlly, right?" Trevon said into the mic. "Well, last year I was cleared of all charges related to Yaffa's death. It's public record of a report filed by the U.S. Marshals and the Metro Dade Police Department that Yaffa's injuries were self-inflicted. Now, if you want to doubt their report, then that's on you."

"But—"

"Facts are facts," Trevon stated calmly. "I know I will always be viewed as an ex-convict by many. But I can't let my past nor how people think of me dictate how I live my life. Yes, it's true Kandi and I were in a relationship, but it didn't work out. That's life and I hold no harsh feelings toward her."

"Good answer." Chanel nodded at Trevon. "That's what we get when we do it live without a delay."

"Oh yeah. Nashlly, be sure to check out my DVD and do spread the word."

"'Cuse me for a second," Grime said, adjusting his mic. "We just got a question posted on our Twitter by one of our listeners. But ah—I'm gonna have to let Chanel read it."

Chanel leaned in Grime's direction to read the question off his laptop. When she sat back up, she couldn't hide her wide grin. "One of your new fans would like to know if you're up to allowing me to ah—measure your dick right here in the studio."

***

"Why the fuck you tell 'em yo' real name?" Swagga shouted behind the wheel of his Bentley Brooklands.

"Because you didn't say not to!" Nashlly complained. "It ain't like they knew who the hell I was anyway! So why are you tripping? I didn't wanna do the shit in the first place."

"Did you block your number out? Did I have to tell you that too?" Swagga glared as he slowed the Bentley for a stop sign two blocks from Nashlly's crib.

She sighed. "Yes, I blocked my number. Now can you tell me what this shit is all about?"

"No! Don't even fuckin' worry 'bout it!"

Nashlly rolled her eyes. "Will I see you tomorrow?"

"I'll think about it," he mumbled his reply.

Nashlly allowed Swagga's sour attitude to slip by without a strong confrontation. She knew it came with the pros and cons of fucking with an A-List celebrity. When she was inside her crib, she stayed tuned into the *"Climax Late Night Talk Show"* on her smartphone. Her curiosity about Trevon turned heavy as Chanel narrated in vivid detail of giving Trevon a hand job in the studio. Chanel announced live that Trevon's dick measured at nine inches. Doubting Trevon's manhood, Nashlly had to download his debut film to see if it was true. Her actions were being repeated by countless other women that needed to see Trevon in action, which spoke louder than Chanel's word.

* * *

Back in Miami, Tahkiyah had everything in place for another one of her private moments. The lights were off inside her lush suite at the Mondrian Hotel. Her nude body tingled with an ache that turned her nipples stiff. She closed her eyes and palmed her titties. This was her secret ritual, and she realized it gained power over her each time she did it. Turning to her side, she flipped her laptop open. Within a few seconds she was back on a porn site listed as Black Sexxx.

Her eyes scanned the list of fantasies she could indulge in.

Theme	Videos	Theme	Videos
Anal sexxx	247	Hardcore sexx	317
Bondage sexx	89	Lesbian sexxx	280
Gangbang sexx	182	Oral sexx	290
Gay sexx	51	Outdoor sexxx	98

Group sexxx 140 Sadomasochism sexxx 32

She clicked *oral sex,* and then she discovered a link to fellatio. All of the videos featured black on black sex. Rolling to her stomach, she previewed a thirty second clip of a video before she downloaded it. Tahkiyah's beautiful face was lit by the screen. She squeezed her thighs tight and pressed her nipples against the soft, royal blue satin sheets. As soon as the download was complete, she touched the play icon to start the twenty minute video.

The film began with a topless big breasted black girl in a hot tub stroking a man's penis. Her titties wobbled with the slightest movements. Tahkiyah stared at the screen and watched the girl twirling her tongue all over the thick headed penis. Her pussy throbbed between her clutched thighs as the girl started sucking on the hard black dick.

"Ummmm, shit yeah! Suck that dick!" Tahkiyah moaned, watching the girl and the dick she was sucking. From a side view the film showed a close shot of the girl engulfing the dick at a stabilized pace. Tahkiyah started touching herself by slipping a hand under her . Whimpering, she circled her hips instinctively while fingering her moist pussy. She would give anything to have a black man in her mouth. Catching her totally off guard, Trevon slid into her thoughts just at the tip of her climax.

***

After the interview, Janelle called Trevon first to offer her congratulations. She informed him that his next film would be moved up to next week. The interview had proven to be a wise choice as Janelle told him of the spike in the number of hits to the AEF website. Tonight alone, she was sure his videos were purchased and downloaded around 800 times. Jurnee later proved that she was serious about Trevon's career. Knowing he would begin his three-day film shoot next week, all sex was halted. Knowing how strong temptation could lure her in bed with him, she made the decision to sleep alone.

Trevon didn't make a big deal about her choice. Besides, there was always tomorrow.

***

LaToria felt a twinge of hope that Trevon didn't hate her. Listening to his voice stirred her emotions for Trevon. Unable to take the hurt, she turned the show off just after Chanel spoke about his penis. Hiding her hurt, she rushed from the tub into her bedroom, where she remained quiet. She dried off and dressed in her pajamas as she slid under the thick green quilted comforter and sheets. Closing her eyes, she squeezed out a stream of tears. *God, please help me make things right with Trevon.* She wiped her eyes in this dark bedroom that she shared with Martellus. Silence later proved that she was alone. Not caring about Martellus' whereabouts, she curled up with the sincere thought of the only man she truly loved, Trevon.

CHAPTER Sixteen

Watch and Learn

January 24, 2012

Tuesday, 12:30 AM – Coconut Grove, Florida

Trevon was outside waxing his XJL in the driveway when Jurnee came out of the house. It was a blue, cloudless day with the temperature in the low 80s.

"You finally got out of the bed, huh?" he said, squatting down to wax the front bumper. When she didn't answer, he glanced in her direction.

She stood with a frown on her sexy face, her arms folded under her large breasts. "You trying to go back to prison?"

Trevon rose to his feet. "What kind of dumb ass question is that? And what's wrong with you?" he said, squinting from the sun in his face.

"Ain't nothing wrong with me!" she snapped.

"Gotta be for you to be coming at me all sideways and shit. Now what's up?"

Jurnee sighed as she fought to manage her temper. "I found that gun yesterday when I was getting Kandi's shoes from under the bed. I should've told you yesterday. But—what are you thinking about, Trevon?" A look of hurt eased into her expression.

Trevon shook his head and then dropped the waxing cloth on the hood of his sedan. "I need it, ai'ight."

"For what?" she said, giving him a slighting look. "I'm all for the gun rights and stuff. But Trevon, you're a felon and—"

"You don't need to remind me about that shit!"

"Obviously, I do since you got the damn thing!" she stated, moving her hands to her waist. "If I didn't care about you I wouldn't be having this conversation with you."

"My life isn't—it ain't all peaceful like yours, okay? I got shit I gotta deal with, and if it comes to me using a gun. Then it is what it is."

"Do you even realize what you're saying? Tell me. If you could do it all over, would you have killed that teacher?"

"Damn right I would! That muthafucka raped my little sister, so fuck him! And no I don't regret it! I did my time. He's dead. So as far as I'm concerned we fuckin' even!"

"You don't mean that, Trevon."

"The hell I don't!"

Jurnee tried to understand his mindset, but she came up short. "How can you become what you want to be by remaining what you are?"

"What the fuck am I, Jurnee?" he said, gesturing. "Can you tell me that since you wanna preach to me?"

"I'm not preaching to you, so don't try to play me like that. Hell, if you don't give a fuck about your freedom then why should I?"

"Shit, I don't remember asking you to!"

"You know what. Ain't got time for this," she said, shaking her head. "Are you going to get rid of that gun or what?"

"No. I'm not gettin'—no!"

Jurnee gasped. "So that's your decision?"

"Ain't gotta repeat myself."

"Fine! As long as you want to be a gangsta and all that, then you can do it by your damn self!"

"And what the fuck is that 'pose to mean?"

"How about I just show you what it means!" She gave him another hard look and then turned, storming back inside the house.

"Whatever! You wanna leave, burn the fuckin' road up!" he shouted. Balling his fist, he turned facing the street and cursed. Then he snatched the waxing cloth off the hood of his Jag, slinging it across the driveway. Holding his head in his hands, he closed his eyes and took a few breaths to clear his mind. Trevon needed his space, so he slid behind the wheel of the XJL and sped off, squealing the rear tires. He didn't give Jurnee a second glance as he left her behind. If she was there or not when he returned, he just didn't give a fuck about it. Driving with no set destination, he was forced to think about his life and the words Jurnee had just spoken to him. Cruising north on 22nd Avenue, he thought deeply on the man he was and the better man he wanted to be.

***

Later around 3 PM, Trevon was pulling from a gas station off 79th Street when he received a call from Kendra. It rang four times before he answered.

"What's up Ms. PO?" he said, checking the lane behind him before he merged into traffic.

"Somebody got some jokes today." She laughed. "How are you doing?"

"Surviving. Just taking it day by day."

"We're all doing that these days to tell you the truth."

"True. But some days shit just seems to get out of hand."

"You should just let some things be. Look. I was wondering if you can meet me at Vic's. It's a new soul food spot on Collins Avenue near the Marlin Hotel. The food is off the chain!"

"Uh, what time you trying to be there?"

"Five thirty. I hope you can make it."

"You paying?"

"Nope. You are. I paid for our first date, remember?"

He grinned. "I see you got jokes today too."

"So will you be joining me?"

"It's a date."

"I was hoping to hear that. Oh, and Mr. Harrison. Don't be late this time, okay? If I have to come looking for you, you won't like it," she said, good-naturedly.

***

Trevon arrived at Vic's ten minutes before 5:30 PM. After parking his car, he spotted the Bentley GT that Kendra drove sitting near the entrance of the restaurant. Hoping he wasn't underdressed, he entered the cozy restaurant wearing a pair of wheat colored Timberland boots, black Gucci jeans, and a white tank top. The eighteen tables were all occupied, and the smell of soul food made Trevon's stomach growl. Scanning the faces for Kendra, he was caught off guard when someone tapped on his shoulder.

"You walked right by me," Kendra said as Trevon turned around. "C'mon, I'm ready to order my food."

"How long you been here?" he asked, enjoying the sight of how her backside was filling out her white jeans.

"Not long."

They took a seat at the green cloth covered table near the tinted window. The wall behind Trevon was covered with framed pictures of prominent black folks. Martin Luther King, Jr., Malcolm X, President Barack Obama, Desmond Tutu, Maya Angelou and many others.

Kendra glanced up from the menu to see Trevon studying the pictures over his shoulder. "Who's in that picture above Nelson Mandela to the right?" she quizzed him.

Trevon turned in the chair. "That's Frederick Douglass. He was a writer and fought to end slavery. In fact, he escaped from slavery." He turned back to the table. "Didn't think I knew that, did ya?"

"I must admit that you're correct." She smiled.

"Ai'ight, my turn. Who's in the picture that's below Oprah?"

"Hmm . . . let me guess. Would it be the author of *Roots,* Alex Haley? Born in 1921 and laid to rest in 1992."

Trevon placed his smartphone on the table. "Okay, we both know our history and stuff. Now, let's order some of this good ass food I'm smelling."

Trevon kept his fitness in mind by ordering the grilled chicken over a fried one. He explained his reason to Kendra by pointing out that the grilled chicken was loaded with protein but low in carbs. Along with the six-ounce grilled chicken breast, he ordered a side of steamed spinach and one baked sweet potato. Since Kendra wasn't too pleased with her size, she figured today would be as good as any to start eating right. She ordered the same as Trevon.

Before the food came, they spoke about the topics of their life. Kendra admitted that she was ready to get back to work. She also told Trevon that she was officially done fucking with Marcus aka Swagga.

Midway through the meal, Trevon watched as a mixed couple entered with two small kids in tow. What Trevon saw was an item that was out of reach. A family. He was still dealing with LaToria and the way she had left him. His choice of emotions were limited, sorrow or anger. He ran with the latter, having more comfort by not dealing with matters of the heart.

"You okay?" Kendra asked as one of the little kids waved at Trevon.

Shifting in the chair, he nodded yes. "I was just wondering what it would be like to have a child."

"It's a major responsibility," Kendra said. "The one heavy burden is trying to be perfect. You know. You trying not to do no wrong in front of your child."

"How's your little one doing? Did she like the canopy bed we put together?"

"She's doing great. Just wanting every toy she sees on TV. And that bed, she treats it like a trampoline with her spoiled behind."

"You ever plan to have another kid."

Kendra glanced down at her plate. "I doubt it." She shrugged.

Trevon waited a few seconds to get his words in order. Clearing his throat, he leaned forward a bit. “How well do you know Swagga?”

Kendra lifted her right eyebrow. “Uh, he’s my baby daddy. I know him very well. Why do you ask?’

“Look. All that shit that happened last year—”

“It’s over with, Trevon,” she said, becoming upset.

“Wait,” he said, reaching across the table for her hand. “Just hear me out, okay? Please. I just need to share something with you.”

“Something about Marcus?”

“Yeah,” he replied after a short pause.

Kendra wanted to pull her hand back but she didn’t. His contact reminded her of the two passionate times they had been together. She would never forget how full and loaded Trevon was when he was deep inside her wetness. Blinking, she pushed the sexual thoughts from her mind, and then told Trevon to speak his mind.

Trevon started from the beginning, telling her about what happened after he left her house last year. Kendra showed no emotion as Trevon admitted that LaToria had popped up at his front door.

“. . . After we had sex, she went home to get some things so she could spend the night. Well, she left her phone at my place and when I found it, I saw a voice message from Swagga.”

“And?”

“He was telling LaToria to turn over some footage of him and Chyna. He assumed LaToria was down with some type of scheme. Told her to leave her phone in the mailbox. Said Yaffa already killed Chyna and Cindy and she was—”

"I don't believe you, Trevon," she said, pulling her hand back. "Swagga ain't shit. I'll tell you that my damn self. But he beat the case, and plus, where is the motive? Yaffa, he just—"

"I got the motive, Kendra," Trevon pressed. "All that bullshit that went down that night was because he didn't want his secret to get out, okay? He tried to burn LaToria alive for something she didn't even know about," Trevon said desperately.

"So how did her name come up, huh?"

"I don't know. Hell, LaToria don't even know."

"So what's the motive? What's Marcus got to hide that I don't know about?"

Trevon picked up his smartphone. "When Chyna and Cindy were killed, there was a guy in the closet."

"And you believe that?"

"This is what I believe." Trevon slid his smartphone across the table. "He sent me these two videos of Swagga and Chyna back on Christmas. You can see it for yourself."

Kendra shook her head, refusing to touch the phone. "I don't care to see him fucking another woman, okay!" she asserted hotly.

Trevon made eye contact with her and slid the phone against her hand. "Chyna . . . isn't a she."

Kendra averted her eyes to the ceiling, sighing. She held a ton of doubt toward what she heard. Since actions spoke louder than words, she picked up the phone to get to the bottom of this bullshit. Whatever secret Trevon assumed was hanging over Swagga's head, she was going to find out. With her mind twisting on what she was about to learn, she pressed *Play*.

CHAPTER
Seventeen
I Know Your Secret

Kendra was dumbfounded after she viewed the two videos of Swagga having sex with Chyna.

"Who else have you shown these to?" she asked, visibly shaken.

"Nobody but LaToria. I told Jurnee about it, but I never got the chance to let her see them."

Kendra pushed the phone back to Trevon with a look of anger and disgust twitching across her face.

"Did you know he was bisexual?"

She tried to think back to any clues or hints that Swagga had a taste for men. "I can't believe this," she murmured with her eyes lowered to the table.

"Were you uhhh—having unsafe sex with—"

"No!" she replied. "He never proved to me he could commit, so even when I was back with him, we used protection. He was upset about it, but now I'm glad I didn't give in."

"That's good to hear," he said, hoping she was being honest.

"What do you plan to do?"

He shrugged. "I was hoping you had some ideas."

"He's the father of my child, Trevon," she reminded him.

Trevon again faced a brick wall. "Well, this sure isn't something I expected to learn today." She refused to look his way.

"Look. He *did* try to kill LaToria for this shit, and now that I have it—"

"You think he'll do something to you," she admitted carefully.

"Something like that."

"What were you planning to do without me knowing this?"

He shrugged. "Everyone keeps telling me that Swagga being gay or whatever won't be such a big deal. Really, I'm thinking about deleting this shit and just moving on with my life."

"What's stopping you?" she asked curiously.

"I hate losing."

"I have a question. Who's your favorite rapper?"

"Uh . . . alive, I'd say Rick Ross."

"And what if he came out of the closet. Would you still support him?"

"Sure. But if you're trying to compare how the public will feel about Swagga, he ain't gonna admit what he did with Chyna."

"Okay, you have a point."

"And that still leaves me at point A. Not knowing what the fuck to do."

"It's personal to me, Trevon," Kendra said quietly as two waiters strolled by their table. "My life was at risk. What if he has STDs? That's my concern. I don't care about his rep or record sales. This is my life!" Tears began to well in her eyes. "I know he was unfaithful to me. But I—I never would have thought that he had gay tendencies."

"What do you want me to do with the videos?"

She wiped her eyes. "I need you to trust me, Trevon."

"You've earned that already. So what's up?"

"I need to download those videos to my phone," she replied quickly.

Trevon struggled with her request. "Maybe I should just delete it," he said finally.

"Don't do that. Like I said, it's personal with me. Let me handle it. Please. He needs to learn what's done in the dark will one day stand in the light."

***

A sudden rainstorm had broken over Swagga's mansion up in Fort Lauderdale and the lower parts of Broward County. Around 8:20 PM, a pair of headlights broke through the thick darkness at the private unguarded back gate to the east of Swagga's mansion. From a distance of two hundred yards, Kendra could clearly see the lit up estate through the bars of the Iron Gate.

Since the back gate was rarely used, it would allow Kendra to make a surprise visit. Using a remote, she opened the gate and then killed the lights. Rain pelted the Bentley with wind-driven sheets as Kendra navigated toward the opulent mansion. Using a second remote, she pulled into the brightly lit garage with her mind contemplating on how she would confront Swagga. Slowing to a stop, she sat behind the wheel with the engine running. Using anger and thoughts of *what if* on the risk of her catching an STD from Swagga, she was fueled. Exiting the Bentley GT, she threw her heart on her sleeve and went inside to face a man she no longer respected or loved.

***

Groupies were a rapper's greatest delight in Swagga's world. It was being proven again up in the privacy of his grandiose master bedroom.

"Mmmm, right there! Ohhhh, keep running it, daddy! Run it hard!" Nashlly moaned with her baby oiled covered ass bouncing back against Swagga. Her small coffee brown titties jerked beneath her as Swagga thrusted his length in and out of her gushy slit.

"Damn, dis ass so soft!" he moaned as he stood behind her caressing her shiny ass. In and out he thrusted hard as she moaned into the pillow she was clutching. The sounds of their raw sex was all the music Swagga needed.

"Yes!" She breathed, pulling the sheets from the head of the bed.

"Who pussy is it?" he asked, slapping her on the ass.

"Yours!" she cried as her butt started to clap. "Mmmm . . . harder!"

Swagga looked down at his bare dick drilling fast inside of Nashlly. Her big soft ass was sweaty and bouncing like Jell-O. He picked up his pace, long dicking her phat-lipped pussy until she tried to crawl away.

"Gotdamn, dis dick so good!" she shouted, coming up on her arms. Baring her teeth, she threw her ass against his every thrust. "Mmmm, you all up in me now! All up in me!" she whined, looking back at him.

"Wiggle that ass!" he shouted with sweat beading up on his forehead.

Nashlly did just that by switching her hips left to right. Swagga fisted his left hand in her fake hair with his right hand tweaking her nipples. Juices flowed freely down her inner thighs. Going hard for another seven minutes, he turned her on her back. He knew she was a groupie, but the only fact that mattered to him: she was *his* groupie. With her banging body and fire ass pussy, he figured he could turn her into a star. Sliding his wet tip up and down her gushy slit, he saw the hunger in her eyes. Hooking her legs over his skinny shoulders, he eased back inside her. She took the dick with her hands clutching his ass. She assumed this was their make-up sex from their argument yesterday. As she humped upward, she hoped deeply that he would cum inside her. Hell, 50 Cent said it best: *Have a baby by me, baby . . . be a millionaire.*

***

"Kendra, what are you doing here?" Rick said after running to catch up with her.

"Uh, I live here, don't I?" she asked, standing halfway up the stairs.

Rick knew Swagga had company in his room, and he now had a choice to make. Protecting Swagga from harm was his job. But as for the bullshit he was putting Kendra through, Rick had nothing to do with that. For the short time he had known Kendra, he had much respect for her. But it was clear that Swagga didn't know the meaning of respect. "I guess you're right," he said, making no effort to stop her.

"Does he have a bitch up there?" Kendra asked bluntly.

"We're not having this little talk, are we?" Rick hinted.

"No, I guess I snuck by you on my way up."

Rick rubbed his face. "Yeah, he got company."

Kendra turned and started to head up to the bedroom.

"Hey wait!" Rick made his way up the stairs. When he reached the stair below her, he glanced at Swagga's bedroom door. "Listen. Don't waste your time fighting that girl. I'll be close by, okay? And um, we didn't have this talk."

She smiled. "Thanks Rick. But I'm not here to fight any of his 'hos. Now, if you'll excuse me. I have an ego to crush."

Rick had to admire Kendra, because most girls would put up with Swagga's drama just because of his worth. Rick wasn't surprised by Kendra and the moral grounds she stood on. She might not be perfect, but the difference in his view was Kendra being a woman and not a girl.

***

Swagga was in the throes of his climax, clutching Nashlly's butt cheeks with her heels bouncing off his ass. He shot off four times, flooding her tight pussy with his cum. She nibbled on his ear, locking her ankles over his ass, forcing him to spew every drop inside her.

"That was sooo good," she purred as he collapsed on top of her.

"Whew! Why you ain't warn a nigga 'bout that good ass wet-wet you got?"

Nashlly unlocked her legs from around his waist, and then squeezed her pussy, gripping his dick that was still inside her. "It's your wet-wet now," she said, sucking on his neck.

"You keep doin' that, and I'ma keep ya ass here."

She tightened her pussy again. "That's what I'm hoping for, daddy."

Swagga kissed her on the lips and then rolled to the side.

"What do we do now?" she asked, reaching for his shiny wet dick.

"Both of you need to carry your ass to the clinic!"

"What the—" Nashlly sat up quickly, crossing her arms over her perky B-cups. Kendra pushed from the wall, her eyes locked on Swagga.

"Who the fuck are you?" Nashlly shouted, and then turned to Swagga. "What the hell is this shit? Who is—?"

"My baby momma," Swagga said in a calm manner. "Yo, go clean yo'self up in the bathroom. This won't take too long," he told Nashlly.

Not caring how Kendra felt, Swagga playfully smacked Nashlly on the ass when she got off the bed. Kendra didn't even give Nashlly a glance as she brushed her arm.

"Who let you in?" he asked, placing his hands behind his head.

"Didn't know I was locked out."

"Well, you see I'm busy. What do you want?"

"Definitely not your sorry ass. I can tell you that!" she told him.

Swagga shrugged, flaunting his nakedness and semi-hard dick in her face. "So what the fuck you want? Ain't nobody tell yo' ass to dip out on me. What? Didn't think you could be replaced?"

"Nigga. I wasn't never in your messed up life to begin with!"

He laughed. "That's how you feel? I didn't care? But damn, why you gotta toss dirt on me? Talkin' 'bout going to the clinic an' shit."

Kendra forced herself to sit on the bed. To her satisfaction, Swagga showed a twinge of fear by sitting up and keeping his distance.

"You know, I was so dumb when I fell for your bullshit when I first met your ass."

Swagga shook his dreads out of his face. "I can say the same fo' yo' thirsty ass! All you wanted was a baby by me!"

"Don't you dare bring Carmelita into this!" she warned with a finger in his face.

"Fuck you!" he said, pushing her hand out of his face. "It's a wrap fo' yo' fat ass anyway!"

She smiled. "Did you fuck that skank in the ass?"

"Why the fuck you worried 'bout it? If I did, so what! Sit here long enough and you can watch."

"No thanks. Besides, I already seen your nasty ass in action," she said coolly.

A sudden silence gripped the room.

"Seen me where?" he demanded.

"Around," she said, looking at her purple fingernails.

"So you wanna play games?"

"Try to play me and watch what happens to your ass!"

"Fuck you!"

"Come up with something new 'cause that term is getting played out just like your dumb ass is!"

"Keep runnin' yo' mouth and get yo' ass fucked up!"

"Ahh." She smiled. "So you do have an ass fetish." She looked across the room at the bathroom door. "It's a she, ain't it?" she whispered, turning back to face Swagga.

Swagga was in a sober mind, so the connection was made. Sliding off the bed, he reached for his boxers. "You remember what happened last year, right?"

"A lot happened last year," she said as he pulled the boxers up over his ass.

Swagga moved around the bed, rubbing his hands together. "So you seen me, huh?"

She didn't answer. Turning, she watched him move over near the dresser.

"You're right about that." He nodded. "She was like—crazy as hell. Motherfuckas were out to put dirt on my name and blackmail me," he said with his back toward Kendra. When he turned, he had a chrome plated gun in his right hand.

Kendra's eyes widened. She made no sudden moves. Fear gripped her, making her regret her choice to confront him.

"Look, yo." He grinned, lifting the piece and a cigarette to his lips. As he lit the cigarette with the gun lighter, he saw relief pouring into her face. "Why you lookin' all stupid and shit?" He laughed with the lit cigarette burning.

Kendra stood, feeling ashamed that she allowed fear to hold her.

"Bitch, you ain't answer my fuckin' question yet, so you can sit yo' ass back down."

Kendra's face turned into a mask of disgust. "Picture that!"

"Don't push me!" he shouted.

"Then don't *shove* me, muthafucka!" she said, matching his tone.

Swagga took a deep pull on the cigarette, and then he pointed at the door. "See your way out if you ain't got shit else to say."

"Why did you do it?" she asked after a short moment.

"Do what?" he asked, balling his face up.

"Chyna."

The cigarette nearly dropped from his fingers. Unable to control his thoughts, he crushed the cigarette out and then stalked up in her face. To his growing displeasure, she didn't back down. "You sure you wanna play this game wit' me?" he warned through his teeth.

"Is it true or not?"

"Fuck you, bitch!" He sneered, inches from her face. "You come here to blackmail me? Is that what dis shit all about, huh?"

"How could you put me at risk?"

Swagga stared at her with pure contempt boiling in his eyes. "For the last time. What the fuck are you talkin' 'bout!"

Kendra's control over her temper was lost. She was giving him the chance to be honest. The chance to say he was wrong or sorry. Instead, he was hiding from the truth. Hiding from the truth that she had seen with her own eyes. "I'm talking about you and that sick shit you did with Chyna! How *dare* you—fucking *it* in the ass. Then get back with me and not tell me shit! I thank God I'm not like that airhead you was just up in. You are so wrong, and you know it! Why didn't you tell me?"

Swagga's worst fear had jumped in his face. *How?* Screamed loudly in his troubled mind. Just like last year, his blame went straight to Kandi. Ashamed of his deeds, he lowered his eyes.

"Look at me!" she demanded. "I saw it, Marcus!" she cried with tears running down her face. "I saw you with Chyna."

Defeated, he had no more fight left. "Yo, lemme explain what happened right quick—"

"That's dead, Marcus!" She shoved him. "I gave you a chance to explain, so now I don't wanna hear shit you got to say!"

"C'mon, baby," he pleaded.

"Your baby is in the bathroom," she said, stepping away from him. Shaking her head at the mere sight of him. "I don't know who you are anymore. I don't love you, Marcus."

"Look, I fucked up. Okay? But let's let that shit stay between us and—"

"That's all you care about is yourself! Did you tell your groupie about Chyna? Huh? Answer me, dammit!"

"It ain't like that," he said, hoping like hell that Nashlly wasn't listening too hard.

Kendra sighed heavily. "Goodbye, Marcus."

"Kendra wait! Please don't tell nobody 'bout this, okay?"

"And if I do?" she challenged. "Whatcha gone do? Try to kill me like you did Kandi? I'm done with you. Do what makes you happy, because it's clear that my *fat* ass can't!"

Kendra turned and left Swagga speechless.

Swagga's world seemed to topple down around him. A past he thought he had escaped was now a strain with each new breath. He was staring at the door when Nashlly glided out of the bathroom butt ass naked, titties swinging lightly.

"Don't let her stress you, daddy," she cooed, dropping to her knees.

"Never that," he said. "And you can bank on that."

CHAPTER
Eighteen
Baby Momma Drama

January 25, 2012

Wednesday 6:20 AM – Denver, Colorado

LaToria feared it was way too soon to be handling sex with Martellus as if it were a chore. Just like yesterday, she was breaking her man off with a taste of her loving.

"Mmmm, mmm, I'm gonna cum," she moaned with her hips moving in a slow circular spin on top of Martellus. Tossing her head back, she lifted her hands to her bouncing titties. In her mind she was back in front of the film crew. Her actions were all for the benefit of the man that was inside her. A man she was losing touch with. Mad at herself, she moved her hips faster, grinding her clit against him. Gasping, she fell over him, her breasts slapping him in the face. Biting her lip, she lifted up on his erection, and then slid back down. Shuddering, she did it again, only higher. Finding a steady pace, she bounced up and down, digging her nails hard into the pillow under his head. Her mounds smothered Martellus in a satisfying enjoyment.

Martellus gripped her soft hips, guiding her up and down his slightly curved erection. Tossing her head back, she screamed out his name, riding the sudden peak of her climax.

Twenty minutes later she watched Martellus leaving for work. She was curled up nude under the sheets, restless. With nothing much to do, she got up and pulled her touchscreen tablet out of her tote bag. Surfing the web, she ended up on her Twitter account where she had 750,000 followers. After a short pause, she posted a tweet.

Freezing my ass off in Denver! Missing MIA soo bad. ☹

Next, she randomly responded to twenty tweets, thanking her fans and true supporters of her films. After she was done, she logged on to her Facebook pages. Again, she responded to messages and posts from her fans. Her heart missed a beat when she came across Trevon's image. She had assumed he would have deleted her as a friend. She was torn with mixed feelings when she saw the change in his relationship status. *Single.* Out of his 3,000 friends, only a handful were men. LaToria could recall how Trevon was planning to ignore two friend requests from two gay men that saw his debut film. She had explained that all money was good money. It didn't matter who it came from. Trevon had to realize that he was in the adult film business, and all of his fans wouldn't be women. Going to his wall, she read his last post.

Ready 2 film next film next week! Hope U all will N-Joy. Shouts out 2 Jurnee!

1/24/12 9:15 a.m.

LaToria closed her eyes, fighting to keep her tears at bay. Holding her fragile composure together, she became curious of what Jurnee was posting on her social sites. Just as she pulled up Jurnee's Facebook page, a knock sounded on the polished solid oak bedroom door. Knowing it was the housekeeper, LaToria turned the tablet off, and then she slid it under the pillow.

"It's open," LaToria said after she lay back and got under the covers. Mrs. Biathrow entered the bedroom with a rosy-cheeked smile. "Good morning, Ms. Frost. Are you ready for your breakfast?"

"Yeah, I guess," LaToria said in a flat expressionless tone.

"Breakfast in bed, or will you be coming down to the kitchen?"

"Uh, gimme a minute to put some clothes on and get myself together."

"I can understand how you must"—Mrs. Biathrow smiled—"feel, speaking on the fun you and Martellus had this morning."

LaToria gasped. "Excuse me! How do you know what we did this morning?"

"I—the walls are thin. I mean, I heard the two of you when I made my rounds this—"

"Get out!" LaToria shouted.

"I'm sorry, Ms—"

"Don't make me repeat myself! Get the fuck out. Now!"

***

"This is so stupid!" Nashlly fumed the moment she slid into the backseat of a '96 Impala. "I told y'all dumb asses that I was gonna call!"

"Well, bitch you didn't!" the driver shouted, twisting in the seat glaring at her.

"I was busy, okay! This shit ain't easy, Art!" She paused, crossing her arms and sinking back against the seat.

"Busy doing what? You had me and Veto sitting in the damn rain last night for almost three fucking hours!" Art shouted with a strong urge to slap the shit out of Nashlly.

"Veto, tell Art that I woulda called if I had the chance to. Since his deaf ass ain't hear me the first time!" Nashlly said, raising her voice.

"Both y'all trippin'," Veto said, shaking his head.

"Nashlly, you need to tighten the fuck up!" Art said, turning back around. "You almost got us killed by not telling us his car was—"

"Art, how the hell I'm supposed to know his car was bulletproof, huh? If you wasn't speedballing so much . . . You shoulda just waited until he was out walking!"

"Better lower your tone!" Art warned, giving her a hard stare in the rearview mirror.

"Or what, motherfucker!" she yelled.

"That fly ass mouth is gonna run your ass down one of these days!" Art said, gripping the steering wheel with both hands.

"Well, today ain't the day! And I wish a motherfucker would!" she retorted.

Veto laughed at the two, and then sung out, "Alright, alright, alright, alright! You gon' learn today!"

Nashlly snickered with a hand over her mouth.

"Shit ain't fucking funny!" Art shouted.

"Look, I gots to go 'cause Swagga is expecting me back within the hour," Nashlly told them. Looking at her watch, she saw it was five minutes past 4 PM. Art turned in the seat. A smile was void on his face. "Next time I call you better answer! 'On't give a fuck what you might be doing with that nigga. Keep playing games, and I'ma leave your ass slumped right alongside Swagga. Now get the fuck out."

Nashlly rolled her fake hazel contact colored eyes as she shoved the door open. Slamming the door, she strutted across the parking lot, keying the alarm off her white 2009 Ford Mustang Boss.

***

"I don't trust that 'ho!" Art told Veto as Nashlly drove off with the system bumping.

"You worry too much, bruh. Shit, we could of had ole boy slumped if it wasn't for that damn tank he was riding in," Veto pointed out.

"Still don't trust her ass."

"You holler at your girl today?"

"Nah, not yet. She told me yesterday he supposed to swing by to see his seed, so you know how that shit go."

"You think she still fucking Swagga?"

"Truthfully, I don't care. I just know her skinny ass better break bread with that insurance money when we slump Swagga."

Veto nodded. "The sooner the better, my nig."

***

At the same time in West Palm Beach, Rick was back on the clock protecting Swagga. He was hoping Swagga would pull a quickie with his baby momma Jamilah and bounce since his son wasn't here.

Back in the bedroom, Swagga was trying to keep his calm with Jamilah.

"Why my son ain't here? I told yo' ass last week that I wanted to see 'im."

Twenty-eight-year-old Jamilah smacked her thin lips. “You ain’t been wanting to see ’im,” she mocked. “How you gonna miss your *only* son’s second damn birthday last month? Explain that!” She rolled her neck.

“I was busy. Damn! You know I had to beat them bullshit charges I had ova my head,” he explained from the edge of the bed where he sat.

“Yeah right.” She rolled her eyes, leaning against the dresser. “I heard you wasn’t too busy to be up under Kendra!”

“Where my son at?”

“My momma got ’im.” She deadpanned.

Swagga jumped to his feet. “You sent my son way up to Atlanta without tellin’ me shit!”

“Nigga, you rich! Catch a jet. And I’m telling yo’ ass now! Ain’t my fault you ain’t never around here!” She gestured wildly with her arms, causing the four 18-carat white gold and diamond bangles to clink on her right wrist.

“’Cause yo’ dumb ass always on some bullshit!”

“Fuck you, Swagga. Okay!” She frowned with her hands perched on her hips. “And why you looking at me all stupid and shit?”

“You got any drawers on?” he asked, lessening the space between them.

She glowered. “You can dead that idea. You been done lost your rights to me!”

He ignored her little tantrum. “Oh, that’s how you gonna handle me?”

“Go and be with Kendra, or your other baby momma, Stephanie!”

Grinning with his dreads hanging in his face, he reached for the first button on her silk orange blouse. "You look so much like Zoe Saldana when you get mad."

"You better get your hands off me," she said unconvincingly, reaching for his belt.

"I know you miss 'im," he teased. "G'head an' pull 'im out."

"Fuck you!"

"Can I get a taste of that good-good?" He unbuttoned her blouse.

"I can't," she whined, rubbing his growth through his jeans.

"Why not?" he asked, palming her small, big nippled breasts. He squeezed the left one while circling his thumb over the right one.

She took a deep shuddering breath. "I . . . got a boyfriend."

Before she could speak another word, he took her right nipple between his lips. "Mmmm, mmmm." He sucked hard on her dark brown nipple while licking it with quick flicks of his tongue. Knowing he had the green light, he grabbed the hem of her miniskirt and then hiked it up her slender hips and waist. A surge of lust filled him when he filled his palms with her tight, honey brown ass. She made no effort to impede him when he took a step back to drop his pants and boxers.

He jerked her around, bending her over the dresser. Even with her legs together, she still had a sizable gap. Bunching the skirt at her waist, he licked his fingers and then started spanking her ass. She rose up on her toes, shaking her ass to encourage him to spank her harder.

"Ahhhh. Maybe we shouldn't be doin' this—since you got a man."

"Boy, stop playing and put it in!" she said, pushing her ass against his penis.

"That's what I thought." Swagga shoved himself deep and hard between her skinny legs. Showing no love nor tenderness, he fucked her thoroughly with a tight grip on her tiny waist.

As much as she hated Swagga, she was infatuated with that meat between his legs. She could recall the night she first met him at the King of Diamonds strip club down in Miami three years ago. Unlike many, Jamilah wasn't on no groupie love. Swagga had approached her while she was leaving the club with her friends. By the time she found out he was only playing with her emotions, she was four months pregnant with his second born. The hurt grew deeper when another girl turned up pregnant two weeks later and gave birth to twin girls. And in the words of truth, Swagga was the dad.

She repeated his name, nearly keeping a cadence with his speedy strokes. With her left leg hiked up on the dresser she strained her neck to look into his face as he fucked her. Her small butt jiggled each time he slammed inside her.

"Harder! Ahhh. You better make me cum!"

"Shut up and take dis dick!"

"Fuck you nigga!"

"Who pussy!" he shouted.

She moaned, "Swagga, please . . . don't stop!"

He kept pounding at her slender frame, trying his hardest to bend her spine. Stroke after stroke after stroke, he long dicked her against the dresser for seven minutes continuously.

Jamilah's climax was triggered when Swagga locked a grip around her slender neck. She mixed her juices with his cum that was poured inside her. Wiggling her tight little bottom, she folded down to the floor after he pulled his penis out. Resting up against the dresser with one titty exposed, she turned angry when Swagga rubbed his dick against her cheek.

"What the hell wrong with you!" she hollered, shoving him with her nose turned up.

"I cain't get no mouth?" he asked with his pants bunched down at his ankles.

"You better get that shit outta my face! Now move and stop playing so damn much!"

"Not even fo' a new Hermes Birkin bag?" He smirked, wagging his dick.

She kicked at his feet. "Stop playing, fool!" She rose, pulling her blouse closed.

"Why you actin' all silly?"

"Shut the hell up!" she said, tugging the miniskirt back over her ass. Shoving him aside, she stomped to the bathroom.

"Oh. I cain't get no head but I can smash?"

Her reply came by slamming the bathroom door and locking it.

"C'mon, Jamilah, you ain't gotta be like that."

She ignored him.

Swagga looked at the bed and then down at his wet dick. Waddling across the room, he picked up one of the pillows, using the pillowcase to wipe himself clean. When he was done, he put it back in place. "Dumb ass 'ho," he mumbled, pulling his clothes up.

"I'ma bounce, yo! And you better have my son here next week too!"

The door eased open. "I need some money," she said with only her cute face showing.

"Get it from yo' punk ass boyfriend. Long as I pay that child support I don't owe you shit!'

"I need new tires for my truck, nigga! Tires that are worn down from me taking and picking up *our* son from daycare."

". . . You better not be lying 'bout that shit! How much you need?"

"Sixteen hundred. And don't bitch about it, because you're the one that bought the rims and tires in the first place!"

Swagga moved his dreads out of his face, and then dug into his front pocket. "Here," he griped, tossing a thick roll of fresh one hundred dollar bills on the bed.

"And how much is that?"

"More than enough. Use some to buy yo' broke ass nigga a hustle, so you can stop asking me for cash." He laughed.

She rolled her eyes. "Thank you."

"Yeah, yeah . . . I'm out."

"Um, where you going?"

"To the studio. Why?"

"Just asking. I might need to see you again later tonight."

Swagga popped the collar on his black and green Louis Vuitton button-down shirt. "I might can swing through. Just gimme a call."

"And be careful, okay? I got worried about our son after you told me about somebody shooting at you."

Swagga mellowed out, understanding her move to send his seed up to Atlanta. Before he left, he assured her that everything was all good.

Jamilah walked Swagga to the front door of the modest three-bedroom crib that was bought and paid for by

Swagga. Standing in the doorway, they shared a brief kiss. She played her part flawlessly, waving goodbye as Swagga and Rick slid inside the back of the Bentley Brooklands.

Not a minute after they left, Jamilah was pacing the plush mocha carpeted floor with her cell phone up to her ear.

"Hey, honey," she said when her call was answered. "He just left."

"Did he suspect anything, baby?" D-Hot asked.

She smiled. "Nope. And FYI, he's going to the studio."

***

Swagga sat behind the tinted glass in the back of his Brooklands in deep reflection. Gazing at the passing landscape along I-95 South, he wanted his focus to be clear before he hit the studio. His manager, Harry Storm was pressing him to get more studio time, and Swagga couldn't say that he was wrong. Swagga wanted to find that drive and true hustle that had earned him three platinum albums. Truth be told, the issue with Kendra knowing about Chyna had him all fucked up in the head. When thoughts entered his mind about going to get tested for any STDs, he would balk, and then dismiss the idea. Too much drama was starting to flood his focus. Rubbing his forehead, he feared the future. When would the next hail of bullets buzz his way? Who else would learn of his slipup with Chyna? At one point along the trip, his mind drew a bead on the melic words bumping from the speakers inside the luxurious Bentley sedan.

Don't trust my lady, 'cause she's a product of this poison.

I'm hearing noises,

Think she fucking all my boys, can't take no more

CHAPTER
Nineteen
I Got a Secret to Tell

It was ten minutes to 5 PM when Trevon received a call from Brooke Vee.

"Hey. What's up?" Trevon answered while behind the wheel of his XJL.

"Um, it's me again," Brooke Vee said. "Whatcha doing, handsome?"

"Heading back to the crib. I just left Chelsea's spot a minute ago."

"The new girl, right?"

"Yeah. We went over the script for our film and got to know each other a little bit."

"She's a lucky girl. Sure wish I could be in her position."

Trevon smiled. "It ain't like this is my last film. But anyway, what's up with your sexy ass?"

Brooke Vee giggled. "Now I'm sexy, huh? You were so dang quiet when you picked me up the other day and took me home."

"Just had a bunch of things on my mind," Trevon replied.

"Hmm. Well, how about you swing by my place for a minute? My little one is with my mom. Maybe this time we can get better acquainted."

Trevon wasn't looking forward to spending the evening alone. Jurnee was still tripping over the gun issue and wasn't speaking to Trevon. "Gimme thirty minutes and I'll be there."

"I was hoping you'd say that. I'll see ya' when you get here."

***

Brooke Vee answered the door with a wide smile on her face.

"Sorry I'm late," Trevon said as Brooke Vee pulled him inside.

She gawked at Trevon, tripping off his handsome looks and muscular build. Everything about Trevon was entrancing to her. His smile, the cleanness and sharp edges of his mustache and goatee, and his all white linen outfit. It all stirred her senses. "Boy, you look so much like Tyrese!"

"You told me that before," Trevon said, taking his shades off. His eyes roamed over Brooke Vee's voluptuous frame, starting at her breasts. She wore a green clingy sundress that molded all of her curves.

"I um, heard your interview the other night. I think you handled the pressure from that hating ass girl, well."

Trevon shrugged as he followed Brooke Vee to the living room. It was impossible for him to remove his gaze from her juicy ass. Being in his line of business, he already knew her alluring measurements. Barefooted, she stood at 5-feet 6-inches and 154 pounds. Her measurements were 34DD-28-42.

In the expansive living room, the two took a seat on a peach leather sofa.

Brooke Vee tossed little hints toward Trevon by brushing her breasts against his arm. "Would you like something to drink?"

"Nah. I'm good."

She settled next to him with her thick legs crossed. She would let Trevon steer the path of their actions tonight. "So um, how do you feel about your next film with Chelsea?"

"Just ready to get it done and over with. The boss said it's a must that I do an interracial film."

"I hope she don't turn your ass out." Brooke Vee laughed. "Them white girls be putting it down on y'all brothers just to have y'all turn on the sistahs."

"I doubt that." He grinned, taking notice of her strong cocoa butter scented skin.

"Okay, enough about her. How are things with you and Kandi? I don't wanna step on her shoes."

"It's just business between us."

"And none of this was planned? Like, y'all two got the porn biz buzzing with all types of gossip. I heard about the big spike in your DVD sales."

Trevon shook his head. "Nah, it wasn't a publicity stunt. But I can see how you and others might view it as being one."

"Are you seeing anyone now?"

"Nah. I think I need to focus more on my career from here on out."

Brooke Vee nodded. "Can I ask you a personal question?"

"Sure."

She cleared her throat. “That shit that went down last year between you and Swagga. Did D-Hot’s name ever come up?”

Trevon looked at her with a puzzled expression. “Not that I can recall. Why? What’s up?”

“Well FYI. I’ve been fucking with D-Hot since last summer. I met him at a video shoot for one of Swagga’s videos. Anyway, you know how some niggas lips get loose when they fall up in some tight pussy. And one day he told me something.”

“D-Hot was Swagga’s producer, right?”

“Yeah. But do you know why they are beefing on the low?”

Trevon told Brooke Vee he had no idea of any beef between D-Hot and Swagga. In truth, he saw no concern in it. Brooke Vee went on to tell him what D-Hot had shared with her one night.

“I’m not in love with D-Hot, so don’t get it twisted. But I’m not gonna allow no nigga to be in my bed and on the phone with another girl. Anyway, I got upset and asked him who the hell he was talking to. Can you believe it was Kandi?”

“And when was this?”

“Right around the time I first met him. Like mid-August. I was sorta jealous but I didn’t press the issue. He told me he was just in touch with her to see if she wanted to be in Swagga’s video. I knew that was a damn lie because everybody knew how Kandi wasn’t fucking with Swagga.”

“Because he cheated on her with that white urban model. Um, what’s her name?”

“Cindy aka Deja Pink. So I knew he told me a lie. But like I said, I didn’t make a big deal about it. This was also the time when you got hired at Amatory and came into the picture. Well, D-Hot never stopped his little talks with Kandi."

"Why you say that?"

"He left his phone over here one night, and I found a bunch of text messages between him and Kandi. And it was a helluva lot more than texts for a damn video."

Trevon shifted on the sofa. "So whatcha saying? D-Hot was fucking Kandi while she was with me?"

"I won't go that far. But listen to this. That night Swagga was arrested at the airport. Guess who called the police and tipped them off?"

"D-Hot?"

Brooke Vee nodded. "I was down at D-Hot's crib that night. He has a big ass crib on Sugarloaf Key. Anyway, he was acting all weird and told me to stay in the bedroom because he was expecting company. Of course, I assumed it was another bitch, so I snuck out when I heard D-Hot talking."

"But it was Swagga?" Trevon guessed.

"Yep. And I heard it all. How D-Hot tricked Swagga into wiring a ton of money to his account."

Trevon took a few seconds to think about what Brooke Vee was telling him. He knew some of her words were true. But what worried him was the link between Kandi and D-Hot. "So you're saying D-Hot tried to steal Swagga's money. And then he snitched Swagga out to the police that he would be at the airport?"

"I saw and heard it with my own eyes and ears. I still don't know why he was in touch with Kandi so hard. When I asked him about it a second time, he got upset so I fell back."

"Does D-Hot know you know about him snitching on Swagga?"

She grinned. "Nope. And I don't think Swagga knows either."

"And why are you telling me?" he asked curiously.

Brooke Vee sighed. "Because I feel sorry for you," she replied timorously, averting her eyes down. "And plus, I think Kandi hasn't been fully honest with you. Again, I don't know what she had going on with D-Hot, but something was up."

Trevon took a deep breath.

Brooke Vee glanced at her watch and then she stood.

"I know this visit isn't what you expected," she said. "But I felt you needed to know what was going on behind your back."

Trevon reached for her hand. "Thanks. But I didn't come here to talk about Kandi or D-Hot."

She smiled as he pulled her down to his lap. "Are you gonna tell me why you came?"

Trevon slid his hand up her smooth thigh when she was seated across his legs. Brooke Vee circled her arms around his neck as his hand inched under the hem of her sundress. She uttered a soft moan when Trevon's tongue traveled up the soft path of her cleavage. Their passion for each other peaked when Trevon discovered she didn't have any panties on. He palmed her pillow soft ass, practically molding it with his fingers. He reasoned his actions with Brooke Vee would prove to himself that he was over the hurt from LaToria. He wanted sex with no emotions. Sex with no strings attached.

Brooke Vee positioned herself with her knees astride his lap, facing him. Lust was clear on her face as she pulled the sundress up over her head. Her fake titties popped freely in Trevon's face. She fed him her left nipple with his hands glued to her wide hips and phat ass. Her pussy throbbed from his tender touch.

Trevon sucked lightly on her cocoa butter scented nipple as his dick pushed up against his linen pants. Her body was new to him, and it excited him. She quickly ended the one-side foreplay by moving off his lap. Tugging at his belt, she licked up and down his neck, wanting badly to free his monster.

"I've been wanting this dick since I first met you," she breathlessly moaned against his ear. "I just wanna fuck, baby. Can you break me off?"

Trevon removed all of his clothes, including his silk socks. Showing his strength, he scooped her in his strong arms and carried her to her bedroom. Brooke Vee turned the light on with her pussy dripping. She began her pleasure with Trevon by asking him to stand while she sat on the bed.

"I want to taste this," she said in a soft, sensuous moan. Leaving her eyes open, she slowly massaged his thick ebony shaft with both hands.

Trevon eased his dick inside her mouth. "Ohhhh," he groaned as her lips circled his flesh. The warmth and wetness of her mouth sent a chill up his spine.

Brooke Vee went to work. Sucking his dick as if the film crew was watching. In and out, his penis filled her wet mouth. "Mmmm, mmmm, mmmm." Back and forth, she swallowed his turgid flesh. Brooke Vee salivated, slurped, licked and nibbled on Trevon's dick from the tip to his balls. She couldn't believe how subjugated her mind and body became for Trevon. In her view, she realized she was living a reality of a fantasy by thousands of woman. While others would only watch Trevon in action, she had him in the flesh. She topped him off with her mouth for nearly eight minutes. His dick was slick and shiny from her slobber.

"Grab one of the condoms, baby," Brooke Vee said with the blunt head of his dick pressed against her cheek.

Trevon figured he would eventually fuck Brooke Vee on film. Being with her now was on a personal level as well as pleasure. When she positioned herself on the bed doggy style, he had to pause and admire her back shot. Like 90% of the women in porn, her pussy was bald. Staying on his feet, he tore the gold package open, and then rolled the condom down his throbbing shaft. Brooke Vee wiggled her hips while looking back at her jiggling ass.

"Don't run from this dick," Trevon teased as he slid his dick up and down the wet entrance of her pussy. He smacked both of her bouncy butt cheeks just to see them shake.

Brooke Vee's mouth dropped when Trevon slowly filled her up from behind. "Ummm, fuck. Gimme all that dick!" she shouted. Balling up the sheets in her hands, she couldn't contain her whimpers as his long dick choked her throbbing pussy. Her dangling titties swung beneath her as Trevon fucked her wet pussy with strong unrestrained strokes. Rocking back against his steady strokes she found a smooth rhythm that had his name pouring from her mouth.

Trevon rode her hard, hypnotized at the sight of her ass slapping back in his direction. The bed squeaked each time Trevon pushed balls deep inside of Brooke Vee. Closing his eyes, he fisted a hand in her hair with thoughts of Kandi forcing its way inside his head. Brooke Vee whimpered with the power behind his long-dicking strokes. Her sopping wet pussy welcomed Trevon's penetration.

"Yess! Fuck meee!" she cried as his meat plunged in and out of her tunnel.

Trevon kept his pace up for several minutes before he slid back out of her.

Brooke Vee took control by telling Trevon to join her on the bed. With the lights still on there was nothing to hide from. Pushing Trevon to his back, Brooke Vee got up on his dick to ride it backward. The sex was intense and hard. Her ass clapped and bounced up and down as she rode him. Her passionate groans poured endlessly.

Trevon later had her legs up on his sweaty shoulders. She clung to his neck and back, moaning and simpering as he fucked the hell out of her. She accepted his entire length inside her, repeating his name over and over with his balls slapping against her ass.

"Ummm, ummmm, Trevon." She licked his ear and then raked her fingernails up his back.

Trevon kept pounding at her tight wetness, beating her into the soft mattress. He was intoxicated off the sight of her big titties jerking beneath him. The sweet new scent of her pussy had him inhaling deeply.

Brooke Vee suddenly felt lightheaded. For a split second she forgot how to breathe. She arched her back off the sheets just as Trevon circled one of her nipples with his tongue. Her climax hit her in three waves back to back.

Trevon's ego was growing by the moment. He continued to fuck Brooke Vee as she came around his dick. Showing no emotions toward her, he turned her on her stomach and then pushed back inside her. Brooke Vee bit the pillow to muffle her moans as Trevon filled her pussy once again. Trevon kept his composure in check when he pounded Brooke Vee to a second climax.

Later in the shower, she slathered his dick with flat licks and noisy slurps until he released his seed on her lips, chin, and titties. Like a true porn star, she rubbed his warm cum all over her breasts and nipples while purring and licking his dick and balls.

CHAPTER
Twenty
Somebody Gots To Die!

A low, dark gray cloud reflected off the glossy black hood of an idling Rolls-Royce Phantom Coupe. D-Hot sat behind the brown leather-wrapped steering wheel leaning against the plush armrest. Picking up his cell phone, he saw it was eight minutes past 9 PM. Sitting up, he looked up and down the dimly lit street. A block away, he spotted two crack heads shambling across the street. Behind him, a few yards away was one of his Toyota Land Cruisers with two of his boys inside. Time was an issue tonight.

D-Hot knew his high-priced coupe would look suspicious in such a shabby neighborhood. It wouldn't matter if he was black or white if the po-po rolled up. The Rolls-Royce would get stopped and searched even if Tyler Perry was driving. D-Hot was clean. It was the Land Cruiser that had him stressed. Sighing, he leaned back against the headrest, wrapping a grip on the black polymer framed .45-caliber five-shot revolver, hoping he wouldn't have to use it tonight in the streets of Carol City.

"Niggas better hurry the hell up!" he grumbled just as the first sheets of rain speckled the windshield. He closed his eyes and then hummed a new beat he was working on. The rain suddenly broke, pelting the fixed roof of the Phantom Coupe. D-Hot jerked up and then glanced at his cell phone again. Only three minutes had slid by, testing his patience. He rubbed his face, yawning and scratching his beard. Just as he settled back in the seat, a pair of headlights grew in the driver's side mirror. He paid little interest to the vehicle, but was able to determine the make, color, and model as it drove past under the pouring rain. D-Hot watched the taillights of the green Dodge Challenger fade out of his view. He was so busy looking ahead that he didn't notice the candy purple Dodge Ram pickup creeping behind the Land Cruiser. His cell phone rang.

"Where the hell you at, bruh?" D-Hot said without raising his voice.

"Y'all niggas sleepin'." Art laughed. "I'm right behind your SUV."

"What the—" D-Hot was made a believer when Art flashed his lights on and off.

"Yo, there's an unlocked warehouse not too far from here. Follow me 'cause it's too open out here," Art explained.

"Alright, man. Whatever—just hurry up so I can get this shit off me."

Six minutes later, D-Hot stood at the back of the Land Cruiser with Art and Veto at his sides. "Y'all better be happy with these, and yes, I got two of 'em." D-Hot pulled the towel off the two brand new assault rifles and then handed one to Art. "It's a—"

"I know what the fuck it is!" Art retorted as he tested the weight and balance of the Smith and Wesson M&P15 M4 tactical rifle.

"Well, these babies had a lil' operation," D-Hot told them.

Art looked at D-Hot. "You sayin' these motherfucka's are fullies?"

"All the way," D-Hot answered as Veto picked up the second illegally converted M4 fully automatic rifle.

"You got ammo?" Art asked.

D-Hot leaned into the back of the SUV and pulled out a large backpack. "Here's four 30-round clips and a 120 rounds. If y'all need more than this then y'all fucked up big."

"We gonna handle our end! Just make sure you handle yours," Art stated.

"We need to get on the road, my nig," Veto said, shouldering the backpack.

"Nashlly call you yet?" D-Hot asked Art.

"Yeah. They all still at the studio. Trust me . . . shit goin' down today."

"You mean tonight," D-Hot corrected him as he closed the liftgate.

"Let's be out, Veto," Art said, glaring at D-Hot before he hurried back to the pickup.

Art sped off, leaving D-Hot and his Do-Boys behind.

"You ready to do this?" Veto asked from the passenger seat, loading the clips.

Art was silent for a moment. "Sumthin' ain't right."

"Speak your mind, my nig," Veto said, loading another brass round into the clip.

"Check it, right," Art said with one hand on the wheel. "Jamilah wants Swagga out of the picture so she can collect some life insurance, right?"

"Uh-huh." Veto nodded.

"An' D-Hot is payin' us, what? Twenty thou' a piece, right?"

"That sounds 'bout right, my nig," Veto replied as Art switched lanes to hit a ramp for I-95 North. "So, what ain't right?"

Art's expression was hidden inside the dark interior. "Bruh, you know that big ass dookie green diamond chain that D-Hot got?"

"Yeah. It um, got that Bigg Dog logo piece on it. What about it?"

Art shook his head as he picked up his speed. "Bruh, I found that nigga's chain in Jamilah's bedroom back on Monday."

"Damn! How the fuck—"

"Ain't say shit to 'er nor his ass."

"Alright, so what's up?" Veto asked after turning the police scanner on.

"We handle our biz, and then I'll get some answers 'bout this fuck shit going on behind my back."

***

Fritz wouldn't consider himself a voyeur since he found no pleasure in viewing others in the act of copulation. Lowering the range finder binoculars from his eyes, he tightened the black poncho over his head and then carefully adjusted his footing in the tree. The steady flow of rain wasn't helping Fritz, but neither would it hinder him. With the binoculars back to his eyes, he read the self-illuminating LED display that told him he was 275 yards away from his target. Scanning the apartment complex, he spotted his target's car 300 yards away, the distance of three football fields.

He smiled, thinking of a name change for the benefit of his trade. "The Mailman" seemed suitable to him since he could strike come rain, snow, sleet or hail. He would strike tonight, quick and fatal.

***

"Yo Rick! You got a call on line four." A studio assistant with a blond Mohawk shouted from the front desk down the hall.

Rick was down on the first floor chatting with a cute Haitian receptionist in the lounge. "Take a message," he said, figuring if it was somebody important they would have had his cell number. "So how long have you been working?"

"Yo, they said they got some info on that I-95 shooting."

Rick quickly excused himself from the receptionist and then hurried down the hall to the front desk. "Hello, who this?"

"Uh, ain't gonna say my name, but I got some info for you."

Rick tried to match the dude's voice with a face but he couldn't. "What kind of news? And what do you know about that I-95 shooting that wasn't on the news?"

"Listen, and this all I'll say about it. I know about that trip you and Swagga made up to West Palm Beach before the shooting and *that* wasn't on the news."

Rick motioned the assistant to step off so he could have some privacy. "Okay, I'm sold. What's this info you got for me?"

"Here's your warning. Two niggas in a purple Dodge Ram are somewhere near the studio waiting for y'all to leave, and them niggas ain't playing the radio."

"And it's real?"

"Ya think? Damn right it's real! Ignore this warning . . . I guess you'll be out of a job by tomorrow because you can't guard a dead man, can you?"

"Alright. I need more—Hello? . . . Hello?" The line went dead. "Shit!" Rick slammed the cordless phone down, and then ran to the elevator making a call on his cell phone. He couldn't afford to ignore the call, even if it wasn't his life that was on the line. As the elevator took him up to the third floor, his call was connected with a posted bodyguard up in the studio with Swagga.

"Whut up, Rick?"

"Yo, Tweet! We gotta code black. I repeat, code black!"

"Ai'ight. I'm moving now!"

Rick made a second call to one of the two bodyguards that were down in the parking lot watching the three vehicles.

"Yo?"

"Hey Rock, we gotta code black an' this shit is real. Tweet and the boys are moving Swagga as we speak. What y'all holdin' tonight?"

"Uh, me and Bobo packing two Glock nines apiece, and I got a Mac-10 too!"

"Ai'ight. Be on point, and y'all know what to do! If it's the same two from the first time, we gotta be heavy 'cause them niggas had an AK last time."

"Okay, dawg. We moving!"

Rick made his last call just as the elevator reached the third floor. He called 9-1-1.

Swagga was in the middle of recording a track when Tweet bullied his way inside the recording booth. Swagga's initial reaction was him snatching his headphones off and shouting, "What the fuck! Don't you see me—"

Tweet uttered two words and grabbed his arm. "Code black!" From day one, Rick had preached to Swagga about the dire seriousness that could initiate a code black. To make sure Swagga knew what to do in such a predicament, Rick had explicitly stated, "Don't ask no questions! Just shut the fuck up and move! Let me and my men do our job, simple as that."

Swagga was sandwiched between two of his bodyguards as they rushed toward the fire exit. He knew shit was dead ass when Tweet paused to check the fire exit with a black 9-millimeter that was fitted with a laser beam under the barrel. Rushing down the stairs, his heavy chains and diamond pieces bounced off his chest and stomach. Reaching the second floor, Tweet shouted for Swagga to hustle faster. Fear seeped quickly inside of Swagga. He wasn't ready to die. Not tonight.

***

Fritz was in his element. Hunting the prey, clad in black boots and matching cargo pants and T-shirt, he crossed the lit parking lot with his head down. He was aware of the surveillance camera positioned to his left on a lamppost. With the pouring rain it would help distort his features. He walked with a fake limp, knowing the footage would later be reviewed by the police. Even without the fake limp, he would be a ghost, coming and going. Out of the range of the camera, he reached his target's high-priced car. Without pausing in his steps, he reached inside the rear left wheel well and removed the quarter-sized GPS tracking device. He dropped it in his front block-shaped pocket, and then moved into the shadows. From his conceded position, he had a clear view of the first door where his target would soon exit.

Fritz ignored the rain that ran down the bridge of his nose and saturated his clothes. This was luxury in comparison to the last locale where his talents were needed.

Down on one knee, he turned stone like, only his eyes moved. Waiting. Not a minute later he saw two silhouettes in the living room window. The tendons in his legs became tight. He waited. Moving only his right hand, he removed the silenced Glock 19 from a custom holster fitted under his left arm. His breathing slowed as he thumbed the safety off.

Fritz came up out of the puddle he was kneeling in. Still in a squat, he watched his target exit the apartment with a dark colored umbrella. *Perfect!* Fritz thought. The rain beating on the umbrella would most surely cover any sounds of his approach.

His target moved briskly down the sidewalk, keying the alarm and remote starting his car. Fritz stood still, hidden in the shadows behind his target. Easing his finger on the trigger, he moved with a purpose. He sped up when he saw the interior light come on inside the target's ride. He darted between two cars, making his approach from the rear. His target slid inside the car, pausing to close the umbrella. Fritz reached him just as he swung his legs inside the car.

"Excuse me, sir," Fritz called out.

His target jerked up in the seat, startled by Fritz's sudden appearance. "Yeah, what—"

Fritz struck. His finger eased back on the trigger twice. His target moaned in agony after two hollow-point bullets pierced his crotch area. Blood pooled from the lethal wound, turning his target's pants red. Fritz watched him, writhing in pain and gasping for a breath that he would never take. Fritz took three deep breaths, and then he nudged his target with the silenced tip of the Glock-19. His target coughed up blood, not understanding that he couldn't move his leg because he was paralyzed from the waist down. Fritz knew he could walk away and leave the chances of survival of his target up to whatever higher power he believed in. *If* he survived, he would never walk again. Fritz held the Glock steady, nudging his target once more. A heartbeat later, their eyes met. Fritz nodded at his target. Then he shot him three times in the face at point-blank range. The body went lifeless, slumped across the center console with three holes above his left ear and cheek. Fritz was closing the door with his elbow when a scream cracked the silence. In a moment's breath he saw the girl his target had been with. She stood six-feet away on the sidewalk holding an umbrella and wearing a T-shirt and jeans. A cell phone fell from her hand. A cell phone that apparently belonged to his target. She was filling her lungs to scream again. Fritz took it all in, and then coldly shot her twice, once in the forehead and once in the throat before the cell phone clattered to the wet sidewalk.

CHAPTER
Twenty-One
I Will Cry for You

Back up in West Palm Beach, Art and Veto were putting as much distance between them and the studio as possible. The decision to haul ass was common sense after they heard the APB over the police scanner. Art was heated as he left the scene. His eyes kept roaming over the rearview mirrors, praying against all hope that no blue lights would appear. He knew he had some bullshit traffic violation warrants over his head, but that wasn't shit compared to having a fully automatic assault rifle. As for Veto, he was shitting bricks just the same.

Art was heading south, leaving the city limits of West Palm Beach. After driving for six minutes on edge, Art reached for his cell phone.

"We should get rid of these guns before we get pulled, my nig," Veto suggested with the mind to toss everything.

"Bruh, chill!" Art shouted, and then checked the speedometer to make sure he wasn't speeding. "We good. Just . . . sit back and chill."

"Look, man. You're the one talkin' 'bout shit ain't right. Now look what the fuck just happened! Who the hell called the po-po and gave 'em the description of your truck?"

"'On't fuckin' know, bruh! Who I look like? A fuckin' psychic or sumthin'! Just . . . we good. Lemme call this bitch right quick."

Veto frowned as Art made a call.

"Yeah, hello? Who's calling?" a female answered.

Art sucked his teeth. "Yo, lemme talk to Jamilah."

"Who's calling?"

Art sighed. "Art! Now put Jamilah on the phone!"

"Damn, Mr. No Patience. Hold on?"

Art turned on the high beams as he drove down a back road leaving the city behind.

"Hey, baby," Jamilah answered a minute later. "What's up with you?"

"Bullshit!"

"Huh?"

"Look, you know I can't say too much over this phone, right?"

"I'm listening." She sounded worried.

"Somebody talking."

"How! Do Swagga know—"

"Nah, just listen. Yo, somebody called the police before we could ah . . . go see our boy."

"Uh-huh."

"And they knew what I was driving."

"Ohh fuck!" she groaned. "Where are you now?"

"Leaving West Palm Beach."

"Where Veto?"

"Right here with me. Look, get my car and meet me at my aunt's house in Opa Locka. And yo, where Nashlly?"

"In the kitchen playing cards."

"She made any calls in the last thirty minutes?"

". . . Ah, not that I know of, baby. I hope you aren't suggesting she called—"

"I just don't trust that 'ho!"

"I don't see her doing that, Art. But damn, somebody had to call."

"This shit is all fucked up, so I'ma lay low for a minute."

"What about Swagga?"

"Jamilah! Didn't you just hear what I said! Somebody tipped the police off!"

"But—"

"But—my ass! I already did that dumb shit the first time and damn near got ran off a fucking bridge! Listen, whatever plans you had wit' Swagga, don't change it."

"Baby, I'm scared. What if—"

"Hold up! Don't start that shit, so stay calm. Okay?"

"I'm trying."

"Look. I'll see you later. Oh wait. Never mind, I'll holler atcha later."

"Okay, bye. Baby, wait. Do you want me to tell Nashlly what's up?"

"Uh . . . no. But bring her with you."

"Okay. I'm leaving now."

Art ended the call as Veto adjusted the settings on the police scanner. "We going to my aunt's crib," Art said, wishing he had a cigarette.

"And then what?" Veto sat up waiting for an answer.

"Between you and me—fuck all this shit. Fuck Jamilah, fuck Swagga, and fuck D-Hot! I'ma hit the stash, gas up my Impala, and go visit my fam' up in New Bern, North Carolina. Ain't 'bout to risk my life or freedom, so fuck 'em both. So what you gon' do?"

Veto scratched his ear, grinning. "Shit, you ain't leaving me down here. I'm goin' with you, my nig."

***

Ariana softly nudged Jurnee on her shoulder, waking her.

"Your phone is ringing," Ariana muttered, flipping her pillow over.

"What time is it?" Jurnee asked with her head under the covers.

Ariana sat up rubbing her tired eyes before she focused on the digital clock across her bedroom. "Um . . . three twenty-two."

Jurnee mumbled a few words before throwing the covers off her head. She answered the call without checking the ID.

"Hello?" Jurnee said, lying on her side.

"Uh, Jurnee, this is Ruby. I'm glad you answered. I was told to call you and inform you that there's been a shooting—"

Jurnee sat up. "Who was shot?"

"All I can say is that you're to meet Ms. Babin at the morgue."

"Ruby! Who was shot? I need to know, dammit!"

Ariana was slipping out of the bed when Jurnee gasped, dropping the cell phone. Things moved with an urgency as the two women got dressed. Jurnee was unable to control her emotions as tears ran unchecked down her face. Ariana was at Jurnee's side to comfort her, showing her compassion even in the early stages of their bond. Since Jurnee was too unstable to drive, Ariana drove off with Jurnee crying in the passenger seat of her SUV.

***

Janelle wiped her wet eyes as the white female homicide detective entered the small office. After they shook hands and introduced themselves, the detective offered Janelle a cup of coffee, which she declined.

"Thank you for making the time to talk to me," Janelle said. "I'm sure it's been a hectic night and all."

"Just the weather," the detective replied, nodding at the rain streaked window behind Janelle.

"Can you tell me what you're at liberty to discuss?"

"Two victims. One female, shot twice in the face area. The male we found inside the car was shot multiple times, and the crime scene is still being processed."

"Do you have an assumption of how it happened?"

The detective nodded. "I think it was a possible robbery attempt that went wrong. I think the suspect was caught in the middle of the act and killed the girl. But what I find interesting is no one heard any shots."

Janelle wiped her eyes again. "I have the next of kin info your partner asked for."

The detective and Janelle spoke for another few minutes before they parted. Janelle's mind was numb. She couldn't come to grips with the pain she had to face. Knowing her tears were meaningless, she was unable to stop them. The events were surreal to her, but yet the moment moved on, regardless of how she felt. She cried. Janelle prayed, asking for strength that she knew she needed in the approaching days.

When Jurnee arrived, she only had three words to say. "Is it . . . true?" she asked Janelle, hoping that a mistake had been made.

Janelle, with a somber expression, slowly nodded yes, and then embraced her friend in need of comfort.

CHAPTER
Twenty-Two
Guess What Happened?

February 8, 2012

Wednesday 2:30 PM South Beach, Florida

Two weeks later . . .

The sultry sun claimed its dominance over SoBe (South Beach) with the aid of the cloudless skies. With the beach beckoning temperature in the high 80s, Janelle and Jurnee lay out tanning on the sand. Both were topless, wearing yellow bikini bottoms. After attending two funerals in the past nine days, both were open to a more upbeat mood.

"How's Victor doing?" Jurnee asked Janelle about her fiancé.

"Working on a new novel," Janelle replied as the heat warmed her back and legs.

"Tell 'im he better still put me on the cover of his next book."

"I will," Janelle said as two Asian women walked by with their small, big nippled titties exposed.

"Been a rough year, huh?" Jurnee said with her arms crossed under her chin.

"Yeah, and it's just the beginning," Janelle added morosely.

"Uhm, about Trevon."

"Don't wanna talk about it," Janelle retorted, brushing sand off her elbow.

"All right. So, you were telling me about that last call you got from Brooke Vee."

Janelle smoothed out the edges of her orange beach towel. Then she lay back down on her stomach facing Jurnee. "She called me like—an hour or so before they said it happened. She said D-Hot was over and that he came to say he was sorry for that stunt he pulled at the office."

"Really?"

"Yeah. Said something about him finding his chain, and she even put him on the line to apologize to me. I told him it was okay and that his main concern should be Brooke Vee since he accused her of stealing his chain."

"I heard what you did for her baby."

"I was there when her baby was born. The least I can do is make sure Brooke Vee's mom won't have any problems financially raising that child."

Jurnee's face suddenly lit up when she spotted Ariana waving at her from the rollerblading path. The two had been inseparable since the day Jurnee left Trevon back on the 24th of last month.

"I see you and Ariana are doing well," Janelle commented as she slid a wisp of hair off her cheek.

Jurnee beamed. “She’s a breath of fresh air,” she said, waving back at Ariana before she took off down the crowded path rollerblading.

“Are you bringing her to the party tonight?”

Jurnee shrugged. “It depends if we can get out of the bed.”

“You are such a big freak.” Janelle laughed.

“Hey! Did you hear about Swagga being shot at?”

“When?”

“Last month. Ariana told me about it. She said there was a small story on it in the *Hip Hop Weekly*.”

“Girl, if it don’t land on my desk, I don’t know about it. But since you mentioned him, he’s been keeping it low for a minute.”

“I think it’s by force since Future and Drake and all them are tearing up the airwaves. It might be over for Swagga.”

“His problem. Not mine,” Janelle replied, welcoming the heat on her skin.

***

“Don’t raise your voice at me, Anthony!” Tahkiyah said firmly as she packed her suitcase.

“Baby, you’ve only been home for twelve days and you’re going back down there! It doesn’t make any sense!”

“That’s because you don’t understand, okay?” she replied as she continued packing.

“I don’t want you to go, Tahkiyah.”

“We’ve already discussed this.”

“Well, I’m not done discussing it, okay!”

“Anthony,” she said, looking at him across the bed, “in the next few minutes I’m walking out that door, and I’m getting in my car and I'm going back to Miami! In truth, it was never up for discussion."

"Why!" he shouted, turning red. "Because you've turned this matter into an *obsession*!"

Tahkiyah took her glasses off her beautiful face. She stared at the man she cared deeply for. She had knowledge of the gossip that her co-workers and employees would remark behind her back about her and Anthony. *"Oh, she like a little cream in her coffee", "If it ain't white, it ain't right for Tahkiyah", "She got money, so only a white man will suit her."*

Tahkiyah had a *reason* for not dating black men, a *reason* that was a pain only she knew. Eyeing Anthony, she spoke clearly. "Are you saying I'm being compulsive and unreasonable about this?"

"No. I just—"

"Yes, you damn well did! Look up the meaning of the word! And while you're at it, Anthony, look up the word finished because that's what we are! Now if you'll excuse me, I have to pack for this *obsession* that is driving me crazy."

"Okay, I get it," he said, pointing at her. "You want to be with a black guy."

"What!" she shouted. "What makes you think—"

He snatched her laptop off the bed. "I saw the videos you downloaded, Tahkiyah. The black sex porn? You didn't have to hide it behind my back! You lied to me about everything!" he rebuked her, shaking the laptop.

"Anthony, I—"

"Save it!" he shouted with an odd grin on his face. "I know what this . . . little trip is all about, Tahkiyah," he said, walking around the bed. "Before we got together, you were dating another white man. Warren, the VP of

Integrated Marking for that automotive magazine. And before him it was that college professor, white as well. And I know of your past love life because you've confided in me, baby." Dropping the laptop back on the bed, he smiled, easing his hands on her waist. "You don't have to leave, okay? If you're missing or just *curious* about being with a black man, bring him here. Let me watch him fuck you. Is that what you want?"

Tahkiyah smiled. "Are you sure?"

Reluctantly, he nodded yes.

"But, baby," she wooed, sliding her hands up his chest. "What about that old adage that people always say?"

"What adage?" he asked as she toyed with his silk tie.

"You know . . ." She grinned. "The one about once you go black, you never go back. Since you've seen the porn. Can you measure up?" She shoved him, erasing the smile on his face. "What the hell is wrong with you? Going through my shit behind my back! Fuck you, Anthony!" she screamed furiously.

"But, baby, I thought—" he began to plead his mistake.

"You thought wrong, *white* boy! This is one cup of coffee you can cancel ever tasting again! Now do this black woman a favor and get the fuck out of my house!"

***

At the same time across the vast Atlantic Ocean, Swagga was ballin' along a stretch of the Autobahn expressway in Germany. He was seated behind the wheel of a yellow Porsche 911 GT3 maxed out at 195 miles per hour with Nashlly filling the passenger seat. In the wake of the GT3 was a jet black Audi R8 being driven by Rick. The trip to Germany was a much needed vacation for Swagga, which had started a day after the code black.

Swagga was getting used to Nashlly's company and super climatic sex. Just two days ago, he had purposefully flaunted her in Paris, France just to get the paparazzi riled up and to keep his name buzzing. She was eating the attention up and keeping her lips or legs wrapped around Swagga every chance she got.

Swagga's mind was elsewhere. He tried to conceal his stress from everyone, including Rick. For some reason he couldn't find peace. Peace of mind is what he seeked. He just wanted to rap and make music. As he sped toward the horizon, he tried to put the bullshit behind him. For starters, his conscience was afflicted ever since his successful plot resulted in D-Hot's murder. Swagga had discovered through his legal team that D-Hot had snitched him out to the U.S. Marshals.

Swagga's plane was never going to Morocco that night. D-Hot had set up his fake escape after tricking Swagga into wiring $75,000,000 to his account. Now, D-Hot was dead, along with Brooke Vee, who was just at the wrong place at the worst time.

***

Back in the state of Florida, Kendra was taking a shower with Trevon. The two had easily rekindled their secret sexual bond, and neither had any objections about it.

"I was just thinking about something," Kendra said, rubbing the soapy rag over his chest. "Remember when we did it at my house that night? Why were you so trusting of me to not use any protection?"

"Trevon was caught off guard by her serious question. "Shit, I guess I just got caught up in the moment."

"Has that happened before? I'm bringing this up because the mess Swagga did behind my back scared me."

Trevon removed his hand from her wet bouncy ass. "Um, since I've been outta prison I only went um, raw with three women. You, LaToria, and Jurnee."

"You're not afraid of the risk you're taking?"

Trevon sighed. "Everything just moving so fast for me. I come home and find myself living a life that I only thought was a dream. LaToria and I hook up, and then we breakup over some bullshit."

"And I popped up," she said, grinning up at him.

"Hell yeah!" he said. "My sexy ass probation officer that looks so much like Jill Scott. One minute you're trying to send me back to prison . . ."

"And the next I'm fucking you like it's my mission in life."

"That sounds about right. But to be honest with ya, I've made a bunch of mistakes since I've been out."

"Including me?"

"Picture that," he said, palming her ass again.

"I'm happy to hear that. And I'm glad you respected my decision about using protection when we hook up."

Kendra had managed to have Trevon assigned to her case load two weeks ago. She would show up at his door no less than four times a week. When she was with Trevon he made her feel desired. Her stance was still the same. Sex with no emotional strings attached.

"I can't believe what I'm about to do with you," she said, stroking his soapy penis.

Trevon licked both of her swollen nipples as she continued to work her grip up and down his manhood. "You sure you want this to happen?"

She nodded yes. "My friend thinks I'm a square when it comes to sex. Doing a threesome has always been a fantasy of mine."

"Who's it really for? You or her? I don't want you to start tripping on me if we do this."

Kendra squeezed his dick. "You're not my man," she reminded him. "Tonight is my night. It will be a one-time affair. Just the three of us, all right?"

Trevon was down to be a part of her fantasy. It was Kendra's kinky idea to invite her BFF Dani to join her and Trevon. She had explained to Trevon how Dani had showed her an unedited copy of his first film.

Telling the truth was easy for Kendra. She openly told Trevon that his first film changed her attitude toward him. Kendra knew about the crush Dani had on Trevon and a few other AEF actors. Not only would Kendra do a threesome. She was allowing the freaky actions to be filmed. Everything was set and ready for Dani to make things happen.

Trevon wasn't surprised when Kendra hit him with a list of rules.

1. Safe sex.
2. No anal sex.
3. No girl on girl.
4. Leave the lights on.

When Dani showed up at his door, she was star-struck and tongue-tied. Kendra felt a

surge of sexual prowess when it was her and not Dani that started things off. After downing two full glasses of gin and juice, Kendra acted out her fantasy as a sexy plus-size vixen. With the camera rolling, she shamelessly wrapped her pink glossy lips around Trevon's long dick.

Tonight was eventful and special for Kendra. As she eased her lips back and forth along his hard dick, she was relieved she had the willingness to do what she had only dreamed about. Everything snapped to reality when Dani finally broke from her trance to join Kendra at Trevon's feet. Kendra held not a stitch of bitterness as she later watched Dani working her lips up and down Trevon's meat.

Trevon fucked both women tirelessly in front of the camera. Dani turned out to be a screamer. Her loud moans and stuttering praises of Trevon's dick was an event itself. She yanked at the sheets, her big ass bouncing all over the place.

Pussy became faceless and nameless to Trevon. He gave his all to both women, showing them the difference between making love and fucking. His focus was on the latter.

Trevon later found himself relaxing alone in the tub. Kendra and Dani had left twenty minutes ago with an hour and a half of their sex on tape. Trevon had his eyes shut, reflecting on his life since he was released from prison. He didn't have much to complain about. He had a big body ride on 24's, a nice ass crib, and money on deck. Porn was his root, his foundation. The women he had been with crossed his mind. LaToria, Jurnee, Kendra, Linda, the cougar he fucked on the set of his first film, Ariana, Dani, Brooke Vee, and Cindy. He wasn't ready to claim Cindy since she had drugged his ass. And he added Chelsea from his second film.

So in truth, he'd sexed eight different women since being released out of the joint on August 17th of last year. A touch of sadness moved him when he thought of Brooke Vee. From what he was told, she was murdered not even two hours after he left her crib. He felt guilty that he knew nothing about her. *Damn. I don't even know the name of her little girl*, he thought. Sighing, he realized that life could hold no promise of tomorrow. Above all, he was through dealing with matters of his heart!

Wanting to get out of the house, he got Coogi down to the socks and then hit the streets at 4:40 PM. The triple chrome Rucci rims twinkled under the XJL as he cruised north along 7th Avenue with the two 15-inch subs bumping in the trunk. Drake's "HYFR" was hitting so hard that he left the song on repeat. His Jag turned heads as he pushed the sedan with one wrist draped over the wheel. He saw his world through a pair of light green Versace shades, and he realized that 90% of the women that looked his way was his own doing. The wet candy paint, the big rims and glossy thin rubber band tires, and the dumping sound system. It all screamed "look what I got!"

For those reasons, he collected eight new phone numbers from ladies that waved him down, hoping to fill that empty passenger seat inside his Jag. He told none of the women about his *job*. All they saw was a black man balling. As dusk began to blanket Miami, he spotted a red McLaren MP4-12C at an intersection at 183rd Street.

Grinning, he flicked the headlights a few times, and then made a call on the hands free phone system.

"Yes, Trevon," Janelle answered with Alicia Keys "Unthinkable" playing in the background.

"I see you're out ballin' tonight. Switched up your Lambo for the McLaren."

"Where are you?"

"At the red light to your left. Behind a taxi. Where you going?"

"I'm still mad at you for changing that script. But since I like you, I'ma let it slide, again."

"You know you can't stay mad at me. But yo, where you headed?"

"Nowhere fast. Just cruising."

"Me too."

"You coming to my party?"

"Wouldn't miss it for nothin'."

"Good, because I want you to meet your next cast mate for your next film."

"Ai'ight I'll be there, boss lady," he promised.

***

Jamilah was moving to Atlanta, and Swagga would be the last to know. Her little insurance scheme was a dead issue, pun intended due to D-Hot's murder. She was alone since Art had bounced out on her without a kiss goodbye. Too much was on her shoulders to deal with. *Does Swagga know I was in on the two hits? Who killed D-Hot? Am I next?* To make matters worse, she had taken a call from Nashlly three days ago. In the simplest terms, Nashlly told her that Swagga was unaware of the shit *they* tried to pull, and it would stay that way. She also admitted that she had her cousin drop a dime on Art and Veto. As for why? This too she was direct and blunt with.

"Swagga is *my* money ticket now, so all y'all bitches can step back!"

CHAPTER
Twenty-Three
Diced Pineapples

Since the weather was permitting, Janelle's RSVP party was being held outdoors under the faint lambent full moon. Greenish lights lit up the palm trees that lined the infinity edge pool, creating a serene ambience. Men and women of nearly every nationality were in attendance at Janelle's Sunset Island mansion.

Lounging out by the pool sipping a lemon daiquiri, Jurnee stood with four other women. She was keeping admired looks her way by flaunting her shapely figure in a gold sequined and mesh dress that clung high above her knees. Her skin had a soft radiant glow of gold that matched the new highlights in her hair. Without being vain, she *knew* she was on top of her game tonight.

Five men and two women had approached her in just an hour of her showing her face. They were all thoughtfully turned down. DJ Kay Slay had the sounds of "Fucking You Tonight" by Biggie Smalls and R. Kelly playing at a respectable level for the swanky partygoers.

You must be used to me spending,

and all that sweet wining and dining,
well I'm fucking you tonight . . .
And another one . . .

Jurnee was telling a story about a blunder that happened to her once during a film when one of the girls nodded toward her.

"Excuse me, ladies." Trevon snuck up behind Jurnee, easing his hands down to her soft prodigious hips. "I need to speak to my manager for a second."

"Hi Trevon," two of the girls cooed in unison. Both were admirers of his debut film.

Trevon didn't speak again until he was alone with Jurnee. "You still giving me the silent treatment?"

"I've been in touch by e-mail and text," she nonchalantly replied without bothering to turn around. "Plus, I sent you a tweet yesterday."

"You still trippin' off that gun?" he asked, brushing his lips against her ear.

"We still cool." She shivered from his closeness. "But I meant what I said. As long as it's under your roof, I won't be visiting you."

"Nah, your sexy ass is just stubborn, that's all."

She shrugged, taking another sip of her drink.

"I got rid of it," he said as he moved around her luscious body.

"When?" She looked at him, shifting her stance in the strappy Manolo Blahnik heels.

"After the funeral," he replied, adjusting his silk and black-green tie.

Jurnee pushed a curly wisp of hair off her cheek. "I might need to check for myself." She smirked, wondering if he realized how bad her body was missing him.

"Ai'ight, we can make that happen as soon as we leave."

"And who said I'll be leaving with you?" she asked with one eyebrow lifted.

"I did," he proclaimed with a grin tugging the corners of his lips. "Where your girl Ariana at?"

"Home. She has a big test coming up."

Trevon looked at her delicious glossy lips, remembering how they felt around his tool. His desire for her was too strong to neglect. "Stay with me tonight," he said.

She smiled at him. "You miss me, papi?" She touched his face as the attraction between them grew by the second.

"Hell yeah," he groaned, easing his hands back on her hips. "I wanna wake up with you in my arms. How that sound?"

She rubbed his earlobe. "It's not *how* it sounds . . . I'm more concerned about *how* it will feel to have you back up in me. And since it's been a while I want it all night long."

"Um, you sho' know how to make my dick hard." He bit his bottom lip and then squeezed her wide hips. "You like that song that's on right now?"

She nodded. Her center became moist between her thighs.

"Good, 'cause that's what I'ma do to your sexy ass tonight."

"Show me better than you can tell me, papi," she said as her nipples stiffened.

Disregarding their public presence, their lips met in an open-mouthed kiss. Jurnee relished the kiss, tilting her head and sucking on his tongue. A soft breeze caressed her exposed arms and legs. Their brief titillating moment ceased when the deejay got on the mic. Trevon kissed her lightly on her nose with his yearning for her written all over his face.

Jurnee noticed a few eyes turned her way as she stepped back from Trevon's embrace.

"You taste as good as you look," he said, adjusting the lapel of his pin-striped white and green single-breasted suit.

"C'mere." She licked her thumb and then wiped off a smudge of lipstick from his sexy lips.

"Where's Janelle?" he asked as DJ Kay Slay made an announcement about the food being ready to serve.

"Somewhere with Victor," she told him. "Um, look over by the rock garden. See the girl in the white backless dress?"

"Uh . . . shit. Who is that sexy lady next to her in that black dress?" he asked, rubbing his chin. "You know I gotta taste for older women."

Jurnee rolled her eyes. "She's married, so stop lusting." She hit his arm with her elbow.

"Who is she?" Trevon checked the woman out.

"That's Jamie Foster Brown."

"Word! Damn, she sexy as hell! What she doing here?"

"She's doing an interview on Janelle for her magazine. Now pay attention. The girl in the white dress."

"What about 'er?"

"How does she look to you?"

"Ai'ight, kinda slim but sexy. Nice little ass. Look like Tracey Edmonds a lil' bit. Why you pointing her out?"

Jurnee reached up and brushed a piece of lint off his broad shoulder. "That's Glaze, and she'll be your next cast mate for your third film. And before you ask, yes, I'm still working a deal out with Cherokee and Pinky. Oh, and Skyy Black is someone else I want you to film with."

Trevon reached inside his suit for his smartphone.

"What are you about to do?" Jurnee asked.

"I'ma go ask the lovely Mrs. Brown if I can take a picture with her to post on Instagram. Who knows? You might see me on the cover of *Sister 2 Sister* one day."

Jurnee laughed easily, reaching for his hand. "Let me introduce you to Glaze."

"And Jamie," he said.

***

Trevon was thrown for a surprise when he was introduced to Glaze. Along with her sexy petite frame she had a strong British accent that added to her sex appeal. Unlike Chelsea, Glaze wasn't an amateur, and her unique talent was centered on her lissome body. Glaze could easily lock her legs behind her head. Add in a tongue that could touch the tip of her nose. She had Trevon ready to work with her. He also learned that she had a man, and she took her relationship seriously. The only time he would see her nude and on his dick would be on the movie set. As for Trevon meeting Jamie Foster Brown, he had to stand in line. Her time was limited, but at least he got his picture and his big kiss on his cheek.

By 9 PM, Jurnee was nursing her fourth martini while sitting by the pool under a row of blue assorted paper lanterns. Her eyes were on Trevon as he enjoyed himself across the pool dancing on the white and blue checkered patio. A new hit by Usher had the crowd buzzing. As long as Trevon was happy, Jurnee's mood was content. She laughed at the sight of him *trying* to keep up with the moves that Chelsea and Glaze were putting on him.

"Looks like he is having a ball."

Jurnee looked up from where she sat as Janelle took a seat next to her. She had her hair down, rocking a white tank-top with no bra and a pair of shiny taupe skinny jeans.

"Hey girl!" Jurnee said.

Janelle sighed, lifting a glass of vodka mixed with pineapple juice to her lips.

Jurnee could tell that something was troubling Janelle. "What's on your mind?"

Janelle lowered the martini to her lap. "Thinking about Brooke Vee. I told DJ Kay Slay to do a moment of silence for her before the night is over."

"That's a good idea," Jurnee said as three bikini clad porn stars slid into the pool.

"I see Trevon has met Glaze," she observed, lifting the martini again.

Jurnee crossed her legs. "I see a bright future for him. I really do."

"I'm thinking . . . nine films in the next six months," Janelle said.

"Think we can get the paperwork done for a film with him and Cherokee?"

"How does he feel about it?"

Jurnee giggled. "I think he's infatuated with Cherokee's big butt. But yes, he's all for it. Oh, let's add Skyy Black to the list."

Janelle ran the idea through her mind for a second. "Send Ruby an e-mail tomorrow."

"Alright. Um, you gonna make Trevon and Chelsea retake their last scene?"

"Nah," Janelle decided. "I viewed the footage and it's good."

"What exactly did he do?"

Janelle plucked the olive out of her empty glass and then slipped it past her lips. "The script called for him to do the money shot as Chelsea gave him some head. But our Mr. Harrison thought it would look better to continue the anal scene."

"He had her outside on the picnic table, right?"

"Mm-hmm. He kept the anal penetration going, but pulled out and came on her breasts and stomach after he took the condom off."

"Were the camera angles good?"

"Yeah, there were two cameras rolling simultaneously, so we got a nice close-up of his climax."

Jurnee set her glass on the round marble table and then glanced up at the moon. "Five years from now, what do you hope is different in your life?"

"God's will . . . I pray that I'll be married and with one or two kids," Janelle replied.

"Really!"

"Yep." Janelle smiled. "I kinda already started on having a baby."

"And I got dibs on being the godmother."

"You know I gotcha on that."

They smiled at each other.

"Heard from Kandi lately?" Jurnee asked as the deejay kept the party jumping with another hit by Kendrick Lamar."

"Not since the funeral. I surmise you two still aren't talking?"

"It's her doing, not mine," Jurnee retorted.

"You need to put whatever issues you got with her aside and call her."

"And why should I do that?" Jurnee frowned.

"Because you're still her *friend*, and I think she needs one in her life. Shit ain't going right for her."

Jurnee crossed her arms. She had too much concern for Kandi to not care. "What's going on with her?"

Janelle stood. "Call and find out yourself, and you better do it."

Jurnee twisted her lips.

"I'll see you later, girl. I got my man waiting on me."

Jurnee giggled. "I knew you was doing the nasty."

Alone again, Jurnee began to feel the effects of the drinks she had knocked down. Smiling, she placed her eyes back on Trevon. She wondered if he ever pictured himself living such a happy life while he was in prison? *I probably care more about his behind than he do himself,* she thought as the party continued.

Her heart started to flutter when he later strolled toward her with that sexy grin on his handsome face. He was stepping past a redheaded, older white girl when the deejay tapped the mic.

"I'd like to get er'body attention right quick. Jus' wanna do a moment of silence for our girl, Brooke Vee. She will be missed and never forgotten, so all y'all need to keep your eyes dry. And your heart easy." When DJ Kay Slay lowered his head, a hush covered the party.

Jurnee stood in her four-inch stilettos as Trevon paused to lower his head. After the moment of silence, "I'll Be Missing You" by Puff Daddy, Faith Evans, and 112 closed the party on a sad note.

"C'mon, baby. Let's go home," were the words that Trevon blessed in Jurnee's ear.

***

"Trevon! Oooohhh, papi!" Jurnee moaned as she strained against the satin restraints that binded her wrists together. Her movements were limited with the bond also being tied to the center of the headboard.

She was up on her knees with her face buried sideways on a green satin pillow. Blindfolded, she was denied the chance to see what treats Trevon had in store for her. At the moment he was tirelessly eating her ass out as she wobbled her velvety ass against his face. His hands palmed her cushy butt cheeks open as his tongue probed in and out of her ass. She whined softly, his electrifying tongue feasting famish-like inside her. Without pause, he picked up a cold diced pineapple off the food tray to his left. He jabbed his tongue inside her ass like a jackhammer. With her guard down, he inserted the chilled fruit between the hot liquescent inner folds of her slit. She thrashed her hips, her pussy walls drawing together against the cold, soft object. Swirling his tongue around her tight orifice, he unexpectedly pushed a second diced pineapple inside her pussy. Then a third, pulling a low susurrus moan from her lips. Her mind couldn't pick which gratifying act to focus on. His tongue? Or the objects in her pussy?

She trembled when he lapped up the length of her ass ten times continuously with deliberate strides of his tongue. Her body melted under his lubricious mouth and tongue.

"Papi, please!" She gasped when he pulled his face back from her juicy ass.

He spanked her cheeks just to see them jiggle. Again he reached for the food tray and picked up a bottle of Dom Perignon. With apt plans to blow her mind, he slid the chilly neck of the bottle all over her ass. When she couldn't stand it any longer, she heard the bottle pop.

Trevon allowed the bubbles to spill on her fleshy ass. Palming her right cheek open, he poured a small amount down her split. The Dom P flowed over her stimulated ass and pulsating kitty.

"Papi—"

"Shut up!" He slapped her ass again. "Raise that ass up! Higher!" He drank from the bottle while rubbing and slapping her ass. "Who ass is it?"

"Yours, papi!" she cried as her kitty turned powerless against his treatment.

Positioning himself on one knee, he grabbed his erection, planting it between her warm butt cheeks. "Be still!" he said before he poured more Dom Perignon on her ass. He shivered when the cold bubbly ran down his dick and balls. Closing his eyes, he moved his hips to ride the length along the valley of her butt. He could tell she wanted his dick in her ass by the way she twerked her hips.

He stopped, but she kept whirling her ass.

"Papi, please do me. Please! I need to cum," she whined.

"Not yet, so stop begging."

She tugged at the bonds when he moved his dick off her ass. She was past ready. Her sex juices were smeared between her thick thighs, and all she needed to calm her was Trevon's loving. She was a breath away from begging when she welcomed his tongue inside her runny center. The tip of his tongue traveled along her outer folds.

"Mmmm . . . yess! Papi, eat good . . . ahhh shit! Awww fuck! Awww fuck!" She pushed herself against his mouth as his tongue sought out the fruit entrenched up her pussy. She squealed when he slurped and sucked the first pineapple out. He chewed it and swallowed it in four bites. She lifted her ass higher in the air when his tongue dipped back between her meaty lips. No man, nor woman had *ever* freaked her this good before. She swore she was going to faint as his tongue chased the second pineapple around and around and around. She could feel the fruit soft texture easing out of her hole. Like the first, he ate it out of her, pausing to lick the pineapple juice that flowed down her inner thighs. The instant he went in search of the third pineapple, she lost grip of herself. Her body shuddered as he foraged laboriously inside her pussy. Jurnee could feel his hands taking control of her nipples. He squeezed them lightly, then hard. His tongue had her speaking in her native tongue. Suddenly, her breath became stuck in her chest. She bared her teeth, toes curled. Her release came in a teaspoon of creamy fluid that pushed the fruit out. Trevon slurped at her slit with two fingers working gently on her clit. Her nectarous release dripped from his bottom lip and chin.

"Mmmm," he groaned, licking the outer folds of her slippery pussy. His ego was on swollen measurements when she collapsed to the bed.

Jurnee's body was weak. With her glossy lips quivering, she spoke his name in a chant. She welcomed the feel of him using his knees to spread her legs apart. Blindly, she lifted her stomach when a pillow was pushed under it. She breathed deeply when he got on top of her, running his tongue up and down the back of her neck. Her breath caught again when he nudged the thick blunt tip of his dick inside her. It sunk deep and slow, breaking the tautness. Submissive to his sex, she whirled her soaked pussy in slow circles all over his extended penis.

CHAPTER Twenty-Four

OMG!

February 9, 2012

Thursday 10:40 AM – Coconut Grove, Florida

Trevon's mood was upbeat since Jurnee's snap back pussy was back under his sheets. She had sexed him before sunrise, bouncing on his morning thickness until they both popped a nut. After a quick shower, she cooked breakfast and then rolled off in her SLS Benz to handle some business.

Now, Trevon was outside shirtless in the driveway rinsing the suds off his big body XJL. The weather was perfect. Hot with clear light blue skies with no chance of any mood-spoiling rain. He was thinking about making a trip to Hooters when he heard a car pulling in the driveway across the street. Tahkiyah's sexy ass jumped dead on his mind as he glanced over the roof of his sedan.

Curious, he watched a clean-cut, casually dressed black man step out of a coconut meat white Audi S6 sedan. As he strode across the manicured lawn, Trevon lifted the yellow spray nozzle over the roof of his car. When the man worked the *for sale* sign out of the front yard, Trevon loosened his grip on the plastic spray nozzle. Trevon crossed the street to get some information from the guy. The dude with the sign greeted Trevon with a small grin as the trunk of the Audi popped open. Trevon spoke first.

"Hey um, I live across the street." Trevon thumbed over his sweaty shoulder. "You just sold this place to a couple from D.C., right?"

The man placed the sign in the trunk. "Ah . . . no. Actually, it's a couple from Tampa."

"Tampa?" Trevon said with a confused expression. "Tahkiyah told me she was from D.C."

"Ah, that name doesn't ring a bell, and I'm sure about that."

"Uh, she's a black woman with—"

"Whoa!" The man smiled, closing the trunk. "Now, I'm sure there's a mistake. The couple that purchased this home is white."

"So you *never* spoke with a lady name Tahkiyah about buying that place?"

"Positive, bruh." The man shrugged. "Sorry I can't be of any help."

Trevon thanked the man for his time, and then he headed back across the street. *Maybe she spoke with another agent or something?* he later thought while drying his car off.

***

Jurnee's Jimmy Choo heels moved gracefully across the glossy brown marble floor at the Turnberry Isle Spa and Fitness Center. Reaching the front desk, she easily gained the attention of the short Asian receptionist.

"Hi. I'm Jurnee Cruz, and I'm here to meet my friend Janelle Babin. Could you check to see which treatment room she's in?"

Since a message was awaiting Jurnee, the information was given without any hassle. The 25,000 square-foot luxury spa boasted all the amenities to pamper the elite women in South Florida. Footbaths, full body massages, aromatherapy, a gym, a cardio room, the list went on.

Jurnee inhaled a strong scent of rosemary when she entered the treatment room. "Hey girl, I got your text," she said as she walked past the bed and out on the balcony. Stepping through the French doors, she rounded the chair. "Why didn't you—" Her words came to a halt when she saw Kandi sitting in the chair.

"Hey. Betcha surprised to see me?" Kandi said with a glass of tea on the table to her right. She nodded to the white padded chair.

"Where's Janelle?" Jurnee asked with an attitude, crossing her arms.

"She's home. She helped me set this up. I kinda figured you wouldn't have come otherwise."

Jurnee remained on her feet as the lush tops of the palm trees swayed in the breeze behind her. Reluctantly, she sat down. "You got ten minutes, so talk."

Kandi was starting to show clear signs of her pregnancy. She was still a diva, rocking a white Prada dress and heels. With the sun warming her skin, she glanced at Jurnee. "Did you sleep with Trevon last night?"

Jurnee sighed angrily. "I know you didn't go through all the trouble just to ask me that! Shouldn't you be concerned about *your man*, Martellus?"

"I'm not with him anymore," Kandi replied flatly, showing little emotion.

"Oh, so now you want Trevon back? Spare me, okay."

"Will you at least listen to me, Jurnee?"

"I am! You're talking, but you ain't sayin' nothin'. And since you want to know so bad. Yes, I slept with him last night."

A sharp sting of jealousy shot through Kandi's heart. "Do you love him like I do?"

Jurnee's mouth dropped. "You call your treatment of him, love!"

"I made a mistake."

"Ya think!"

"Look, I don't want you nor Trevon to hate me. I just need both of you to know the truth," Kandi confessed as a cloud slid in front of the sun, throwing a blanket of shade on the balcony.

"Truth about what!" Jurnee asked with anger laced in her tone.

Kandi drew in a deep breath before she spoke. "About the baby."

Jurnee's face softened. Whatever beef she had with Kandi she couldn't include the child. "Okay, I'm listening. What's wrong?"

"Please don't judge me," Kandi murmured, tears welling in her eyes. "Remember when I asked if you ever did something you regretted?"

Jurnee nodded. She was too concerned about the baby to speak.

"Well, I did something I deeply regret doing." Kandi's voice broke. Tears raced down her cheeks. "I loved Trevon so much, and you know that. But I'm not mad at you, Jurnee. I know I caused all of this trouble myself. A part of me died when I left Trevon." Kandi tried to smile through the pain that filled her.

"Kandi. Please tell me what's going on."

"I was really planning to have an abortion," Kandi admitted as she wiped her eyes.

"Why? Why were you going to—"

"I didn't want to live a lie," Kandi told her. "I couldn't do it to Trevon. Not after I learned the truth."

"Learned what truth? Just tell me what in the hell is going on, Kandi. Please."

Kandi glanced down at her lap. "I was already a month pregnant before I had sex without a condom with Trevon."

Jurnee gasped, her hand moving involuntarily to her mouth.

"It was a mistake. It wasn't supposed to happen," Kandi continued. "I was going to have an abortion, then lie to everyone and say it was a miscarriage. I just couldn't tell Trevon the truth."

Jurnee shook her head, filled with disbelief. "Why?"

"I . . . was so lost. I didn't mean to hurt Trevon like I did. When I was with him, I was true to him. If I had known the baby wasn't his I would have never put him through this," Kandi cried softly. "When I went to the doctor back in late November, I found out I was fourteen weeks pregnant. I knew right then that Trevon wasn't the father. I didn't know what to do. He was so happy about being a dad."

"So, you've told no one else about this?" Jurnee said as she came to grips with the pain that Trevon would have to face.

Kandi shook her head.

"And you think you've made your issue better by leaving Martellus? You know he'll put up a fight for the baby. Kandi, you need to get your shit in order because this is a mess. I mean—"

"Martellus isn't the father either," Kandi interrupted.

Jurnee slid to the edge of the chair. She stared at Kandi, wondering how bad off things had turned for Kandi. "Who's the father?" Jurnee asked.

A sheet of silence covered the balcony for a moment before Kandi spoke. When she told the truth, it sent Jurnee into the treatment room with tears slipping down her face.

CHAPTER Twenty-Five

Swagga Like Us

"What in the hell is wrong with you, Marcus? You don't make no surprise visits to my job!" Kendra said as Swagga sat down across from her desk.

"I just got back in town. Just wanted to see what you up to," he said with five different colored diamond chains around his neck.

"And somewhere in that head of yours you figured my place of work would be a good spot? Who are you trying to impress by barging up here with your clique?"

"Ain't nobody wit' me but Rick," he said, taking his black 4119 Burberry sunglasses off. "Do I look high?" He grinned with red eyes.

"What do you want? If you want that car back you—"

"Ain't worried 'bout that car, okay?"

"Alright. Speak what's on your mind." She leaned back, crossing her arms.

"Yo, that bread I wired you last year. Why you give it back to me?"

"Marcus, I told you why already. I was not with you for your fame or money. I gave it back because I assumed you would need it for your legal fees."

"That was some real shit you did. I thought I was gonna be broke until I got my bread back from D-Hot. Yeah, he did some grimy shit, but I hated what happened to 'im," he said in a sullen tone.

"Speaking of which, why didn't you tell me about what happened last month?"

He frowned. "A lot happened last month, so—"

"The issue you had on the road. The shooting where somebody tried—"

"It ain't shit to stress ova'. Just some hatin' ass niggas. And I *couldn't* tell you because you ran out on me, remember?"

"I know we're not on the best of terms, but I want you to be careful out there, Marcus. And when are you coming to see your daughter?"

"This weekend if you'll let me."

"I'll never stop you from seeing your daughter and you know that, so stop trippin'."

Swagga glanced at his new $22,000 Jacob white diamond watch. "What time do you get off? It's uh, ten minutes to one."

"Later, around ten. Why?"

"Maybe we could go out to—"

"No, Marcus. We are *not* going back down that road again, okay?"

He shifted on the chair, realizing Kendra was one in a million. She was special. "It's about the videos you saw, huh?"

"Listen, Marcus. I don't trust you no more. Even if it was a onetime thang or whatever. It happened, okay? The fact is that you didn't tell me you had sex with that she-male. You weren't supposed to keep things like that from me. How could you put me at risk?"

Swagga had no words to explain his actions. He was about to tell her about his doctor's appointment set for next week when the phone on her desk rang. He stayed quiet, watching a woman that he knew *had* love for him. With Kendra he knew the true meaning of making love, which was different from sex and fucking. In truth, he couldn't explain his spontaneous urge to see her. Maybe he could fix things *if* his HIV test was what he hoped it would be. Negative. Nashlly crossed his mind for a second. *If* his test was positive she would be given a rude awakening for her gold digging ambitions. His daze of thoughts were broken when Kendra stood up, smoothing her shirt in place. His eyes roamed over her soft plump figure.

"I need to run down the hall right quick. Can you wait here for a minute or two or what?"

"I'll wait." He settled back in the chair.

Kendra nodded and then made her way around the desk. Once the door was shut, Swagga slid his fingers through his long dreads. If he could be with one woman, it would be Kendra. Glancing back on her desk, he saw her iPhone beside her coffee mug. *I wonder if she still got the same code?* Knowing he was in the wrong, he leaned up and picked up the pink iPhone.

When the five digit code unlocked the iPhone, he immediately touched the video icon. There were only five videos.

My baby's B-day party
YMCMB @ Club Liv
Untitled

Untitled

My fantasy cum true

Swagga touched the icon to view the first untitled video. He only needed to view five seconds before his stomach tightened at the sight of him and Chyna. The second untitled video was his second time he was caught on film with Chyna. *I wonder how the fuck she got this shit.* Moving fast, he pulled out his new cell phone and quickly downloaded the two videos. And just for the hell of it, he also downloaded the fantasy video, just to be nosey. He downloaded the two untitled videos of him and Chyna to find out *who* sent them to Kendra. Placing the iPhone back how he found it, he tried to relax so Kendra wouldn't be suspicious of anything.

When she returned minutes later, he made a comment on her lemon scented perfume. She ignored him, keeping a wall up around her emotions.

"Marcus, for future reference. Please don't visit me at my job again, okay?"

He slid his shades back on. "Fine. I won't. Shit, why you slavin' at this bullshit job anyway? Ain't like you need any gwop."

"I was working when you met me and—"

"Yeah, yeah, I know. You're an independent woman." He rose, adjusting his palm-sized Gucci belt buckle. "Here." He dug inside his front pocket and pulled out a band of cash. "Put this unda' my princess' pillow." He dropped four one hundred dollar bills on the desk. He knew she would never turn down any money for their daughter. As he turned to leave, he paused at the door. "Um, yo." He looked back at her. "For all it's worth. I'm sorry fo' all the bullshit I put you through."

Kendra wasn't moving backward anymore. What she had with Swagga based on her emotions was a done deal. All she could do was maintain her position to ensure he had a relationship with his daughter. That was the best she could do. When he left, she thought of his secret. Like she told Trevon last week after she confronted Swagga, exposing him was pointless. Damn near every month or so, a rapper or some celebrity was coming out of the closet. *Hell,* even President Obama was for gay marriage. Being politically correct, she took a lax view on gay relations, but it was *not* okay for her private life. She had no need or want to be with a bisexual man. And it didn't matter if he was out of the closet.

***

Swagga's exit from the downtown building was a coordinated movement that guided him out the back door. Rick ran the security team hard as they placed Swagga in the back of a custom stretch Cadillac Escalade ESV. The ivory ESV limo was brand new to Swagga's fleet. It sat on chrome 28's and could seat four in the back, side by side seating. Swagga slid back into the black leather six-way adjustable reclining chair as Rick sat across from him.

"What Kendra talking about?" Rick asked as the limo pulled out of the parking lot.

"Same old shit," Swagga replied, staring pensively through the tinted window.

Rick could see the troubles weighing down on Swagga. "I know you're not worried about that D-Hot problem. We clean on that. We got nothing to worry about, trust me."

"Fuck that snitchin' ass bama!" Swagga mumbled.

"Your mind right to hit the studio?"

"Yeah, let's go. I'm good."

Swagga's mind was glued to the bullshit about Kendra holding the Chyna issue over his head. They were cruising along I-95 North when Swagga pulled out his cell phone. He pulled up the *sender's* information on the first video of him and Chyna. A 305 number showed up. He also learned that Kendra had gotten the video on the 24th of January, last month. His stomach was twisting in knots at the thought of someone else other than Kendra knowing about his secret. Pulling up the second video, the *sender's* information was the same. Swagga came up with an idea. He could block his number out and then call the sender's number to find out who the third party was. Taking a deep breath, he made the call. Instead of a ring, the sound of Lost Boyz' "Me and My Crazy World" filled his ear. A short loop of the late '90s hit played twice before the voicemail kicked in. Swagga became tense.

Yo, whut up? Yes, you've reached Trevon Harrison, but I'm kinda busy at the moment. Ain't nothin' changed, so leave your name and number, and I'll get back atcha. Peace.

Swagga was stunned, hiding his emotions from Rick. Ending the call, he laid his head back on the headrest closing his eyes. His grip tightened on his cell phone. He could deal with Kendra having the videos, but with Trevon *back* in the picture it was a different story. *So that bitch Kandi had the fuckin' videos all along! Knew I shoulda killed that 'ho when I had the chance to!* Swagga thought, with his anger boiling to the moon. *Okay, so she fuckin' wit' Trevon. He gave her the two videos, which he got from Kandi. They must have a reason to be keeping 'em.* Swagga's mind raced. In the end he knew their reasons for keeping the two videos would only turn to drama for him. He could explain the first night when he took Chyna to his crib. Swagga had believed that Chyna was just a bad ass Asian jump-off. It was the second, third, and fourth times that ate at him. Swagga lowered the volume and then viewed the video.

The scene started with a clear shot of Trevon sitting on a bed wearing a pair of boxers.

"Dis nigga again!" Swagga said under his breath. *Okay, so this bitch gotta fuck flick of dis nigga on her iPhone. Ain't no big deal. He's a porn star*, Swagga reasoned as the video continued. *Wait a minute. That's Kandi's bedroom!* Swagga noticed when Trevon stood.

He averted his gaze from the scene as Trevon slid his boxers off. For a few moments the scene was unchanged until a second person ambled up to Trevon.

Swagga jerked upright in the seat, his eyes bugging out.

"Yo, dawg. You okay?" Rick asked.

Swagga was stunned at the image he saw. A sour pill turned his stomach at the sight of Kendra deep throating Trevon like a true bitch in heat.

CHAPTER
Twenty-Six
The Truth

Jurnee had finally pulled her emotions in check. She was seated on the bed next to Kandi in the treatment room. *Why, why, why!* was bouncing off the walls in Jurnee's head. "Of all the men, why him?" Jurnee asked with a wad of tear-soaked tissues in her grip.

"He was convenient at the time, and it was just a spur of the moment thing," Kandi told her with the intentions to come clean about everything. She was tired of trudging alone with her burdens. By telling the truth, she was trusting Jurnee would understand.

"How did it happen?" Jurnee pressed with the need to know.

"I drove over to confront Swagga at the studio, but he wasn't there. I was just so mad at him for cheating on me. Anyway, D-Hot was there, and I was on some bullshit."

"How?" Jurnee asked impatiently.

Kandi didn't reply right back. The memory of what she did still put knots in her stomach. "I knew how tight Swagga and D-Hot were. Both business and friendship. I just wanted Swagga to feel my pain. I knew by me just fucking D-Hot wouldn't hurt Swagga. So I gave D-Hot something that Swagga never had the chance to do."

Jurnee shook her head. "And that was to let D-Hot do it without a condom?"

Kandi nodded weakly. "I was gonna throw it all up in Swagga's face, but I changed my mind. Plus, D-Hot wanted it to remain just between us. He didn't want any beef with Swagga."

"How many times did y'all do it?"

"Just once. He was the one that tipped the police off. He told me everything when Swagga was arrested."

"He did it for the baby?"

Kandi nodded. "It's all a mess."

"So nobody knows—"

"We kept it a secret."

"And now you got Trevon thinking the baby is his. But in truth it's D-Hot's and he's no longer with us."

"I didn't want this to happen, Jurnee. I didn't expect to fall in love with Trevon and not know I was already pregnant. I wanted Trevon to be happy with me, but I screwed it all up."

"It ain't what I thought," Jurnee admitted. "I thought you were just on some bullshit. I mean, I can't even imagine having to deal with your problems. Kandi, I know what I'm about to say is, well . . . easier said than done. But you should've told Trevon the truth when you first learned the baby wasn't his."

"I couldn't, Jurnee. That man was beyond happy. I just couldn't break his world like—"

"You crushed him when you left. . . . Face it. You took the easy way out by running and not dealing with it. It was *my* shoulder that he cried on because of you," Jurnee stated, unconcerned if Kandi's feelings were hurt.

"You're right," Kandi said. "I can't face him."

"That ain't an option. You *have* to woman up and tell him the truth, okay?"

"And what about the fact that I'm still in love with him?"

Jurnee stood and paced the floor in front of Kandi.

"I did all the wrong things for all the wrong reasons," Kandi said with tears building in her eyes again. "I didn't know what to do, okay? I never had a *real* mother to teach me this . . . shit! All I wanted. All I needed was Trevon, and I messed it all up." She broke down crying into her hands.

Jurnee wanted to run to comfort Kandi, but she couldn't. Knowing the truth had filled Jurnee with a small plate of compassion. Kandi had just made some dumb ass life-changing decisions that she didn't think all the way through. Jurnee felt pity for Kandi.

"Where are you staying?" Jurnee asked, forming an idea in her mind.

"At the Mondrian," Kandi said, wiping her watery eyes.

"So it's really over with you and Martellus?"

"Hell yeah," Kandi murmured. "Go ahead and say 'I told you so'."

"About what?"

"I caught Martellus fucking his housekeeper. I just needed a reason to leave his ass, and he gave me one."

"And what if you hadn't caught him. Would you still be with him?"

Kandi looked down at her feet. "I never stopped loving Trevon. I just want to make things right."

"You have to face Trevon. He needs to know the truth, okay?"

"Will you help me?"

Jurnee had to set aside her own emotions and deal with the truth. Kandi hadn't meant to hurt Trevon. It was just a fact of life that stood true through any type of issue. Life is only what you make it. "Yeah, I'll see what I can do."

Kandi stood. "I don't wanna be alone, Jurnee. Please help me."

Jurnee left Kandi behind with a promise that she would call her later. It was Jurnee who cried silently when she got inside her Benz. Again, she fought to pull herself together and she did. Driving away from the Turnberry Isle Spa, Jurnee tried to picture how Trevon would react to the heart-crushing truth of the baby. Realizing that assuming, wondering, nor hoping would give her the answer, she knew what had to be done. If Kandi didn't like it she would have to deal with it.

***

Trevon stepped out the front door on his way to Hooters when Tahkiyah pulled up behind his XJL. She waved at him with the top down on her 650i coupe. Trevon was caught off guard by her sudden appearance. When he reached back to lock the door, she stepped out of the Beemer.

They met at the rear of Trevon's Jag. They both eyed each other from head to toe under the bright Dade County sun.

Tahkiyah had her hair down, giving her an added pinch of sex appeal. A pair of gold wishbone earrings adorned her ears. Gold trimmed aviator sunglasses hid her eyes. She was killing it with a black embroidered silk-chiffon top and a flesh-clinging blue, white, and black silk pencil skirt. Her award winning legs and calves were enhanced by a pair of Gucci patent leather black pumps.

Trevon was thugging today wearing a fresh pair of wheat colored Timberland boots, slightly baggy True Religion jeans, and he topped it off with a white tee and a Gucci bucket hat.

"Uhhhhh, Tahkiyah, right?" he asked, checking her over. *Damn, ain't no way she fifty something! She fly as hell. Hair done, nails done . . . er'thang did.*

"Yes." She smiled.

"Ah, what brings you around today?" he asked.

"I was just in the area, so I thought I'd drop by."

"Where you coming from?" he asked.

"I have a suite at the Mondrian."

"Oh. You and your husband?"

"Actually, I'm not married." She watched his reaction closely. When he crossed his big arms, she read the doubt he expressed.

"Is there anything else you lied to me about?"

Tahkiyah took the sunglasses off. She didn't feel comfortable being untruthful. "I was never moving in across the street."

"And?"

"I only have one child—"

"Lemme see some I.D."

"Really! You're going to card me?"

"Damn right. You may be fine and all that, but it ain't good to lie."

Tahkiyah turned and breezed back to her car to grab a quilted white leather Versace shoulder bag. "Let's make a deal," she said as her fingers brushed against the chrome 9-millimeter in her bag.

"What kinda deal?" he asked as she removed her driver's license from the small bag.

"If my driver's license proves something you think I lied about, I owe you one wish."

He thought it over for a second. "And if I'm wrong?"

She smiled. "Then you owe me a sensual *full* body massage at my suite. Today."

Trevon viewed the bet with this woman as a win-win chance. "Ai'ight. You *said* you were fifty something. Prove it."

"Mmm." She grinned, giving him the license. "I hope you're good with your hands."

Trevon saw it in print on the D.C. driver's license.

Tahkiyah Lloyd Bradford. HT: 5'4" WT: 120* Eye: Hazel * Race: Black * DOB: 8/11/58*

"A bet is a bet, Trevon." She smiled, sliding her sunglasses back on.

"How do I know you're not crazy?"

She laughed, strolling back to her car. "If somebody is going to be crazy it might just be you," she said over her shoulder. As she slid behind the wheel, she motioned him over.

"And what will I be going crazy over?" he asked, feeling challenged by her.

"I'll let my actions speak louder than words." She lifted her sunglasses and boldly looked between his legs. "But I'm willing to bet *again*." She lowered the sunglasses. "That this sugar is so good and sweet that you won't last no longer than . . . five minutes."

Trevon's dick was already making its choice known by growing under his jeans. He had never met a woman in her class. He couldn't back down.

"I'm in need of some attention, Trevon. Come to the Mondrian. I'll leave a note for you with my room number. And *if* you are man enough to show up and honor your bet, I'll be waiting." She revved the engine twice and then backed out of the driveway leaving Trevon speechless.

Her challenge and bet flooded his mind. On his way to Hooters, he was compelled to prove Tahkiyah wrong.

***

Around 3 PM, Trevon's ego had him at the front desk at the Mondrian Hotel. As promised, a message in a sealed perfume scented envelope was handed to Trevon by the staff.

***

Tahkiyah was given a five minute heads up of Trevon's arrival by the same hotel staff that had slid the message to Trevon. Her body tingled with excitement over the possibilities that could happen between herself and Trevon. She moved quickly, spraying the scent of her perfume in her wake. *I have to go through with this,* she thought for the hundredth time. By the bed she checked to make sure the ice hadn't melted too much in the shiny chrome bucket. The bottle of Moscato wasn't her top choice of drink, but today it would suit the moment. The two wine glasses were spotless, the bed was made, the curtains were shut with the lights down low and most important, Tahkiyah was wanting, open to dealing with her sexual needs. She viewed Trevon as an object. Being with him would simply be mixing business with pleasure. Stopping to view her reflection in the mirror, she checked her hair too.

A knock at the door was sudden, making Tahkiyah's heart miss a beat. Rushing to the door, she had to lift up on her barefooted toes to peek through the viewing glass. Her nipples grew at the sight of Trevon out in the hallway. Taking a quick deep breath, she opened the door.

Trevon knew the 4-1-1 when he laid his eyes on Tahkiyah. He viewed her as a temptress that he couldn't resist. Her body was coated with a sheer white teddy, black lace trimmed panties, and a black garter set that connected to some black knee-high fishnet stockings. Even her glasses added to her charm and sexiness.

"I see you came," she said softly.

"Not yet," he replied, making her smile.

"Well, come on in." She motioned him inside.

Trevon stood by the TV as she locked the door. He couldn't take his eyes off her pert, light brown ass. The panties bit enticingly into her flesh.

"Do you know the key to pleasing a woman, Trevon?" she asked, crossing to where he stood.

"Yeah, communication," he said, playing it cool.

She came to a stop in front of him. His size alone made her pussy moist. "Good answer. And can you explain it?"

"All women don't like the same thing. Some like it rough, some like it soft and slow."

"Continue," she said, reaching under his white tee. What she felt was a rippled sea of hard muscles.

"Knowing what a woman wants makes it easier to take care of her needs."

"And which is more important? The want or the need?" She trapped his nipples between her thumbs and index fingers.

"The need," he said, sliding his hands up the black elastic strap running down the front of her leg.

Tahkiyah pulled his white tee up. "Oh my gosh!" she moaned, licking her wet lips at the sight of his chiseled stomach. Unable to control herself, she took his left nipple in a soft grip with her lips.

Trevon stayed calm, but lowered his hands to caress her ass gently. Not once did her age cross his mind. She painted his hairless chest with licks and kisses. Her hands explored his chest, arms, stomach, and back. His white tee came off first. No more words were needed to explain what they both wanted.

"I'm not a fan of wearing bras," she moaned as he inched the hem of the teddy up her waist.

Trevon was dying to get between her legs and crush. Precum stained his boxers, and she had yet to touch him below his belt. The passion between them moved to another level when Trevon cupped her pussy through the thin panties. She was hot and damp. Tahkiyah's knees got weak as he massaged her sex while sucking her ear.

"Take—" she moaned, clinging to his wide shoulders, "a shower with me first."

***

"Pick up the phone, Trevon!" Jurnee muttered as she sped west along the East West expressway. When his voicemail picked up, she ended the call by voice command. Switching lanes, she mashed the gas, rocketing past a green SUV in the right lane. The throaty exhaust note matched the 563 horses under the hood. Jurnee wheeled the attention grabbing SLS over the posted speed limit without thought. At her speed, the chrome rims turned into a blur, giving an illusion of them spinning backward. Her state of mind didn't register the speedometer creeping past 90 miles per hour. She kept pushing the SLS, jumping lanes without using the turn signal. Horns sounded in protest in the wake of the speeding Benz. Trevon was thick on her mind. A single tear broke from the corner of her eye. She gripped the wheel, her foot still adding pressure to the gas pedal. Smoothly, the SLS broke the triple digit barrier.

"Call Trevon!" she shouted at the voice activated Bluetooth system. Tears started to blur her vision. *I have to tell him,* she thought. *If I don't, I'm no better than Kandi, and he—*

Before she could finish her thought, two things happened simultaneously that broke her concentration on the road. First, Trevon answered her second call. And with his voice in her ears, a Florida State Trooper appeared behind the SLS with its light bar flashing. Jurnee gasped at the police, and then her speed. For 3.5 seconds, her eyes had left the road while she was moving at 102 miles per hour. When her mind snapped to the present, she stood up on the brakes only five seconds before she rear-ended a moving van.

***

At the same time, Trevon didn't have the time to wonder why Jurnee had hung up. Shrugging, he pulled his socks off and then joined Tahkiyah in the shower.

***

Unbeknownst to Kandi, she was two floors above Trevon at the Mondrian Hotel. She felt troubled with having to face Trevon. Jurnee was right. Running away from Trevon wasn't the answer. Sulking alone in the suite, she lay back on the large bed gazing at the ceiling. Needing *something* to do, she reached for her laptop on the bedside table. She placed it on her stomach, opened it, and then powered it up. Once she logged on, she saw a new e-mail waiting to be read. With a soft touch of the e-mail icon, she waited a mere one second for the e-mail to fill the screen.

To: Kandi@aef.com

From: Tbradford@aol.com
Subject: You and I
Date: 2/8/12 11:10 p.m.

God's will this message will reach you. I've been meaning to sit down and type this ever since I got your e-mail. There are things I need to tell you face to face, and all I seek is your understanding, for we all make mistakes that we have to live with. In my case, I lived with mine for too long. I hope to hear from you soon. Here's my # 202-914-2018

Tahkiyah Bradford

CHAPTER
Twenty-Seven
I Ain't a Killa . . . But Don't Push Me

Fritz looked at his Swiss Hublot timepiece when a knock sounded at the door of his suite. His guest was on time, not a minute late at 4:30 PM.

Getting up from the table, he filled his hand with a new silencer fitted 9-millimeter pistol. The Glock-19 he had used on D-Hot and Brooke Vee was in three pieces, rusting at the bottom of the Biscayne Bay. He treated his used weapons like used condoms. They were only good for a onetime use. Knowing the security was tight at the Fontainebleau, Fritz would still keep his guard up at *all* times. To his surprise, he saw Swagga standing alone out in the hallway. Just to be sure, he looked through the peephole again. Clicking the safety off, he waited to open the door until a middle-aged couple cleared the hall.

"Where's Rick?" Fritz asked Swagga as he motioned him inside with the gun.

"We don't need 'im," Swagga replied, looking at the piece Fritz held in plain view.

"What's in the bag?" Fritz glanced in the hallway and then closed the door.

"Money."

"Get against the wall so I can pat you down and I won't ask twice."

"Chill, yo! Whut the fuck!" Swagga complained, shoving his hoodie off his head.

Fritz roughly shoved Swagga up against the wall. "Drop the bag and *don't* move." Fritz held the 9-millimeter against Swagga's spine, while moving the blue leather Louis Stewart bag with his foot. "Why did you come alone?" Fritz asked, frisking Swagga with one hand.

"I can handle my own gotdamn business. And, yo, I thought you was from the islands. Where yo' accent?" Swagga asked with his face against the wall.

"I'm bi-accented," Fritz said sarcastically. "Turn around and keep your hands on your head."

Swagga turned to Fritz, masking his face with a mean grill. He stiffened when the tip of the silencer pressed against his throat. It stayed in that same spot as Fritz thoroughly patted Swagga down. Once he was sure that Swagga was unarmed, he relaxed.

"Dis how you do business?" Swagga said, fixing his gear.

"I hate rap," Fritz told him. "How much is in the bag?"

"Thirty thou."

"Dump it on the bed. If it's all there—*then* we can talk business."

"And if it ain't?"

"Then I'll consider you a threat, and you won't live to see tomorrow."

Swagga snatched the heavy LS bag off the floor and stomped over to the bed. Fritz kept his gun on Swagga until the money was spread out over the bed.

"Okay, have a seat at the table," Fritz said a few minutes later. Being patient and true to his threat, he *forced* Swagga to count every single bill.

Swagga adjusted his Gucci headband as he joined Fritz at the table.

"I had a flight leaving tonight," Fritz began. "But I must assume you need something taken care of?"

Swagga nodded while trying to give off the right vibes. Sure, Fritz was looking like a preppy dude in the dress shoes, black slacks, and a green linen shirt, but Swagga wasn't fooled. "It's a nigga by the name of Trevon. He's a porn star."

Fritz nodded. He picked up a black felt humidor. "Would you enjoy one?" Fritz had opened the humidor, revealing six cheroot Havana cigars.

"Hell yeah!" Swagga picked one out, looking at the square cut on both ends.

"It's a cheroot. It's the way its cut that makes it a cheroot. For example, if it was tapered at both ends, it's a perfecto," Fritz explained.

"You know your cigars, huh?" Swagga asked.

Fritz smiled. "Every man has his joy. And yours?"

"Phat booty 'hos," Swagga said as the Gucci headband slid down his forehead. "So whut up? Can you help me?"

Fritz reached for a gold plated lighter. "When do you need it done?"

"ASAP," Swagga said, nudging the headband back up as Fritz lit his cigar.

"Why the rush?" Fritz pushed the lighter across the table.

"I'll pay extra if needed." Swagga lit his cigar. He leaned back in the chair, filling his lungs.

The two Cuban cigars burning, quickly scented the room.

"What has this man done to you?" Fritz asked, surrounded by a thick cloud of smoke.

"A lot. I just need 'im gone. Done wit'. Period," Swagga said with the cigar in his mouth.

"If you want it done tonight, it will be ten thousand extra." Fritz tapped the cigar over the ashtray.

"Not a problem. Just let me know when and where to break you off wit' the rest. Hell, you can still catch your flight tonight." Swagga held the cigar out. "I think I need to invest in these."

"We can do a bank wire for half on my laptop," Fritz suggested.

"Say no more. Let's do it," Swagga replied eagerly.

Fritz placed his cigar in the ashtray and got up from the table. Swagga took a deep breath, thankful for the cigar helping to calm his nerves. When Fritz left the room, Swagga reached behind his head and under his mane of dreads.

Fritz returned to the table about a minute later with a thin laptop computer. He oddly sat with both hands on the table, looking directly at Swagga.

"You ai'ight, yo?" Swagga asked, smoke flowing from his nose and mouth.

Fritz picked up the silenced 9-millimeter he had left behind. "There was a hit on me once. Back in ahhhhh '06. A guy came to see me, sorta like this. I left the room and left my piece on the table."

"And what happened?" Swagga asked with a wall of fear building.

"He was armed, but he figured he would get more . . . how you say—street rep by killing me with my own gun."

"He missed?"

Fritz smiled. "My gun didn't work. I allowed that mistake to ride him for three seconds before I killed him with my second piece that did work." Fritz laid the 9-millimeter next to the laptop. "You can't trust no man."

"Man, I'm here to do *bidness*," Swagga explained. "Fuck all that other shit."

"I see that now," Fritz said, opening the laptop. "I'll need your account number. Do you have it?"

"Yeah. Lemme get my wallet."

Fritz fingers flew over the keyboard as Swagga slid back from the table. "I'll need your—" Fritz froze when he looked up from the screen.

Swagga's tight grip on the Smith & Wesson .22 caliber pistol had it shaking. Fritz slowly raised his hands up. A sense of failure tore at him for underestimating the young rapper.

"Where did you hide it? Oh, the headband." Fritz smiled. "Behind your head. Under your hair. I'll have to keep that in mind for next—"

Swagga lunged across the table, popping five quick rounds into Fritz's face. With his adrenaline thumping, Swagga ran to the bed and stuffed his bread back inside the leather Louis Stewart bag. He tried not to look over his shoulder at the lifeless body slumped face down on the table. Blood pooled around the laptop edging to the end of the table. Only the sounds of Swagga's heavy breathing sounded in the room. On his way out, he paused to snatch up the box of cigars.

"Won't be no next time, muthafucka!" Swagga pulled the hoodie back over his head. He slipped out the door with the LS bag slung over his shoulder.

***

Nashlly was waiting for Swagga inside her Mustang Boss filing her nails. He scared the piss out of her when he yanked the door open.

"Boy, damn!" She jumped as he slid inside, closing the door and tossing the LS bag in the back.

"Let's roll, baby," Swagga said with his hands shaking.

He settled low in the seat as Nashlly slowly pulled out of the Fontainebleau parking lot. He was buzzing off that new taste of power. That rush of being invincible had flowed through him when he popped Fritz's top. Killing Fritz would tie up the loose ends. Fuck the bullshit of having to worry about Fritz coming back to blackmail him. Swagga was done with paying others to do his dirt. Yeah, Fritz had taken D-Hot's grimy ass out the scene, but that was over with. If you wanted shit done right, do it yourself! Swagga assumed things would've been done differently, had he done shit *his way* on that Chyna bullshit last year. Bringing Yaffa in the fold had fucked everything up.

Swagga was keeping Nashlly in the blind about killing Fritz. He threw her off by telling her he was hustling that *white* girl on the side. She fell for it, thinking she had a platinum meal ticket in Swagga. Her rapper/D-Boy. Swagga was moved now. He had broken his fear of killing. Next on the menu, Trevon.

CHAPTER Twenty-Eight

If He Only Knew

Trevon had fulfilled his end of the bet by giving Tahkiyah a full body massage that left her sopping wet. It was forty minutes past 4 PM when she motioned to take things to another level. Her youthful C-cup titties sat upright, circled by large areolas that Trevon tasted with his tongue. At her request, he had rubbed her down from her neck to her feet, butt ass naked. Kneeling on the bed, he took her in his arms, sucking on her nipples. She grasped the stiff flesh below his waist, stroking it up and down. Being somewhat kinky, she still had her designer glasses on.

Trevon *knew* she was a stranger to him. They had just met. To cope with the doubt of whether to fuck her, he saw his actions no different than bagging a chick at a club. Her sexiness was too thick for him to pull away. He molded her breasts in his hands, flicking his tongue like a whip across her bulging nipples.

Tahkiyah's thirst for Trevon flooded her morals and the lines she knew she was crossing. She couldn't tell him that he was the first black man that had touched her since 1988. She couldn't tell him how she was raped while married to another man. She couldn't tell him how she deceived her husband by causing false troubles in their marriage. Nor could she tell him how she managed to stay away from her husband and subsequently give birth to a child she didn't want. She held it all in. After she gave birth to the child that was *forced* inside her, she tried to return to her husband a year later. The marriage failed two months later. Tahkiyah couldn't erase the face of her rapist out of her mind. She came to detest black men, even her innocent husband of nine years.

She trembled in Trevon's arms from her fear and pleasure. The mix of emotions had her head spinning. She needed him to break the bonds to her past. Tahkiyah squeezed and stroked hard between his legs, smearing the slick fluid over his tip and up and down his shaft. Filling her palm with his balls, she enclosed him, pulling a deep moan from his chest. The room was spinning. Her breaths were rushed as she made him lie back on the bed. Her tongue and lips left a wet trail down the middle of his stomach. She swirled her tongue in and around his navel while her hands fondled his hard mast of meat.

Her tongue left a wet path around the hairless base of his erection. She felt the heat of his dick against her cheek warming the side of her face. With her eyes closed, she gently licked upward, pressing her tongue flat against his map of veins. While on her knees, her nipples swayed against his upper thigh.

Trevon was propped up on his elbows, chest heaving as her tongue caressed the underside of his manhood. When her lips reached the tip, she swirled her tongue in his gel of precum, giving him the pleasure he so badly wanted.

"Oooohhh shit!" His head dropped back to the pillow. Her warm mouth sent a stream of tingles from his balls to his toes. She took the blunt head of his tool to the back of her mouth. He raised his head just as she tightened her lips around his dick. She consciously lifted her head, unhurried, causing her lips to stretch from her face. The sight and sensation curled his toes. The instant she reached his tip, she went back down then lifted her mouth again, stretching her lips.

Tahkiyah kept both hands at work. His taste was new and delicious. Up and down, she slobbered on his dick, turning and shaking her head.

"Mmmm, mmmm, mmmm, mmmm." She lost herself for a minute by sucking hard and fast. Pulling back in control, she took his balls inside her mouth, sucking them gently.

"Shit!" Trevon's ass sprung up off the bed.

She released his balls. "You enjoy that?" she whispered with her hands still working his saliva coated dick.

He nodded, struggling to catch his breath. "You got skills, baby."

"You ready for some of my knockout?" she asked, stroking his dick.

Trevon didn't answer right away. Her hand job was just as good as her head. "Just tell me how you want it," he said, sitting up.

When she released his dick, it flopped hard against his stomach. "I don't want to have sex with you." She smiled, walking her fingernails up the length of his dick. "Nor do I want to make love to you."

"Mmm, so I guess that leaves one thing." He reached out and cupped her left breast, running his thumb around her areola without touching her nipple.

"Do you still wish to bet against your endurance inside me?"

"I don't back down from nothing." He slid off the bed and picked up a condom.

"May I do the honors, please?" She crawled in his direction, licking her lips.

Trevon handed her the condom as his gaze fell on her ass and the two sexy dimples above it. As he stood, she slid him back inside her wet mouth and started sucking. Her titties jiggled back and forth just like her head. Trevon rode the high waves of the continuous ecstasy of being inside her mouth. When she started wiggling her ass, he couldn't stop his urge to spank her. Each time his palm warmed that tight soft bun, she would whimper and moan around his dick. He punished both of her cheeks as her slurps grew loud between his legs.

Tahkiyah stayed up on all fours, sucking longingly with her soft lips. She balled the sheets up in her hands when his fingers slid up and down the moist cleft of her ass. Her pussy was throbbing, and it seemed to gush an ounce of juices when Trevon inserted two fingers between her thin-lipped sugar walls. If Trevon hadn't learned by now, Tahkiyah was clearly showing off her cunning skills of fellatio. In truth, it was a strong fetish that she couldn't go without.

Trevon pushed his two fingers deeper in her hole, stirring them in a quick circle. Her gushy sex popped and snapped around his digits.

"Fuck!" she moaned with spit all around her lips. She slipped him back inside her mouth, rolling her pussy against his hand.

Trevon knew he couldn't last another minute in her wet mouth. When he pulled out of her jaws, she tried to pull him back. They both took a second to settle down.

"You taste too good." She smiled with her pretty titties dangling.

It took all the self-control she had to keep her lips off his dick as she rolled the condom down his enlarged stick.

"Stand up on the bed," he instructed her.

Tahkiyah shivered at the amount of moisture smeared between her thighs. Fingering her long hair over her shoulders, she rose to her feet. Trevon slid his hand down the sides of her svelte frame.

"Put your arms around my neck. I don't need no bed to beat that pussy up."

She did as he asked, gasping when he smoothly picked her up, slipping his strong arms up under her legs.

"Awww fuck!" She threw her head back, suspended against him as his slab pushed up between her syrupy pussy lips. "This dick! Oooohhh fuck! This dick! Yesss."

Trevon palmed the bottom of her ass, and then he broke her walls down. He went hard, bouncing her up and down his span, digging deep and fast. Her titties wobbled in circles as he fucked her on his feet. With her arms locked around his neck she moaned in his ear, bouncing and whirling herself against his dick. Their wet bodies slapped together in a steady tempo.

"Ooohhh fuck! Oooo God! Trevon, please!" she cried as his dick kept punching up inside her frame. "Mmmm . . . fuck me! Ooohhhh fuck. Mmmm."

"My pussy now!" he moaned as her titties shook against his chest. "Dis pussy good! Mmmm!"

Up and down, she slid along his dick with sweat forming all over her body. She had lost the bet three minutes ago, but she was oblivious to it. He carried her to the sofa, fucking her pussy every step of the way. She sucked hard on his neck as her soft ass bounced against him. He lowered her on the wide, soft arm of the sofa without pulling out.

With her feet on his shoulders, she cried out his name. Trevon palmed her tits while mashing her out. He long-dicked her gushy hole, bouncing his balls off the back of her ass. She couldn't stop moaning. Her pussy clung to him, smacking and sucking. She reached down to grip her own ass as his dick kept plowing between her legs. With his powerful constant strokes, her glasses finally came off.

He left her speechless with his moves. Before she could utter his name, she was face down and ass up on the sofa. She couldn't toss her ass back hard enough. Her first dick-induced orgasm popped inside her about twenty minutes inside their session. He was drilling her on the floor with her calves pushed back, corkscrewing his hips until she creamed all over his stick.

When they finally made it back to the bed, she drew her knees up beside his hips and bounced on his dick with her mind in a trance. Time meant nothing to her as she begged him to fuck her. Ecstasy. Pure, raw ecstasy filled her body as Trevon banged smoothly at her bushy center. Her fear was gone. It was now replaced with a hunger, and thirst, and a yearning. She later stared up at the man fucking her lights out. This was not a part of her plan. Releasing her grip off her chrome 9-millimeter under the pillow, she used that same hand to kill Trevon with pleasure. She gently cupped his balls and held him in her hands until he could give her no more.

***

Tahkiyah refused to let Trevon leave. After his first nut, she waited with her hazel eyes on the clock for him to rise again. Their explicit marathon of sex continued without pause. Tahkiyah took Trevon inside her again after licking him to his fullness. Her heels bounced off his bare ass as he groaned above her. She met his hard thrusts by jerking her pussy up against him. Biting his shoulder, she gripped the back of his arms and then she fucked him back. Their bodies slapped together loud and repeatedly. His dick drilled in and out of her gushy sex. Rubbing his black skin, she looked down at the flesh that filled her.

"Ohhh fuck! Trevon! Baby, yess!" She rolled her hips, wanting all of him inside her.

Trevon pumped her steadily. On looks alone, Tahkiyah was by far the finest woman he had fucked. Her pretty face was coated with a gleam of sweat beneath him.

With no emotions, he kept throwing himself in and out of her sweet pussy. They mated like animals all over the bed. Never in Tahkiyah's life had a man made her feel irresistible. Chanting his name, she shuddered around his dick and reached a climax that snatched her breath away. Floating in a blissful moment, she tickled his balls when he later groaned in her ear. Her nude body was wet with sweat. They lay together entwined, leaving the room scented with lust and sex.

"You were marvelous," Tahkiyah whispered breathlessly. "What time is it?"

Trevon reached blindly for his smartphone on the night table. "Um, fifteen minutes past seven."

She sat up, sliding her fingers through her hair. "Well, I lost the bet." She smiled at him. "And it was sooo good to lose. How long did we do it?"

"Shit, don't ask me." He shrugged, sliding his hand back and forth across her hip. "But I know one thing. It was longer than five minutes."

"So um, are you in a relationship?" she asked, rubbing his chest.

"Nope. I'm single and free."

"Really? Yes, I want the truth."

"Ain't gotta lie to you about nothing. So let's get that straight. You're the one that came at me with all that game."

"It wasn't game." She pouted.

"Okay, so tell me how you ended up at my crib? I know now that you didn't plan on moving into the spot across the street."

Tahkiyah wasn't ready to tell him the truth. She couldn't make her next move until one or two things happened:

1. She could find LaToria.
2. Find out more about Trevon and his link to LaToria.

"Does it really matter? Hell, I don't think you're being honest with me. What's up with you and that woman back at your place?" she asked, purposely putting Trevon on the spot.

"Who, Jurnee?"

Tahkiyah nodded. "I saw the way she was looking at you that day. You're fucking her and I know it."

"Whoa." Trevon sat up. "What does it matter to you? Seriously, I don't know you. You don't know me . . ."

"I apologize, baby," she said. "I guess I just lost my mind. What you did to me was so good. I'm sorry. I had no right to question you like I did. Can you forgive me?"

Man. I hope this chick ain't on no bipolar shit. Pussy was good. But it might be time for my ass to bounce. "It's all good," Trevon replied with an easy smile.

"Can we exchange numbers?"

"Yeah." He grinned. "You know where I live, so what difference does it make?"

"Are you leaving?"

"I have to get home to feed my dog." Trevon stood and then he picked up his clothes.

"Wait." Tahkiyah crawled toward him. "Before you leave. Can I have you in my mouth again?"

They grew quiet for a second.

"When are you going back home?"

"Soon," she replied, kissing his stomach. A second later, she took him back inside her mouth.

With her body refreshed and cleaned, she slid up under the new clean sheets. The room service had changed the sheets and left a single long stem rose on the pillow. Tahkiyah was giddy when she realized the romantic gesture was from Trevon. Inside the small card was written:

You're the best I ever had

She smiled, feeling no regret for fucking him. For tonight, she would sleep well and happy. *I should send him a text. Or a picture of my pussy.* She reached for her phone just as her laptop pinged, signaling she had an e-mail. Reluctantly she got out of the bed.

To: Tbradford@aol.com
From: PIstaton@aol.com
Subject: Trevon
Date: 2/9/12 7:55pm

Sorry for my delay. His name is Trevon Harrison no known aka. DOB 7/25/79. He has a criminal record and is currently on probation. Did 15 years for 1st degree murder. I dug deep and I found something that's best for you to see for yourself. I found his connection to LaToria.

See Attachment file

The rose fell to the floor. *Murder . . . I slept with a convicted murderer! Tahkiyah read the e-mail twice. This can't be true. And what's this connection with LaToria?* Sitting at the foot of the bed, she moved the cursor over the *open* icon to view the attachment file. Her heart pounded in her chest as she waited for the file to open.

"What the hell?" Tahkiyah murmured when an opening credit scene for an adult film filled the screen. She quickly assumed that it was a sick joke. Her mind went numb five seconds later when Trevon's face popped up on the screen. In a minute's span, her world was turned upside down by the sight of Trevon and LaToria aka Kandi. She exploded off the bed, losing the contents from her stomach before she reached the bathroom.

CHAPTER Twenty-Nine

This Can't Be True!

Trevon didn't think of Jurnee until a little after 8 PM. Sitting on the edge of his bed with Rex lying at this feet, he placed a call to Ariana.

"Hey Trevon!" she answered after the first ring. "What's going on?"

"Nuthin' much. Ain't wake you up, did I? I know you got a bedtime since it's a school night," he said with a grin.

"Nah, you're good. But it's close to me turning in." She laughed.

"Um, you seen Jurnee?"

"Not since she left for Janelle's party last night."

"Hmm. I just tried her number right before I called you."

"Ain't nothing wrong, I hope."

". . . I'ma call her again and leave a message this time."

"When did you see her last?"

"This mornin'. She said she was gonna swing by to see you after she did whatever she had to do."

"I'm worried."

"Chill with the negative thoughts," he said, trying to quell his own uneasiness as well as hers. "She know damn near everybody in Miami, so ain't no telling where she at. Well, lemme get off this phone, and *when* I reach Jurnee, I'll make sure she calls you. So don't be stressin' yourself out over nothing, ai'ight."

"Okay. But promise to have her call me. No matter what time it is. I'll leave my ringer on."

"Ai'ight, and you do the same if you see or hear from her before I do."

"I will. Bye and good night."

"Ai'ight, take care."

Trevon tried Jurnee's number again. Just as the first ring sounded, the door chimed. Rex, as always, sprung to his feet and shot out for the front door barking. Trevon was right behind Rex with his iPhone ringing in his ear. *I know it ain't Jurnee 'cause she got a key and the code to get in,* he thought as Rex went crazy at the door. Trevon's heart dropped in his stomach when he saw the red and blue light flashing through a gap in the curtains. He ended the call when Jurnee's voicemail kicked in. *What the fuck the police doing here?* Trevon was slow to answer the door. A fear of going back to prison had him stressing like hell. Rex kept barking and looking back at him. The doorbell rang again. Trevon felt like his feet were mired in thick brown mud as he moved to the door. *I know I ain't done shit. God, I hope it ain't nothin' 'bout Yaffa.* "Rex sit!" he said, peeking through the curtain. *Shit. Ain't but one police at the door. Fuck it.* Trevon grabbed Rex by his collar and then tugged him back to the bedroom.

Trevon hurried back to the door with his worst fears forming in his head. Taking a deep breath, he turned off the alarm and then opened the door. The female cop greeted him with a curt nod. "I'm looking for Mr. Trevon Harrison," she said with a stoic expression.

"Uh, I'm Trevon."

She glanced down at a notepad she held. "Do you know a Ms. Jurnee Cruz?"

Trevon's heart began to thump. "Yeah, I know her. What—"

"Sir. She was in a real bad car accident, and we need—"

"Where is she!"

"Jackson Memorial. She's in critical—"

Trevon ignored whatever else she had to say. All that mattered to him was reaching Jurnee. *C'mon, baby, hold on! Hold on! God, please let 'er pull through this.* Trevon sped off in his XJL hoping his prayer was heard.

***

An hour later, Swagga was laid up with Nashlly preparing to call it a wrap for today. He was sitting up watching old reruns of *Martin*.

"Nigga funny as hell!" He laughed with a bottle of Moet beside him.

Nashlly had her face glued to her cell phone tweeting to her friends on Twitter. She was topless, wearing only a pair of blue cotton panties.

"How much longer you gon' be on that shit?" he asked, hoping she would top him off like she did yesterday.

"Just a minute," she replied without looking up from her screen.

He leaned over, trying to see what she was doing. "You been on that shit for almost an hour," he complained. "Here, post this tweet. In bed wit' da KOM, Swagga." He laughed, thumping her nipple.

"Oww!" she said. "And you better stop before I tweet it for real. And then all your groupies gonna get mad. And what does KOM mean?"

"King of Miami. Hell, I might need to buy the rights for that. But yo', tweet it and take them drawers off."

"Wait, baby." She reached between his legs. "You know I'ma handle my shit in this bed, so relax. It's just some big news buzzin' on Twitter."

"'Bout what?" he asked as she managed to get his dick hard with one touch.

"That porn star, Honey Drop, was in a two-car accident today. Fucked up real bad too. People tweeting that she might not make it."

"Word?" Swagga said, losing interest with the TV.

She nodded, hiding her sigh of relief when he rolled over to get his own phone. "Swagga, the bottle!" She caught it by the neck just as it started to spill.

"My bad, yo," he said, grinning.

Swagga was easily drawn into the news about Honey Drop aka Jurnee. She was an A-list star in the world of porn. He saw Nashlly had told the truth. All the big names were posting heartfelt tweets in support of Honey Drop. When he saw tweets from Birdman, Rick Ross, Uncle Luke, Trina, Wale, and Tyga, he knew it was time to add his two cents.

@ Home hopin' that Honey Drop will pull through

He didn't mean one word, just wanted his name in the mix. Shit was turned up a notch when a picture of Jurnee's crumpled up SLS was posted. All of the AEF porn stars were showing their true support for Jurnee. Some were still speaking on the unsolved murder of

Brooke Vee. Swagga was about to log out when a tweet from Trevon popped up.

@ Jackson Memorial showing love for Jurnee. Pray!

His face balled up instantly. "I need to use your car!"

"Huh? Where you going?" She looked up as he jumped off the bed.

"Don't ask too many questions. Not tonight."

She laid her cell phone down, sliding off the bed with the bottle of Moet. She set it on the floor and then stared at him shoving his legs in a pair of black slim-fit Carhartt jeans. "I'm going with you!" she stated with her fists on her hips.

"No you ain't," he said, reaching for his hoodie.

"Why?" She stomped, making her brown titties wobble.

"'Cause I fuckin' said so, bitch!" he shouted at her from across the room.

"Why I gotta be all that?" She matched his tone.

"Listen," he sneered, dropping the blue Louis Stewart bag on the bed. "Get dressed and get the fuck outta my crib!"

Nashlly was about to get fly at the mouth, but held her heated words when Swagga pulled a gat from the LS bag.

"You think I'm playin', yo?" he said, placing the .22 in his pocket.

"This is fucked up. I know you're going to the hospital to see your ex!"

"Fuck you talkin' 'bout?"

"I just saw the tweet by your ex bitch, Kandi! She's on her way to the hospital too."

Swagga flopped on the bed to put his $525 black Mark McNairy boots on. "You don't know what the fuck you talkin' 'bout, so shut the fuck up!"

"So you gonna do me like this!" she screamed.

Swagga's mind was twisted around knocking off two birds with one stone. He wouldn't pass up the chance to catch Trevon and Kandi at the same spot. All his troubles would end tonight! Fuck any talking—wasn't shit else to say. Since they wanted to hold that Chyna shit over his head, they would die for it. When he was on his feet, he stared at Nashlly. "Don't be here when I get back!"

Nashlly saw her future of living the *ballin' life* fading quickly. "Swagga, wait. I'm sorry, I'll—"

"Bitch, it's over. Get yo' shit and get missin'!" He started for the door.

"Swagga!" she called after him. "Swagga, please!"

She was left alone in his bedroom, shocked at how fast things had turned from sugar to shit. The flashy LS bag was still on the bed. She waited a second, thinking he was coming back to see if she was leaving. Instead, she saw the light flick on outside the huge window. *I know this dumb ass fool ain't leaving for real?* she thought, rushing across the floor to look outside. She stood at the window looking down at Swagga's multi-port garage. Nashlly waited a minute before she saw his ass running toward the garage. He couldn't take her Mustang because the keys were over on the dresser. A minute after he slipped inside the garage, she saw him pulling off with no lights on, behind the wheel of Rick's 760Li.

"This fool done crossed the wrong bitch!" She fumed, turning from the window. She made a quick dash for her cell phone on the bed. Clinging to a hope that he wasn't dead ass serious, she called him to see what was really up. Hell, she could deal with the shit talking and his bitches on the side as long as he kept her laced up. *But nooo, this muthafucka trying to bump me to the curb! Oh, really!* She stood by the bed waiting for him to pick up.

"What the fuck you want, bitch!"

"Baby, why you buggin' out on me? Listen, we can have some freaky sex when you—"

"Yo! Why are you asking like I care or need your ass? It's two things ain't ever seen. One is a UFO and two, a bitch I need!"

"So you gonna shine on me like this?" she asked, getting upset.

"Bitch, you don't even exist to me no more!"

Nashlly was one on one with the dial tone a second later. Steaming mad, she got her shit together and snuck out past Rick with a tight grip on the money-filled LS bag. She had a trick for Swagga, one that would put his ass on the cover of *XXL* and *Hip Hop Weekly*!

***

Trevon sat alone inside his XJL talking to Janelle on his iPhone. "Ain't nobody telling me nothing!" he said in a state of frustration. "All they keep saying is that she's still undergoing a bunch of operations and shit! I don't even know if she's breathing on her own or not. She had to be airlifted from the accident, so I know her condition ain't good," he said.

"Trevon, listen to me," Janelle's voice broke from the pain she was dealing with. "I know what we *do* for a living isn't viewed as righteous. But tonight it's really based on what you and I believe in, okay? We have to pray for her and I mean *hard*." She sobbed. "We are all the family she's got right now, so we have to stay strong. But know that whatever happens it's for a reason and it's God's will, so—"

"She gonna make it," he stated firmly, refusing to listen to any negative talk about Jurnee not pulling through.

"I know she will."

"How soon can you and Victor catch a flight from New York?" he asked, wiping his eyes.

"I hope by noon tomorrow. If I can get a sooner flight, I'll take it."

"Ai'ight 'cause I'll be here. Ain't goin' no fuckin' where till I can take Jurnee home."

Trevon was patient with himself as he struggled to control his emotions. He was unconcerned about the bullshit he thought was so important. He didn't care if his rims were shiny. He didn't care which model had the biggest ass. He didn't care about fucking a new female. *All* he cared about was his friend, Jurnee.

A car parked next to his sedan pulled off, its headlights briefly filling the dark cabin of his ride. He saw the wetness around his eyes in the rearview mirror. Shedding tears wasn't helping Jurnee. When he slid out of the XJL, he eased the door shut and reluctantly made his way back inside the hospital.

He was drained, walking with his head down. Trevon couldn't forgive himself for being in bed with Tahkiyah while Jurnee was fighting for her life. He had learned from the police that her last phone call was made to him. He was on the phone with her at the point of contact. All he could do was hate himself. Stopping at the front desk, he spoke to a black male RN and was again given no news. Tonight he wasn't going for that 'no news is good news'. Leaving the front desk, he ended up finding a seat in the waiting area. He tried to sit away from everyone else. Alone was what he wanted to be.

***

Kandi swallowed the lump in her throat when Trevon walked by her. *He didn't even notice me,* she thought with her eyes blurred. Part of her wanted to sit and just stay silent. *I have to do it.* She shouldered her black leather Fendi tote bag and then rose up in her ankle strap pumps. A small kid ran by with an older sister giving chase. Kandi left her tears in place as she closed the space between the man she so deeply loved. He sat with his head down, his once strong shoulders slumped.

". . . Hey, Smooch," her voice broke.

He didn't move an inch. Kandi waited, her heart jumping. After what seemed like forever, he looked up at her. His face showed no emotion. Each time he blinked it sent a new line of tears down his face. Kandi shifted her eyes away, hoping he didn't hate her.

"What are you doing here?"

She fidgeted with the strap on the tote bag, unable to look him in the face. "I'm . . . here because of Jurnee," she whispered.

"I guess your *man* put you on a private jet, huh?"

"I'm not with him anymore," she replied quickly, and then added, "I been here in Florida since yesterday."

His expression stayed the same. *Beefing with her now ain't the time nor place,* he reasoned.

"Do you know anything about Jurnee's condition?" he asked, sitting up in the chair.

"Not much. I just got here about ten minutes ago."

He scratched his chin. "You can sit down if you wanna."

Kandi had all types of feelings still locked inside her heart for Trevon. If she could, she wanted to just be in his strong arms again and just be. Just be one, together. As it stood, her life was turned upside down with the blood speeding to her head with a dizzying quickness.

Silence bounced between them for a moment as they sat inches apart. Out the corner of her eye she saw the pain in his slack posture. She couldn't stomach the act of adding more hurt in his life by telling him the truth about the baby. That's what she wanted to do. But in truth, going off her talk with Jurnee, she knew she *needed* to tell Trevon the truth. She had to do it, even if it ran the risk of Trevon hating her.

"Trevon, can I talk to you?" she asked nervously.

"You ain't gotta explain nothing to me."

"Yes, I do," she said. "Do you remember when I said you couldn't understand why I—"

"I remember everything you told me! I remember you said it's over, so why try to—"

"Trevon, please!" She laid her hand on his knee. "Just listen to what I have to say, okay? I *never*—I swear I never meant to hurt you."

"Well, you did. And like I said, it is what it is."

"No, Trevon. It's not what you think—"

"It never is!" He finally looked at her. "You wanna talk. G'head and tell me why I deserved this shit you put me through. *Make* me understand!"

She held her useless tears at bay. "Trevon, I didn't cheat on you, okay? I was already a month pregnant when we met, and I didn't know it."

Trevon stared at her as her words sunk in. "So what you saying? The baby ain't mine!"

"I swear to God I didn't know I was pregnant when we met, Trevon."

"This some bullshit," he muttered. "How the fuck—yo, this shit here is—"

Cutting him off, she told him everything. She left nothing out, speaking the truth, just as she did with Jurnee. He didn't know how to feel when she explained how she planned to have an abortion. "I was wrong, Trevon. I should've told you back in November after I learned I was fourteen weeks pregnant." She wiped her eyes with her lips quivering.

Trevon had to face his reality. D-Hot was the father, not him. Did it hurt? Yes, a hole was widening in the center of his chest.

"Please don't hate me, Trevon." She sobbed quietly.

Finding the right words to say eluded Trevon. He didn't hate her. He couldn't hate her. Staying silent would not solve any issue in this case.

"So, you thought I would . . . not love you anymore had you told me this last year?" he asked with no anger in his tone. If anything, he was loaded with misunderstanding her actions.

She nodded weakly.

He sighed, feeling pity for her. "Life ain't perfect, LaToria. If you had told me back then, yes I would've been crushed just like I am now. But it wouldn't have changed how I felt for you."

She looked up. "I'm so sorry, Smooch. I just didn't know—"

"How's the baby?"

She blinked, and then glanced down at his hand on her belly. All she could do was cry. Trevon sided with staying calm. What would him going off in anger help? Nothing. What shook him were the memories of all the good times they shared. Their issue was defined easily. A mistake on LaToria's part that they would have to settle together. Trevon knew what would have happened had he known the truth last year. He would've stayed with her. He was in love with her for the present and the future. Her past didn't form who she was today. Trevon wouldn't judge her, not tonight, not tomorrow, never.

On the strength of keeping it real, he eased his arm around her shoulder. "Stop crying, okay? We gon' talk about this, but right now we gotta be strong for Jurnee."

She nodded against his chest, thanking God that he didn't hate her.

CHAPTER
Thirty
Bustin' Shots

Back at the Mondrian hotel, Tahkiyah was doing her own research of LaToria's whereabouts. At the time noted on her laptop, 10:18 PM, she hit a patch of luck. By visiting the AEF webpage, she caught the news about the accident involving Jurnee. Tahkiyah, at first, didn't make the connection of Honey Drop being Jurnee until she came across her picture. On a hunch, she then logged on to Twitter and saw the last tweet posted by Kandi. She didn't waste any time getting dressed to make a ride to the hospital. On her way out the door, she turned back and added one certain item in her purse. Her mind was set, and there would be no other alternative, other than finding and facing LaToria. Once she was seated insider her BMW, she checked the 9-millimeter inside her purse to make sure it was loaded and ready.

***

Swagga killed the headlights after he found the closest parking spot to Kandi's black Escalade. From his position, he could see the front end of her SUV to his left.

He had also found Trevon's XJL, but it was too close to the hospital entrance to do anything crazy. He would wait and form a plan now with the .22 placed on his lap. He sunk lower in the seat when a Metro Dade police van rode by. *A plan! I need a fuckin' plan! Ai'ight. Cappin' that bitch out here might get my ass life. Gotta snatch her ass up somehow.* He picked up the light .22 just as it dawned on him of his fuck up. "Damn!" he vexed through his teeth, popping the clip out. He only had six rounds left out of the ten he had loaded earlier with gloves on. In his rush to catch Trevon slipping, he had forgotten to reload the .22. *Shit! Three for Trevon and three for Kandi. Fuck it.*

***

Kandi was back on Twitter making an update when a frugal dressed middle-aged dude shuffled into the waiting room. It was easily seen that he was homeless.

"'Scuse me," he said with his hands in his pockets.

No one seemed to pay him any attention. The only reason Kandi looked up was because she could smell a funky odor coming off his body. She moved her purse under her seat with her foot, ignoring the white bum like everyone else. Kandi looked past him, hoping that Trevon would return with some good news about Jurnee's status.

"Um . . ." the bum continued. "Anybody in here drive an uh, black Escalade truck?" He pointed over his shoulders. "Been a little fender bender, and the other—"

"Sir," Kandi said with hopes he wasn't talking about her SUV. "Did you say a black one?"

He nodded. "Yeah, an' it got dem big ole chrome rims. Real nice-looking too."

Kandi muttered a curse under her breath and then got up to find out what was going on. *Damn! Of all nights, this is the last thing I need!*

***

Back in Fort Lauderdale, Rick was shoved out of his sleep by Tweet. He sat up with his eyes heavy. "What's up?"

"Dawg, we got major problems!" Tweet exclaimed.

"Talk." Rick shoved the covers off as Tweet looked over his shoulder back at the door.

"Feds at the front gate."

"Feds!" Rick shot up and grabbed his six-shot Sig Sauer Sub-compact 9-millimeter.

"FBI, and they ain't playin'."

Rick rubbed his face. "Fuck! All right. Where Swagga?"

"Uh, that's another problem. I checked all over the place, and he ain't here."

"Fuck you mean he ain't here?" Rick shouted.

"Nigga bounced. That 'ho Nashlly gone too. I think Swagga took yo' Beemer 'cause it's gone and so is Nashlly's whip."

"Call—"

"I already tried calling Swagga like . . . five times. He ain't picking up."

"Yo, let the Feds in. . . . They might . . . shit—just let 'em in. I'ma be down in a sec."

By the time Rick reached the first floor, the Feds were stationed around the living room ten deep. A tall suited black agent looking like Cuba Gooding Jr. met Rick at the bottom of the stairs.

"Your name, sir?"

Rick looked at the three other bodyguards on duty with Tweet. All four were seated on the sofa with worried looks. "Uh, Rick."

The FBI agent frowned. "Your government name."

"Rickey Terrell."

The agent glanced across the room at an agent standing by the lamp. They exchanged a quick nod that went unnoticed by Rick. "Ah, repeat that please."

Rick sighed. "Rickey Terrell."

"Mr. Terrell. I have a search warrant for this property."

"Can I see it?"

Rick was shown a legalized federal search warrant that he couldn't dispute. The only thing that seemed odd was the fact that the warrant didn't list what the Feds were looking for. When Rick took it upon himself to ask, the agent said he would soon find out. Shit got weird when one of the agents pulled out a small handheld scanner. Once he turned it on, he waited a few seconds and then left the room.

"Mr. Terrell, can we step into the kitchen?" the suited agent asked Rick.

"What's this all about?"

"I'll explain in the kitchen."

Rick knew he had no choice. *Fuck! I hope Swagga ain't leave no weed or nothing lying around.* Rick tried to play it cool with the agent following him to the kitchen. Once they were seated at the table, the agent introduced himself.

"My name is Lorenzo Thompson, and I'll get to the point, okay. I have a picture of a man I'd like to show you. Here's the first one." Agent Thompson reached inside his jacket and removed two 4 x 6 glossy pictures.

Rick's stomach dropped to the floor when the agent slid a picture of Fritz across the table. It was clear the picture was taken without Fritz knowing it.

"His *real* name is Ronald Bleibtreu. Born in Germany and he has a *very* interesting military background, which I can't speak on. He's fluent in six different languages, and you might know him simply as . . . Fritz."

"Never seen 'im before." Rick slid the picture back.

"Are you positive, Mr. Terrell?"

Rick scratched his neck in a nervous fit. "Yeah, I 'on't know dude."

Agent Thompson slid the second picture across the table. It was a close shot of Fritz lying face down on a table. "We found him at the Fontainebleau today. He was shot four times, close range with a twenty-two caliber."

Rick stared at the picture. *Shit, I'm good! Ain't kill the nigga.* Rick started to relax a little. "I don't know 'im."

Agent Thompson adjusted his brown tie and then sat back crossing his arms. "The FBI has been aware of Ronald for quite a while . . . five years to be exact. He's an expert at taking care of things. Making people take permanent naps, if you know what I mean."

"Nah, I don't."

"Anyway, our agency got word that Ronald had created too many enemies abroad. We heard he was bringing his uhhh *talent* to the U.S. By then we had a nice thick intelligence file on Ronald, and with that, we came up with a plan."

"Yo, why are you telling me all this? I don't know the dude." Rick was getting irritated.

"I'm almost done. Well, one of our agents met Ronald in parts of Portugal and gave him a gift. A gift we *knew* he would keep. See, we could allow him to roam freely in the U.S. knowing what we knew about him. We allowed him to move as he pleased because we were *always* on him."

Rick cleared his throat. "Yo, this is a waste of time because—"

"Do you know the charge for conspiracy to commit murder, Mr. Terrell?"

Rick shifted his position in the chair. Shit wasn't looking too good for him. Things took a turn up shit's creek when the agent with the handheld device entered the kitchen with a bagged object. Agent Thompson stood as the second agent handed him the evidence bag.

"This look familiar to you?" Agent Thompson asked.

What the fuck! That's Fritz's black cigar box! How the fuck that shit get here?

"It was in the master bedroom," the second agent told Thompson.

"Who sleeps in that room, Mr. Terrell? Care to tell me?" Agent Thompson pressed.

Rick stuck to being hood. "I don't know." He shrugged with a straight face.

Agent Thompson was tired of the games. "Look, this cigar box is the gift we gave Ronald. It's a tracking device *and* a listening device, okay? Now, do I need to repeat word for word of you talking to Ronald about hiring him to kill David Reed aka D-Hot on the twenty-first of last month at the Fountainebleau?"

Rick knew the deal and how the Feds got down. "Ain't got shit else to say. I wanna call my lawyer." Rick eased back from the table, gripping the Sig Sauer.

Agent Thompson nodded, giving the signal to arrest Rick, just a split second before Rick took matters into his own hands.

***

Trevon couldn't hide his letdown after his brief talk with one of the RNs. There was still no information being released about Jurnee's status. All that was being said is that her condition was critical. Rounding the corner to the waiting room, he saw a face that slowed his steps. *What the hell is she doing here? And where is LaToria?* He walked by a row of occupied chairs to where Tahkiyah stood by the water fountain.

"You following me?" he asked, touching Tahkiyah on her shoulder.

"Trevon!" she said when she turned. "I see we meet once again." She forced a smile, her hazel eyes darting around the waiting room.

"You looking for somebody?" he asked.

Tahkiyah pushed her glasses up on her nose. She had to come clean and tell him what was really going on. "Indeed I am," she told him. "I'm looking for—"

Her words were halted when Trevon's iPhone started ringing.

"Uh, hold on for a sec. I gotta take this call." He turned his shoulder to her and then answered LaToria's call. "Hey. Where are you and why did you—"

"What up, playboy!"

Trevon took the phone from his ear to double check the caller ID and number. As clear as day, LaToria's name, number, and a small image of her face showed on the screen. He recognized the voice, and it turned his stomach inside out.

"Don't get all quiet on me, nigga!" Swagga jeered. "Shit gonna *almost* be like a déjà vu fo' yo' ass tonight! Only this time, ain't gon' be no tricks, feel me? Well, I don't know if you still care fo' this 'ho, Kandi or not. But yeah, I got 'er and you know what I want!"

"What type of shit you on?" Trevon's temper came sudden like a lightning strike.

"I'ma be on this bitch's *ass* if you don't do what I fuckin' tell you! And trust me, dawg, I don't give a fuck 'bout this bitch being pregnant!"

"Look, just tell me what you want. Ain't no need to do no silly shit."

"Nigga, didn't I just say it's gonna be a déjà vu! I want them two videos you got since you an' yo' bitch played me the first time. Don't know how the fuck you got 'er off the boat, but shit goin' my way tonight!"

"Swagga, I'll give you the shit, ai'ight? Just don't hurt—"

"Listen up, nigga! You gon' see me tonight. See, I can play games too. I guess you think shit just gon' fly 'bout you fuckin' Kendra and shit! Nah, muthafuckas takin' my kindness fo' a weakness ends tonight!"

Trevon wasn't in a position to beef with Swagga. "Yo, I hear ya'. Just tell me what to do."

"Oh, so you do care. Even after this bitch been fuckin' around behind your back! You's a sucka fo' love ass nigga. Listen, and I won't say it twice. I want you to come alone to the same spot where this shit went down between us last year."

"The warehouse?"

"Right. Come alone so we can talk. Settle this shit like men. Just you and me."

"What time?"

"Midnight. That will gimme some time to have fun with this big booty 'ho I got wit' me. Shit, I know you don't mind me runnin' up in it. Not with how you fucked Kendra an' her fat ass friend."

Trevon glanced at his watch. It was ten minutes to eleven. Every second LaToria was with Swagga would tear Trevon apart. He felt helpless, having no one to turn to. Calling the police would only make matters worse.

"Midnight, nigga!" Swagga said and then killed the connection.

"Trevon, what's going on?" Tahkiyah had stood near Trevon taking in the one-sided call. He ignored her as he rushed for the exit. She called after him once more to no avail. Sighing, she took an empty seat and prayed for a face to face meeting with LaToria. She had her own issues to deal with.

***

"Take *all* your clothes off and hurry the fuck up!" Swagga shoved Kandi on the small bed inside a cheap motel off of Biscayne Boulevard. He moved along the chipped green painted wall with the .22 aimed at Kandi. "And I mean er'thang. I'ma have me some fun, and bitch, you can bag them tears 'cuz they don't move me."

Kandi hated Swagga so much that she couldn't even look at him. She removed her shoes first and then reached behind her back to unzip the dress.

Swagga sat down on a dingy looking brown chair beside the night table. He watched her tugging the expensive dress down her super thick frame. Seeing the swelling of her belly had him boiling with envy. *How she gonna let a broke ass jailbird ass nigga bust raw over me?* His hating thoughts grew as she slowly took her bra off. *Damn, that bitch bad. Titties big as hell. Hmm, look at that cat!* His dick grew hard. "Turn around and take them drawers off. And do it slow. Show that phat ass!" he said, undoing his belt. He wanted her to feel like shit. When he had his dick out, he fumbled with his cell phone. "Act like your ass at the King of Diamonds, bitch."

Kandi shook with pure humiliation as Lil' Wayne and Drake's "Maybe She Will" sounded from Swagga's phone.

"Dance, bitch! And keep that ass facing me. That's all I wanna see. Now, do what it do and bounce that ass." He laid the .22 on the table and then enjoyed the show. All the love and lust he once had for Kandi was now hate.

Kandi kept her eyes shut, moving her wide hips off beat. She couldn't find a rhythm no matter how hard she tried.

"Now turn around," he said, midway through the song. "And open yo' eyes! Look at my dick. Yeah, now rub your nipple and rub that pussy." He stroked his dick at the sight before him. "Now, get down like a dog—"

"Swagga, ple—"

"Now, bitch!" he sneered, lifting the .22 up to her face.

Kandi held her hands out with tears streaking down her cheeks. Sobbing, she got down on her hands and knees.

"Now, crawl yo' ass over here and suck my dick. C'mon, bitch. Ain't got all fuckin' night!" He gestured with the gun. "You do it fo' a livin', but tonight it's fo' free."

Fear of not seeing tomorrow gripped Kandi's soul. She was afraid of Swagga. She saw the hate etched across his face.

"Keep yo' hands on the floor!" He pressed the gun against her forehead and grabbed his shaft with his free hand, forcing his dick past her lips. "Work, bitch!" he moaned, fisting his hand into her voluminous hair. Without caring, he filled her mouth to the hilt, making her gag. Swagga kept the gun against her neck as her lips pulled up and down on his dick. "This all yo' ass is good fo'! Aaahhh yeeaa . . . fuck. Suck it, bitch! Suck it . . ."

He settled back in the chair as her head bounced below his waist. He didn't want to cum in her mouth for a reason. He didn't want *any* DNA left on or in her since he was planning to body her ass tonight. For several minutes his dick tingled inside her wet mouth. He ignored her tears that flowed in heavy rivers down her face.

"Ai'ight . . . stop!" Swagga shoved her hard after she got off his dick. "Go in the bathroom and rinse yo' mouth out! An' do it good!"

It was a rough urge to turn down the act of fucking her big ass, but Swagga was able to hold back. "And leave the door open!" He got up to his feet, fixing his clothes. *I gotta dead this 'ho soon. Ain't no need to take any kind of chances tonight.* Swagga thumbed the safety *on* then *off* then back *on.*

"Hurry up, 'ho! Put yo' shit back on. We 'bout to take a ride." Swagga slowly lifted the .22, aiming at the back of Kandi's head from across the room. Licking his dry lips, he clicked the safety *off.*

***

At the same time, a manhunt was in its early stages for Rick. He had bodied the two Feds in the kitchen and then hauled ass out the back door. It was true of a person being able to hear bullets whizzing by. Rick could personally attest to it from the close rounds that nearly popped his top. The remaining Feds had opened up a barrage of lead on his black ass. A Florida Highway Patrol helicopter was the first to respond to the Feds frantic plea for assistance. Swagga's mansion resembled a police convention with local, state, and federal law authorities amassed on the property.

Rick had run north until he shook the Feds in the dense woods. He knew they wouldn't cease chasing, so he wouldn't cease running. As he sprinted across an open field, he tripped and stumbled in the dark. Rolling to his back, he struggled to catch a grip on his breath. The star-lit sky gave him no sense of peace. Pulling out his cell phone, he called Swagga. *Dis nigga better answer!*

"Yo, whut up?"

"It's over, dawg," Rick said, rolling to get up.

"Whut the hell you—"

"Nigga, shut up and listen!" Rick took off at a jog as he gave Swagga the scoop. "We fucked up. Feds been listening since day one. And if you can't explain how you got Fritz's cigar box without poppin' him, it's over for you." Rick sped up when he heard the dogs barking in the distance. "Swagga! I need your help—" Rick took his phone from his ear. "Bitch ass nigga!" he vexed at seeing how easy Swagga had turned his ass around for him to kiss. The line went dead, but Rick kept moving.

CHAPTER Thirty-One

Feel My Pain

Kandi shook uncontrollably as Swagga shoved her back inside the trunk of the BMW 760Li. Her hands were tied behind her back, and her own panties were stuffed in her mouth. The ripped bed sheet Swagga tied around her face kept her quiet. A fear laced moan sounded as the trunk slammed over her. All she could think about was the baby and Trevon. She was afraid that both would suffer because of her. Thoughts troubled her mind, fearing that Trevon wouldn't be able to save her tonight. She was thrown against a hard object when the 760Li sped out of the motel parking lot. She cried hard, finding it easier to give up. Just as it seeped into her mind, she forced that thought out.

Minute after minute, mile after mile, her trip in the trunk grew. Something wasn't right. When she cleared her mind she realized the trip to the warehouse should have been short. Focusing on the sounds around her, she judged the BMW was speeding along a highway. The sedan had been rolling nonstop for at least ten minutes.

Reality slapped her hard. She wasn't being taken to the warehouse.

***

Trevon didn't know what to do anymore. Showing no fear of Swagga, he had driven his XJL to warehouse 7210 at two minutes to midnight. His sedan sat with the engine running and the lights off. He waited, feeling it was pointless to pray since he was a sinner. When his watch showed twenty minutes past midnight, he stepped out of his car. He dialed LaToria's number. It wasn't answered, not even a voicemail. At the end of his rope, he looked up at the sky above. "Why gotdamnit!" he raged to the world. He tried her number again. Nothing. Sliding down to the ground, he leaned his head back against his car. He was defeated. If Swagga were to walk up and catch Trevon slipping, he wouldn't care. Jurnee crossed his mind. He couldn't do shit for her, and it pained him that it stood the same for LaToria. Just as his mind lost grip with reality, his iPhone rang.

***

Rick was winded, pausing for the eighth time to catch his breath. Leaning up against a thick tree, he wished he could redo his past. His life was fucked up over $20,000! "Fuck!" he muttered, kicking at the high weeds.

Suddenly he heard voices to his left. He ducked, moving around the tree with the baby 9-millimeter gripped tightly. With only four shots left, a shootout was being suicidal. He peered in the direction of the voices, hoping like hell they hadn't heard him. His heart thumped in his ears. He eased down to one knee, his finger on the trigger. The voices grew louder but dropped silent not a second later. Rick stayed motionless, only moving his eyes. Remaining in one spot was not aiding his escape. He *knew* someone was close, but he couldn't take the risk to give his position away.

"Rickey Terrell!" A loud voice came from his left followed by a bright spotlight. "This is Broward—"

Rick let off two quick shots over his shoulder and took off running. He made a life altering choice by falling for Swagga's plot. He allowed Swagga's troubles to become his downfall. Running hard, he oddly stayed in the spotlight. This time he didn't hear any bullets whizzing by. He didn't hear the sporadic shots of gunfire behind him. Closing his eyes, he sensed the final period of his life. It came a split second later in the form of a 5.56 full metal jacket round that punched him an inch below the base of his skull.

***

The phone call Trevon had received led him to an abandoned trap house in Carol City. The caller was a dude's voice that was new to Trevon. He gave the address and then said four words that crushed Trevon.

"Come see the body."

Trevon parked behind a white 760Li and a brown van. The trap house was unlit and sitting at a dead end street. He stepped over broken wine bottles and crushed beer cans. A pit formed in Trevon's heart when he neared the BMW. Under the faint cast of the moon, he saw streaks of blood on the trunk lid and bumper. There was no fear filling Trevon. He was too numb, yet he went on. Taking a step on the concrete and wooden porch, he prepared himself to face whatever awaited him. Pushing the creaky door open, he saw blood at the entrance. A light was on, a single lamp without a shade over it. Trevon stepped inside the odd smelling house. To his right sat a black couch with several tears in the seat cushions. All of the windows were covered with black thick curtains that reached the floor. Drug use was apparent by the broken needles and empty clear vials. The piss stained colored walls were bare, marred with ragged holes along sections of the baseboard. Trevon's attention fell to the stain of blood trailing from where he stood that marked a path down the dark hall.

"LaToria!" he called out. Dreading the silence, he took a deep breath and then moved along the line of blood. He wouldn't allow thoughts of LaToria being dead to enter his mind. He refused it. There were three doors along the narrow hall. Two were on the left and one on the right. The blood continued past the first door on the left only to turn and go into the second. A light was on. Trevon's steps came quicker. All he wanted was for LaToria to be safe. He was not a man of great need. He called her name again. No reply. Sliding a hand down his face, he opened the door. What he was met with sent him stumbling back against the wall. His eyes told the truth, but his mind was having trouble grasping the sight.

CHAPTER
Thirty-Two
Baptized in Eternal Fire

"Who are you?" Nashlly asked Trevon with a chrome and black .380 at her side.

"Trevon," he replied.

Nashlly stared at Trevon with a mean expression. "He good, Art. You can put it down."

Art lowered the pistol grip Remington 12 gauge pump from Trevon's face. "Anybody else come wit' you?"

"Nah," Trevon said, shaking his head. "You the one that called me?"

"Yup," Art said with the pump pointed to the floor. "Yo." He turned to Nashlly. "I'ma go outside and make sure we don't get no unexpected visitors."

Nashlly nodded, her eyes never moving off of Trevon. "C'mon in." She waved Trevon inside the small bedroom. "Watch out for that puddle of blood," she said, wiping a sheen of sweat off her forehead.

Trevon looked at the bed and the dingy bloody mattress. "Where's LaToria?"

"In the bathroom. She's okay and lucky."

"I want to see 'er!"

Nashlly frowned. "Tonight ain't a good time to be lifting your voice at me. If it wasn't for me and my dude, your girl woulda—" Nashlly paused when the bathroom door to her right came open.

"LaToria!" Trevon rushed across the room, taking her in his arms.

Nashlly watched them, wishing she had a man that would love and care for her. *Nah, fuck that shit 'cause niggas ain't shit!* she thought as Trevon continued embracing LaToria.

"What the fuck is going on?" Trevon asked with LaToria sobbing against his chest.

"We both got beef with Swagga," Nashlly said. "I had a little issue wit' him today. Long story short, we followed him and just waited for a chance to kidnap his punk ass. We caught him slipping at a motel. He had your girl tied up in the trunk. After she told me what he had done, we called you here."

"All this blood?" He looked at the floor.

"It's from Swagga," Nashlly told him.

"Where is he?"

Her eyes looked across the room. "In the closet."

When Trevon tried to release LaToria, she clung to him tighter. Nashlly brushed by them and then yanked the closet door open. Swagga was naked and tied with wide strips of duct tape on his mouth. His nose was bloody, and he had seeping gash along his hairline.

"I exist now, huh!" Nashlly kicked Swagga on his knee. She looked at Swagga with solid hate in her eyes. "Jamilah said she wished she could be here, but she'll settle for the loot when we body your ass!"

Swagga strained against the tape with fear in his eyes. When Trevon stepped up next to Nashlly, he stopped struggling. Swagga stared at Trevon, knowing the outcome wouldn't be in his favor. He recoiled back against the back of the closet when Trevon squatted near him. Trevon had no pity for Swagga. He slowly pulled the duct tape off his mouth. Swagga dropped his head on the dirty floor, breathing hard through his mouth.

"Why we have to go through this shit again?" Trevon wanted an explanation. "You risked all that you got . . . for what?"

Swagga ignored Trevon. If Rick had told him the truth about the Fritz issue, he knew a murder case was now over his head. So what, Frank Ocean came out of the closet. Swagga couldn't do it. He couldn't face the shame.

Trevon stood back up just as Art reentered the room with a red plastic gasoline jug.

"Nooo, nooo, nooo, please!" Swagga moaned. "Nashlly, baby, I'll make it up—"

"Save it, nigga!" Nashlly shouted. "You're worth more dead to me!"

Trevon didn't feel right with what was about to go down. He tried to build off his dislike toward Swagga, but pity slowly began to set in. When LaToria squeezed his waist, it was then the vision of Swagga's burning yacht popped back in his head.

"You were right 'bout this night being d jà vu," Trevon said as Art opened the jug of gasoline. "Only this time it's your ass that's getting burned!"

Gasoline fumes filled the bedroom as Art began sloshing the gasoline around the room.

"FUCK YOU!" Swagga screamed. "Fuck all of y'all."

Trevon turned with LaToria in his arms and left the room. Swagga's screams and loud cursing followed them down the hall.

Nashlly moved aside as Art poured the remaining gasoline on Swagga. His anger was now reduced to pleading tears and choking sobs. When Art pulled out a lighter he looked at Nashlly.

"G'head and—"

"No." She took the lighter from his hand. "I'll do it. Go ahead and get the van started."

"You sure?"

She nodded. Once she was alone, she wiped a tear from her face.

"It ain't have to be like this, Swagga. I *tried* to save your ass from Jamilah, but you didn't want me, so—"

"Please shoot me, Nashlly! Please, yo! Don't let me burn alive . . ." he cried, banging his head on the floor. "I'm begging . . . please don't make me suffer like this."

***

Trevon was backing out the yard just as a single gunshot went off. Three seconds later, Nashlly ran out of the trap house as flames engulfed the bedroom. Trevon watched it burn for a few seconds before he left it all in the rearview mirror. He sped off in silence with LaToria curled up in the passenger seat. His night wasn't over, Jurnee. Was she dead or alive? He drove directly back to the hospital as his heart stirred for LaToria.

***

Tahkiyah was minutes from going to bed when her cell phone rang. She was intending to ignore it until she saw it was her private investigator calling.

"Hello," she answered, rubbing some cocoa butter lotion on her breasts.

"Ah, I know it's late, but I don't think you'll mind this late call."

"What do you have for me?"

"My guy in Atlanta that works at that credit card company. He just sent me an e-mail. LaToria's name popped up when she used her credit card. She's back in Miami."

"I'm aware of that," she said, rubbing the lotion into her nipple. "I just don't know—"

"She has a room at the Mondrian," he told her. "She checked in on Thursday."

Tahkiyah's hand fell from her breasts. "Are you sure!"

"Positive. I went ahead and called down there to see if she's still checked in and she is. She's in room 214."

Tahkiyah got up off the bed and looked at the time. 1:38 AM. She thanked the private investigator, and then sat back down to calm herself. Her mind was made up a few moments later when she rushed to get dressed. Again she left the room with the 9-millimeter concealed in her purse.

***

LaToria was numb as she rode the elevator up to her floor at the Mondrian. She had convinced Trevon that she was okay. She left him at the hospital with a promise to return after she showered and got her mind right. As for the bullshit Swagga had forced her to do, she kept it from Trevon. Her feelings of Swagga's murder was blank. She was neither happy nor sad. Stepping off the elevator with her head down, she wondered if Trevon would give her a second chance. Would he accept her child? All she wanted in life was to be happy.

"Excuse me."

LaToria lifted her head and saw a beautiful woman standing across the hall. What struck LaToria as odd were the tears welling in the woman's eyes behind her glasses.

"Are you LaToria Nicole Frost?" Tahkiyah dropped her hand inside her purse.

LaToria had been through too much shit tonight to be scared anymore.

"Yeah. And who are you?"

Tahkiyah closed her eyes. *I have to do it! I have to do it!* she chanted in her head. Opening her eyes, she took the first step in reaching peace and that sentiment of closure that left her heart torn. "LaToria," she said. "I'm . . . Tahkiyah Bradford. I'm your mother."

CHAPTER Thirty-Three

A Night to Remember

The burning trap house in Carol City had nearly burned to its foundation by the time the police and fire department arrived. An APB was already out for Swagga and the white 760Li. Once the Feds got word of the BMW's location, they rushed to the scene ASAP. Many weren't surprised when a charred body was found in the closet. For what it was worth, the coroner pointed out the single bullet hole in front of the skull. Until a DNA test was done to identify the body, the cause of death would be listed as a gunshot wound.

Swagga's life came to an end due to his jealousy and fear of how others viewed him. His demise also centered on him being enthralled with things he didn't have while ignoring the items he possessed.

***

LaToria had to practice what she wanted to preach to Trevon. She had to give Tahkiyah a chance to speak the truth. Tahkiyah tearfully told LaToria how she was raped, and gave birth behind her husband's back. She pleaded for LaToria to forgive her for putting her up for adoption.

Tahkiyah sobbed deeply, asking for forgiveness and a chance to make things right.

LaToria had known of Tahkiyah by her first name only, since she was ten. She cried with her mom, choosing forgiveness over hate. She told Tahkiyah of her unfair past and what pushed her to do porn. Together they cried for both hurt and joy. LaToria knew she wouldn't be alone anymore when her mom promised to never leave her again. As for Trevon, Tahkiyah had sent him a text message that same night before she left the room with LaToria.

I hope you will take this with an understanding that even I myself find hard to grasp. Our night. Let it stay between us. I was wrong to let it happen and had you known who I was, I doubt it would've happened. I'm sorry, but building my bond with my daughter is all I live for now. TTYL

Tahkiyah, LaToria's mom.

***

Trevon had read Tahkiyah's text message twice, but was too numb to show any reaction. It was too much to add to his troubles. With his head back against the wall and his eyes shut, a black female surgeon entered the waiting room.

"Is there a Mr. Trevon Harrison here?" she asked softly.

Trevon shot to his feet. He had waited for this moment since he first learned of the accident. "How is she?" he asked, full of concern.

***

At the same time, LaToria and Tahkiyah walked up on Trevon and the surgeon. LaToria watched closely as the two spoke quietly. *Please God. Let it be good news.* She was coming up behind the surgeon when Trevon had an outburst of grief that caused LaToria to prepare her heart for more pain.

CHAPTER Thirty-Four

Things Done Changed

May 25, 2012

Friday 3:45 PM – Miami, Florida

Three months later . . .

Trevon's career had shot past the moon and risen to a status of A-list stardom. With a new manager at his side and two new films on the market, his life was nothing like he dreamed of. His name was buzzing from New York to Hollywood, California, with rumors blowing up left and right about who he was dating or fucking. He made the threesome film with Cherokee and Pinky that was currently his bestselling DVD. His appearance on *The Wendy Williams Show* had caused his Facebook page to max out with friend requests only five minutes into the show. Porn was his true hustle. He was now getting appearance fees to show up at clubs, and a buzz grew instantly when he was spotted with Maliah

Michel on his arm at Club Liv. Because of his hustle and the team behind him, Trevon was a star. *Any* woman he was seen with, the media easily speculated he was fucking them. In some cases they were correct, but in truth, he was 100% single and focused hard on his career.

The sun had its chest out today with the roasting temperature up and around 89 degrees. Trevon slowed his outrageously painted light green Aston Martin Rapide in front of a modest fenced-in home. Trevon's new sedan sat mean on a set of chrome 22-inch Strappo Rucci rims. The ride was a gift to himself, and of course, he broke his mom and sister off with money for GP and love. With the engine running, he tapped twice on the horn and then muted the music. Pulling out his iPhone, he sent a quick text message to Kendra.

Hey u! Hope all is well wit u and lil one. Just had u on my mind. Be sure to call me as soon as you have the time. Take care.

Trevon's conscience was a little troubled over Kendra's daughter having to grow up without a father. The day it was proven that it was Swagga that was shot and burned, Kendra and her daughter moved up to Raleigh, North Carolina. With the money left to her from Swagga's estate, she had no reason to ever work again. Trevon would never tell her of the role he played in Swagga's death. As for the video Swagga had downloaded of the threesome with Kendra, it was deleted. The same was done with the videos of Swagga with Chyna. When a shadow moved over Trevon, he looked up from his phone.

"Y'all ready?" he said, getting out of the Aston Martin sedan to help Ariana with the bag she carried.

"You're the one that's late," Jurnee said as she moved slowly toward him. Trevon smiled at his best friend. The accident had caused her to lose her left leg from the knee down. Though her walk was slow in the prosthetic limb, she was alive and deeply in love with Ariana. Trevon tried to help Jurnee inside the car, but she slapped his hands away.

"How you feeling?" he asked Jurnee when they were all inside the car. Jurnee leaned across the center console and kissed Trevon lightly on the lips. What had troubled her mind on the day of the accident was the issue of what *she* had to tell Trevon. She was going to tell Trevon the truth about Kandi's baby, but it would've come after she told him about hers. Jurnee was three months pregnant by Trevon, and there were no doubts about it. The bond Jurnee and Trevon shared was beyond unique. As for people that didn't understand it, they dared not to even waste their time to explain. As long as they were happy, fuck what everyone else thought about it.

"I can't believe Janelle is getting married today!" Jurnee said when Trevon pulled from the curb.

"And she's two months pregnant," Trevon added. Rick Ross' "Hold Me Back" lightly thumped in the trunk.

"Hey," Ariana said from the backseat. "You two come up with a name for the baby yet?"

Jurnee smiled, looking at Trevon and caring so much for him. She had mad love for him, but it was Ariana that she was in love with. She could still recall the day Trevon was at her side, nine days after the accident. The doctors had already told Trevon about Jurnee being pregnant, but he still took it as new news from Jurnee herself. As a true friend, he was the rock she needed when she faced hard times during her period of healing. When she was physically able to have sex, she did so with Trevon until she could barely move. She needed to *feel* alive, and yes, she called him papi while he pounded at her sweet wetness. As for life with a baby, they would deal with it and take it day by day. And most important, there would be no regrets.

***

Nashlly was still in Miami and living off those five minutes of fame she had by dating the late Swagga. *Hip Hop Weekly* and *XXL* had done big stories on Swagga's unsolved murder. Nashlly flawlessly played the role of a broken-hearted lover in both magazines. It was *rumored* that she was dating/fucking a baller in the NBA, but he was remaining nameless.

Jamilah collected a check for $7.5 million, only half of what Kendra got. Jamilah knew Kendra was always number one out of his three baby mommas. Reluctantly, she gave Nashlly $800,000 just to keep her out of her face. As for Art, he was back up in New Bern, North Carolina thinking of ways to triple the $500,000 Jamilah had dropped in his lap.

***

LaToria and Tahkiyah had stayed true to their word. They both gave each other a chance, and through time they became inseparable. They lived together in a five star condo on Miami Beach and became what many people take for granted, a family.

"This doctor needs to hurry his tail up!" Tahkiyah said, losing her patience while sitting in the obstetrician office with LaToria.

"Something's wrong, Ma," LaToria whined from up on the examination table.

"Hush girl, and stop all that worrying. He's just running some tests and—"

"My baby is too late, Ma. I shoulda had her two weeks ago!" LaToria had done the math in her head. *I was fourteen weeks pregnant back in November, so my nine months is . . . now! Please God. Let my baby be okay.* Lying on her back, she caressed her swollen belly with fresh tears pooling in her eyes. She *knew* something wasn't right. Her soul was telling her so. Listening to her mom, she thought of Trevon, so she wouldn't worry herself too much. She was still in love with him, but she understood his choice to take things slow. He showed his care for her and the baby by attending a few Lamaze classes with her. Back in February she had visited him on Valentine's Day. Emotions that were once hidden were shown openly. They had sex twice that day, but a wall still stood between them. They spoke daily, for neither could go on and ignore the feelings they still shared for each other.

Now in truth, LaToria was happy that Jurnee had pulled through. But in secret, she had cried her eyes out when she learned that Jurnee was pregnant by Trevon. There was no hate, only a hurt that left an aching pain on LaToria's heart. With her effort to gain Trevon's love back, his connection to Jurnee would forever be unique and special. Jurnee would give Trevon his firstborn.

LaToria needed to know what was wrong with her baby. A call suddenly came through on LaToria's cell phone that her mom answered.

"Hi Trevon."

LaToria wanted to hear his voice, but she didn't think she could hold herself together. Instead, she motioned to her mom that she didn't want to talk. She settled to listen to her mom talking.

"Yeah, we're still at the doctor's office—okay—well, we shouldn't be here much longer and no, we won't miss the wedding and—" She paused when the doctor walked back in. "Trevon, let me call you back. The doctor just got back in. Okay . . . bye-bye."

The white male doctor stood by the examination table with an iPad in his hand. "We have a problem here, Ms. Frost."

LaToria moaned, causing Tahkiyah to come to her side.

"Relax, baby." Tahkiyah rubbed LaToria's face, feeling scared of the pending news herself. "Please tell us what's wrong with the baby," Tahkiyah said.

The doctor sat down. "The baby is in great shape. All of the tests are fine."

"But . . . you said there's a problem," LaToria cried.

"Ms. Frost, when you went to see that *other* doctor back in November, he made a mistake."

"What kind of *mistake*?" Tahkiyah asked sharply.

"Ma'am, your daughter isn't late at all. The mistake came in the form of your daughter being told she was fourteen weeks pregnant. The truth is she was only eight and a half weeks pregnant. You're only eight months pregnant, Ms. Frost. Your baby isn't due until June."

Only the sound of the air conditioner running filled the office. Kandi was pulled back to reality as her mom started crying.

"Baby," Tahkiyah cried. "You hear that? The baby is Trevon's!"

It was true. A small mistake had sent LaToria on a path of destruction that tore up her happy home. LaToria had no doubt who the father was. Trevon Harrison!

CHAPTER Thirty-Five

The Last Scene

One year later . . .

There would be no embarrassing moment on *The Maury Povich Show* for Trevon to learn the truth of his firstborn. He was at LaToria's bedside back in June of last year when she gave birth to a baby girl. Then a week before Thanksgiving, he repeated the special event again with Jurnee. She gave him a baby boy.

Trevon was still doing porn while finding a balance in his life around being a father and his expanding career. He took things slowly, putting nothing before his kids. To be the man he wanted to be, he had to be willing to face his faults. He understood his fears in life, for no man or woman stood without fear. He understood the pain of having missed out on fifteen years of his life behind bars. Facing it, he made the choice to put it in his past. With each new day it was a challenge and yet a gift for Trevon.

As for dealing with his heart, he was able to forgive LaToria for her misguided actions without blame or fault.

The two met halfway on their trip back to commitment. Nothing in Trevon's sight would push him from his course in life.

In private he had a long mature talk with Tahkiyah to speak on the secret they shared. They both understood how lust proved to be their only link. What happened between them, they promised each other to take it to their grave. Trevon also promised that he would treat LaToria right and gladly welcome Tahkiyah as his mother-in-law when that day came. He found his balance by being himself and not what others expected him to be.

"Smooch!" LaToria shouted from the kitchen. "The baby is crying again."

Trevon was already making his way to the bedroom with Rex on his heels to check on the little ones. By the tone of the high-pitched cry, he knew it was his daughter. Reaching the crib in the bedroom, the crying stopped once his daughter saw him. She was spoiled and hated being alone. Her brother was wide awake as well, sharing the crib with his sister. Seeing his kids gave Trevon a purpose to live. A reason to be something that was taken for granted by many men, a father.

The End . . .

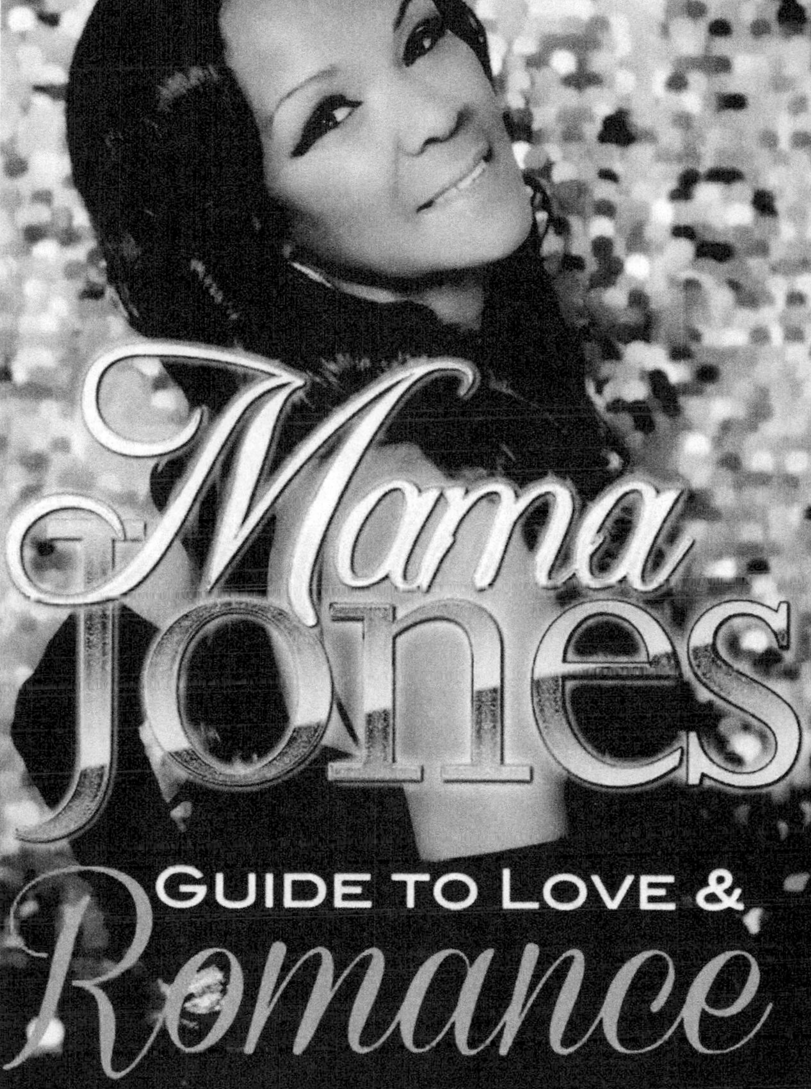
WAHIDA CLARK PRESENTS
Mama
Jones
GUIDE TO LOVE &
Romance

New York Times Bestselling Author of *Justify My Thug*

Honor Thy Thug

WAHIDA CLARK

WAHIDA CLARK PRESENTS

The Devil's GAME

A NOVEL

SHAWN 'JIHAD' TRUMP

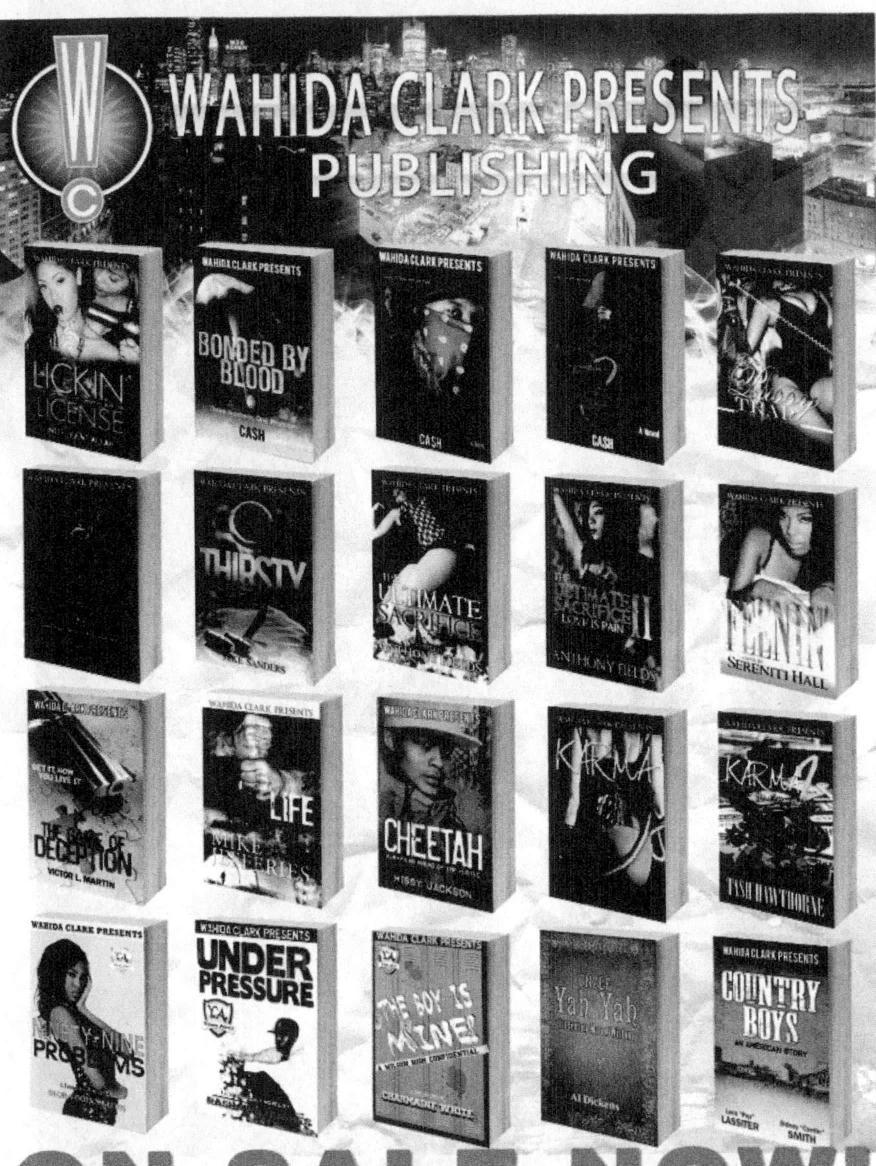
WAHIDA CLARK PRESENTS
PUBLISHING
WAHIDA CLARK PRESENTS
BONDED BY BLOOD
CASH
WAHIDA CLARK PRESENTS
CASH
WAHIDA CLARK PRESENTS
CASH
A Novel
THIRSTY
THE ULTIMATE SACRIFICE
THE ULTIMATE SACRIFICE II
LOVE IS PAIN
ANTHONY FIELDS
SERENITI HALL
GET IT HOW YOU LIVE IT
THE GAME OF DECEPTION
VICTOR L. MARTIN
WAHIDA CLARK PRESENTS
LIFE
CHEETAH
KARMA
TYSH HAWTHORNE
WAHIDA CLARK PRESENTS
WAHIDA CLARK PRESENTS
UNDER PRESSURE
WAHIDA CLARK PRESENTS
THE BOY IS MINE!
A WILSON HIGH CONFIDENTIAL
Yah Yah
Al Dickens
WAHIDA CLARK PRESENTS
COUNTRY BOYS
AN AMERICAN STORY
LASSITER
SMITH

CPSIA information can be obtained
at www.ICGtesting.com
Printed in the USA
LVOW04s1739021216
515533LV00009B/595/P